HEIR TO MALLA

HEIR TO MALLA

Book 1 in the Land of Magadha series

ANNA BUSHI

July Publishing

Contents

Dedicated to my parents for instilling the love
of reading in me

www.annabushi.com

Library of Congress Control Number: 2021900201
ISBN 978-1-7364103-0-1 (paperback) — ISBN 978-1-7364103-1-8 (hardback)

First Printing, 2020

Map of Magadha

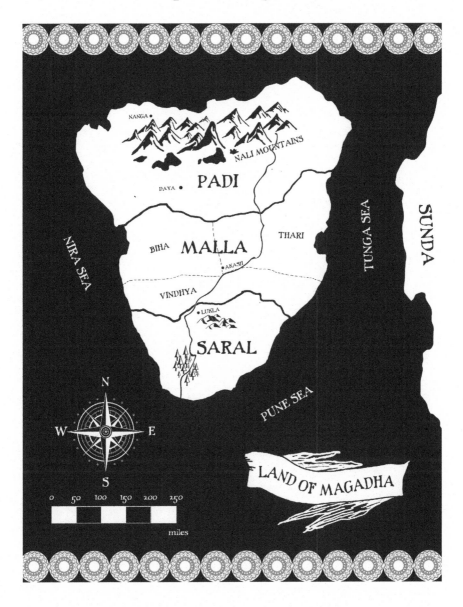

I

Troubled Times

I hummed a song as I scrubbed my body with sandalwood paste. The clear water and wisps of steam rising from the bathtub reminded me of being in a boat with Rish. He would row while I picked the water lilies blooming in the large palace pond. I would see him this morning, and the thought caused flutters in my stomach.

"Princess Meera, is Prince Jay coming back? I have not seen you this happy in a while," said my maid as she washed my hair.

"No, Kantha. My brother remains in Saral. I thought of visiting my grandmother today." I probably did not fool her. While I loved Queen Mother Priya, my maid understood I would not be this joyful in anticipation of seeing her.

I stepped out of the bathtub, dried myself, and went into my room. The white-washed walls gleamed in the morning sun. Gold, silver, and brass lamps hung on the walls and from the ceiling, glinting in the rays, their light long extinguished. My armoire stood in a corner in the shadows, over five feet tall, and carved with a wing-spread peacock on the door. I opened it and scanned the array of saris in every color. I chose a ripe mango-colored fabric, embroidered with a mango leaf pattern in silver thread, to wear.

Kantha helped me drape the sari. "The color brings out the golden glow in your skin, my lady."

As Kantha worked her magic on my hair, my thoughts shifted to the potential dangers of my interest in Rish Vindhya. As the Princess of the Malla kingdom, I knew he would not be my equal. Yet the fluttering in my stomach urged me to ignore my duty and follow my feelings.

Recently, my attraction to him threatened to overwhelm me, filling me with a longing to touch his face and to press my cheek against his chest. Yesterday, as I climbed into the boat with him, I stumbled, and he gently pressed his fingertips to my waist to steady me. My body came alive at his touch, causing me to lose my footing again. He held me tighter, his arms wrapped around me as he guided me to my seat. My breathing sounded like wind blowing through a hollow bamboo stick, and his breath came in short gasps when he released me.

Kantha pulled my hair, causing me to break out of my reverie.

Equals among royalty were few and far between. Princes were not exactly lining up for my hand. Prince Amar of Padi had recently married a local girl. The stories I heard of his misdeeds caused me to rejoice in escaping this union. That girl could have easily been me had the marriage been arranged. As for Prince Nakul, we currently warred against Saral, so his thoughts on a union remained a mystery unless Jay miraculously brought an end to the war. Though I did wonder if an alliance between the two of us might be suggested as a way to bring about peace.

My inner voice argued that Rish was no commoner. He hailed from the Vindhya house, the richest and most powerful house of the Malla kingdom, and was the cousin of my stepmother, Queen Charu. A union with him would allow me to remain in my beloved Malla kingdom, and help Jay rule.

Rish's face floated into my mind, agreeing with me. My feelings clouded my judgment. *A second son of the second son, could not claim to be my peer*, I scolded myself.

Kantha finished and stepped back. "I braided your hair with five strands and weaved in a single string of jasmine garland, my lady. It matches your festive mood."

Yesterday's jasmine flowers plucked at night, filled the room with a heady scent. She laid out gold earrings, bangles, and a necklace with the same mango leaf pattern as my sari, and I put them on. As a finishing touch, she pinned a gold chain on my hair, and the mango leaf ornament at the end of the chain rested on my forehead.

As I strolled into the palace gardens, I heard the cries of myna birds, parrots, and crows as they left their nests in search of food. Rish waited by the lily pond. He stood under a ficus tree with thick foliage that blocked the sky. My heart skipped as I approached him. He wore a white silk *dhoti* draped around his waist and a loose-fitting upper garment, our traditional garb. He had gold earrings, armbands, and a gold chain around his neck, symbolizing his high birth. He stood tall, his hand on his sword hilt.

A light breeze rustled his hair, causing it to fall across his forehead. I wanted to reach out and smooth his hair. On looks alone, he would be a match for a princess. Such thoughts were beneath me; I reminded myself. As I came nearer, he did not turn to greet me with a smile, as I expected. Instead, his eyebrows drew together, giving me pause.

"Princess Meera, I have some news to share. News better received while seated, so please," he said and guided me to one of the benches.

"Rish, what is it?" I asked, my mind racing. I saw my father yesterday, and he'd appeared in good health.

"As I broke my morning fast with Uncle Kasu, one of his men came with news from Saral."

My heart stopped beating, and I silently prayed. *Please gods, let no harm have come to Jay.*

"General Devan is on his way to Akash and—" He hesitated and gazed at me. "Prince Jay is missing."

My stomach tightened, and I stammered, "Missing? How can Jay be missing? He has five personal guards who would not let him out of their sight."

"The Vindhya man did not know the details, my lady. We must wait for the General to arrive. He should be here in a few days."

Tears filled my eyes, but I blinked them back. I was a Malla princess, and I would not give in to fear like a common girl. I tried to slow the beating of my racing heart.

Rish extended his hand as if to touch me. As I looked up, he pulled back. Part of me longed for his touch to ease my fear, but I knew if he did, I would lose my composure.

He regarded me kindly. "My lady, Prince Jay is beloved among his men. And Saral would not want to incur King Vikram's wrath by harming him. I am sure he is safe."

I took his words to heart. No harm would have come to Jay. I pushed aside my personal feelings as a sister and thought about the impact on our kingdom. News of his disappearance could not be allowed to spread.

"Rish, make sure the Vindhya man does not tell his tales to others. News such as this takes wings of its own. We must clip these wings till the General arrives and tells us the true story." As I spoke, I wound the end of my sari around my index finger.

"Princess Meera, I will make sure no one repeats the tales. We cannot keep this buried for long, though. Any news about the Prince is bound to spread like smoke from an extinguished torch."

"But try we must; I will go to my father and see if he knows more about Jay."

Rish took leave, but I remained on the bench for some time. Hot tears I'd held back until now flowed down my cheeks. This would not do. Jay may not be lost, and I could not give in to despair yet. I dried my eyes with my sari and walked to my room. I splashed cold water on my face, trying my best to hide any trace of tears and anguish as best as I could before seeing my father.

Father was conversing with Chief Kasu Vindhya and Chief Guard Mano Biha when I entered. My father sat at the head of a large rosewood table with carvings of a tiger family on it. Tigers represented the Malla kingdom, our protectors, so the carvings represented the king protecting his subjects. A female with her cubs and a male tiger roaring nearby were depicted beautifully.

My father no longer bears any resemblance to the menacing beast, I thought. Once majestic, my father now appeared frail and gaunt. Since his fall from a horse during the battle in Lukla months ago, the king's road to recovery proved slow. His tall frame appeared thinner, and his hair and beard were peppered with grey.

The morning sun poured in through the large windows, but a chill from the night still lingered. My father gestured for me to come forward and sit beside him.

"You have heard the news, my child?" he asked.

I nodded.

He turned to the others. "Mano, how could the Crown Prince disappear? Were his guards with him?"

Chief Mano, head of the city guards and the guards for the royal family, was not a tall man, but he trained every day and could easily beat men half his age in a fight. He shook his head and mused, "King Vikram, we must wait to hear what happened from one of the men present at the scene. My brother, Devan, is on his way, but he will not reach us for quite some time."

"He has sent the prince's chief guard, Balan, ahead to the capital. He should arrive here by tomorrow."

Heat coated my father's next words. "My chief of guard, Veera Vindhya, died saving my life. Here Balan is coming to tell me he failed his duty to protect my son. If the prince is indeed lost, shouldn't he be leading the search effort?" None had an answer for him. "Bring him to me as soon as he arrives." My father furrowed his brows and relaxed his clenched fists. "In the meantime, make sure this remains a secret until the General arrives. Chaos is our enemy in times like these. Uncle Kasu, if that means you have to throw your man into the dungeons, so be it. Mano, I don't want the city guards spreading any rumors about the prince."

Chief Kasu, my stepmother's father and the treasurer of Malla, ruled the prosperous Vindhya house. He ranked as the most powerful man in the kingdom after my father and brother. He replied dispassionately, "Yes, your Majesty. I will chop off their tongues if needed."

My father inclined his head. The men bowed and left.

Then he turned to me, and the pain in his eyes hit me like a brick. "A king needs to be cold-hearted, but the father in me cannot. The news I heard, if true, will throw this kingdom into despair. A father's past deeds now haunt the son. The mistakes I made in my youth have cast a shadow on this family."

Confused by his words, I tried to reassure him. "Father, you have been a just, benevolent, and noble King, and the kingdom has prospered under your rule. Your deeds could not possibly be responsible for Jay's fate."

My father dropped his gaze. A whisper tinted the edges of his words. "My child, I wish I could agree with you. I married a woman betrothed to my brother for the sake of duty. And I neglected that duty. A king needs many sons to hold his power, and your stepmother is childless."

I found it strange hearing my father talk of marriage, while I'd contemplated my own earlier in the day. Royal marriages were arranged for many reasons, producing heirs being the most important one. I set aside my thoughts about marriage.

"Father..." I hesitated, dreading to utter the words aloud. "How could Jay have disappeared? Do you think..." Sudden waves of agony and pain rose from my stomach into my throat, and I gasped for breath.

Hearing the anguish in my voice, my father shook his head like a beast waking from slumber. He transformed from a grieving father to a mighty king, his eyes focused, his lips drawn into a determined line. He put his arms around me and declared, "Don't despair, Meera. We will find him. I command the biggest army in the land of Magadha, and I will summon all of our men if needed."

Before Jay had left for Saral, we stayed up late one night and talked about our forefathers who had ruled the three kingdoms. Jay, at sixteen, yearned to explore the world. Just like his namesake, King Jay, he wanted to bring the three kingdoms of Magadha under one umbrella. Caught in his excitement, I shared his dreams, and we built this magical kingdom out of thin air. He sent me letters from Saral, filled with youthful exuberance and desires. I had pinned all hopes for the future on his young shoulders, and now I feared for Jay, Malla, and myself. I heard footsteps outside. I took a deep breath to steady myself. The door opened and in marched the Queen.

Her gaze fell on us as she strode in our direction. I glanced at the woman my father married for the welfare of the kingdom. My grandfather wanted to secure the allegiance of Kasu, as well as gain access to their wealth. At first betrothed to my uncle, crown prince Rudra, she married my father instead when my uncle and grandfather perished at sea. Though not a traditional beauty, she had a pleasant face.

She observed us, then said calmly, "My lord, I heard the news from my father. I don't think any harm will come to Jay. I will ask the priests all over Malla to pray for the prince."

"Charu, till we hear from Devan, I don't want the news to spread. Pray all you want, but do it here in Akash. And do so silently."

My stepmother then turned to me. "Meera, are those tears I see? Did I raise you to be such a coward? Wipe them now. Your father wants us to hide our grief, and we will do justice to his request. Come with me."

I tasted the bitterness of her words. I glanced at my father. He nodded before he settled back into his chair, his eyes closed, and forearms crossed. I also desired some quiet time alone to come to terms with my grief. Instead, I followed the queen to her chambers.

Queen of Malla

When we reached her chambers, the queen sat down and gestured for me to sit next to her. Paintings on her walls dominated her large sitting room. One depicted Vindhya women who became Queen of Malla, another Vindhya palaces and temples, and on a third, deities in their fierce forms, engaged in battle, destroying demons. As a child, these paintings filled me with terror, and I avoided her chambers. Now, I wish these gods would fight our battles, instead of sending our fathers and brothers, to be maimed or killed.

My father married two women, one for love and one for duty. He married my mother, Kayal, a Saral girl he had fallen in love with before he ascended the throne. As king, he married Charu Vindhya, to secure the Vindhya alliance and to access their coffers. While Charu remained the Queen, my mother ruled the king's heart. Queen Charu bore two daughters, but they died soon after birth. She begrudged the presence of Jay and me in her life. We represented all that she sought but had been denied her.

More than a decade ago, when my mother died in childbirth, I resented my stepmother. There were many a night when I wished she had died instead.

After my mother's death, Charu grudgingly accepted Jay and me into her life. Recently, I came to realize it must not have been easy being a mother to the two children of her rival. When my mother lived, she would sing songs to us and narrate stories of both Malla and Saral. She asked my father to teach me how to ride a horse. I loved to ride with her along the river, the wind blowing in my hair. After she died, my stepmother frowned upon horse riding as not an activity suitable for a princess and tried to put an end to it. She stayed out of the affairs of the crown and spent most of her time in prayers and feasts. She wanted me to follow in her footsteps.

During my childhood, playing the role of our mother did not come easily to her. She appointed various teachers to enrich our minds and bodies and left our day-to-day care to servants. As I grew older, she more easily fell into a counselor role.

I wondered if my life would take a similar path, where I would be a pawn in a royal chess game, marrying for duty. Rish's face drifted into my mind, and I pushed the thought away.

Queen Charu looked at me and said, "I know you love your brother very much. I wish I could comfort you and say he will return safely, and your life will be filled with happiness. But that would be a lie. As a young girl, I held naïve ideas. You are a princess and the only daughter of the Malla king. While your father cares for you, pursuing the wellness of the kingdom must lie ahead of pursuing your happiness."

I watched her and saw a sadness in her eyes. I remembered father's words of his marriage. Strangely, I felt pity for her and wondered what she aspired to as a girl my age. Before I could stop myself, I blurted out, "What were your dreams before you married?"

She sighed and said, "I dreamt of being queen. My wish came true, but at a price. My father wanted to betroth me to Prince Rudra, your father's brother, and I allowed my head to be filled with silly ideas. Ideas of being a queen and sitting on the throne. The Prince rode into the Vindhya palace on his horse, and I watched him from the terrace. He looked tall and handsome and everything a girl could dream of. As he entered the palace, my friends and I showered him with flowers. He glanced at me and smiled, and my heart went into a flutter. Not being a traditional beauty myself, his appearance enamored me. He had taken after his mother. Queen Mother Priya still is beautiful today, and many considered her one of the loveliest girls in her youth."

She paused and examined me and said, "You have inherited her looks and beauty."

A blessing or a curse, I did not know yet. "Mother, tell me what happened in Vindhya," I prompted. I had always called her that, even when my mother lived. A royal tradition of how the offspring addressed all the king's wives.

She continued a faraway look in her eyes, "My father spared no expense, and my betrothal to the prince took place in a grand ceremony. The prince spoke only a few words to me, but I remember them as if it was yesterday. *My lady, wait for me with a wedding garland when I return.* I waited impatiently for his arrival from the Sunda kingdom across the Tunga Sea. Having won a hard-fought victory, your grandfather, King Karan, and Prince Rudra would head back to Malla in a few months. I kept my promise to him and picked delicately scented white lilies to create my wedding garland. News of Rudra's bravery in the battle reached the shores, and the entire kingdom waited with thousands of victory garlands for their crowned prince. But my joy suffered a short life. A storm hit the ships on their way back, and the prince and king drowned. We were all plunged into despair."

She paused and contemplated her clasped hands on her lap. "Your father, Prince Vikram, the second son, came back to Malla to be crowned the king. My father asked me to marry the new king. I obeyed. I became the queen. My dreams were fulfilled, though not in the way I thought. Dreams may come true, but be sure you fully understand what you want."

My stepmother had never talked me to about her marriage before, and I sat in silence, not knowing what to say.

I thought about my father's side of the marriage. My uncle, Prince Rudra, had died tragically, and my father ascended the throne among the chaos that arose from losing both the king and the crown prince.

My father wed his brother's betrothed, a woman he had not laid eyes on, and she married him, mourning for the Prince she lost. Kings arranged royal marriages for the welfare of the kingdom. And yet, I let my heart pine for a young man with no titles. If Jay was not found, I would have no choice in the matter. I would be wed to secure our kingdom.

Queen Charu straightened her shoulders and turned her attention back to me. "Save your tears, Meera. If something has happened to Jay, you would need all your wits about you."

Tears welled in my eyes anyway for the mother I lost, the brother whom I raised, and my stepmother who got her wish to wear the crown but knew no real happiness.

That evening Queen Charu and I left for the temple to pray in secret for Jay. The temple stood on a hilltop in lush green surroundings, and I would have preferred to ride on an elephant or a horse to view the stunning vicinity. My stepmother chose to ride on a palanquin, and I followed her lead.

We sat across from each other as four men carried us on their shoulders. Along with our usual guards, it surprised me to see Rish ride in front. Throughout the journey, he rode in ahead of us and did not glance in my direction at all. I had opened the palanquin curtains, so I could see the passers-by. A few people stopped and greeted us, and I acknowledged them. News of Jay had not spread, and the people moved about their daily business. It felt strange to me that the kingdom kept running smoothly while its fate hung in the balance.

Once we reached the gates, the men placed the palanquin gently on the ground. I got out first and stretched my hands to help my stepmother out. Rish jumped down from his horse, his gaze darting around us for signs of trouble. He ordered two men to wait outside and asked the others to accompany us.

The black granite temple, built over two centuries back by a Malla king, fell into neglect many years ago. Recently, I donated some lands, so the temple could be maintained from the farm revenue. As I walked in through the gates, I inspected the repairs being made with immense satisfaction. The outer wall ran around the temple. Inside, a small courtyard held some magnificent beech and neem trees. The flowers had fallen on the ground, creating a carpet of purple and white. I saw a peacock in the courtyard that had arched its tail feathers into a graceful fan of blue, green, and other hues. I have a few of these beautiful birds in the palace gardens as well. My maids would often collect their feathers and make them into fans. The feathers also sometimes found their way into a hairpiece crown or a dancer's skirt.

The main temple structure shone in the sunlight. I scanned the tapering rectangular dome, carved with divine sculptures of the gods and goddesses in various dance poses. Some of the sculptures were recently restored, their hewn rock brighter than their counterparts. As I stepped into the main sanctum, the priest seemed delighted to see the queen and the princess and performed a prayer for us. After that, he came out of the inner sanctum and gave us some milk from the offering to the god.

"Princess Meera, you grace this temple with your presence. Please also grace us with a song about Krishna in your divine voice. That would make this devotee's day."

My stepmother responded. "She is a princess—"

I interrupted her, "In the presence of the gods, all are equal, mother." Having never grown up as a princess, Charu had a lot of opinions on what a princess could and could not do.

Rish stood in the temple's main hall, examining the sculptures depicting Krishna's early life as a cowherd, and spun when he heard the priest's request. I usually had my companions with me, so we could sing as a group. For some reason, singing by myself in front of him disconcerted me. I tried to push those feelings aside and focused on the serene face of God Krishna. Once I started, the song took over me, and I forgot my surroundings. As I sang the divine hymn about seeking Krishna's blessings, my mind silently beseeched him to protect Jay.

When I finished, I realized several of the devotees had stopped to listen.

An older woman with tears in her eyes came up to me and said,

"Princess Meera, your song evoked a devotion I have not felt in years. May the gods grace you with all that is good."

The priest offered me flowers and blessed me. "I pray that you soon marry a husband as strong and wise as Lord Krishna himself." Rish came nearby at that point, and I blushed while receiving the flowers, though I had been blessed similarly for a few years now.

I recovered quickly and told him, "I have heard these blessings many times before. Our royal astrologer even told me a year ago that the time neared for my lord to come riding on a horse to claim my hand. I see no use for these blessings. Bless my father, brother, and this kingdom instead."

"Mark my words, princess. The man who is fortunate to marry you is not far away. The kingdom will prosper under your brother and will see many glorious days. You will live for long years to see this."

Imagining my wedding to Rish, I turned a deep red at these words. It served me well for engaging the priest in this conversation. I could sense Rish's gaze on me, and I stole a glance at him. His eyes watched me intently as I proceeded around the inner sanctum, scarcely sensing the scenes around me.

3

Chief Guard

Jay's head guard, Balan, arrived the next day, and Rish came to fetch me as he had promised. As we entered, I noticed my father, Queen Charu, Chief Kasu, Minister Kripa, Chief Guard Mano, and Balan assembled in the small throne room. The silver throne had only one chair next to it for the Queen.

Balan uttered, "Princess Meera," as he saw me, then caught himself. He looked like he had ridden without any rest from Saral, his face weary and his clothes dirty. He must have come straight from the stables. I stood behind my father and waited for Balan to deliver his news about my missing brother, my heart pounding.

Chief Guard Mano had handpicked Balan for the newly crowned heir's head of guards. A few years older than Jay, tall and well-built, my brother needed someone like Balan on his side in a fight. Level-headed and a stickler for rules, he ably commanded the young men under him. Jay's five guards had all sworn an oath in front of Goddess Durga to protect him with their lives. If they failed, they swore to cut their own throats. In one of Jay's letters, he sounded exasperated by their diligence. He wrote, "*I get the feeling that if Balan thought I would be safe locked up in a cell with guards all around me, he would do it.*"

Glaring at Balan, my father thundered, "What happened to my son?"

Balan rubbed the back of his neck. "King Vikram, my tongue trembles to say this. Maram celebrated Buddha's birthday with a festive procession, and Prince Jay wanted to mingle with the commoners to hear what they thought of the invasion firsthand. I tried to dissuade him, but the Prince said, '*In Akash, my sister and I have gone on rounds in disguise. We would dress up as ordinary folk and attend temple festivals mixing in with the crowd. The opportunity presented a truly great way to gauge what the subjects were saying and feeling. I would like to do the same here. I want to attend the festival as a commoner and mingle with the locals.*"

I could see out of the corner of my eye my stepmother's disapproving glare. Jay and I never let it known we'd gone out in disguise before.

"Fool," yelled father, shocking me. "Mano and I knew about their jaunts and his men dressed as peasants followed, never letting them out of sight. You thought I would let my heirs wander unprotected?" he snarled. I stood stunned.

"I did not know," stammered Balan. Under father's scowl, Balan continued, "In the end, Kapil Biha, Shiv Thari, and I dressed as Malla traders and Prince Jay and Vasu as our servants. I thought once he'd dressed as a servant, I could keep him hidden and draw attention away from him. We joined the milling crowd waiting for the parade of the idols. Though the area remained partially under Saral control, it pleased the Prince to see the people going about their daily lives and partaking in festivities. Soon we could see the elephants with the Buddha idols on their backs making way through the crowd. Monks walked along with the elephants, singing songs in praise of Buddha and Saral. The crowd showered flowers at the elephants and joined in the chanting. Prince Jay sang along, and I felt foolish for having worried earlier."

He paused and hunched up. Chief Guard Mano cleared his throat, causing Balan to look up like a deer caught among hunters. Taking a deep breath, he continued in a low voice. "When the procession moved on, and the crowd dispersed, we walked back. We passed through a wooded area when an arrow came whistling by. It narrowly missed us. Before I could react, a second one came my way, and I pushed the Prince aside. The arrow hit Kapil instead and embedded into his upper arm. We all drew out the swords hidden in our clothes and ran further into the woods with the Prince in the middle."

I clasped my hands tightly to keep them from shaking. Father leaned forward on his throne and peered at Balan. Balan's voice quavered with emotion as he continued, "Soon, I saw about ten men on horses riding towards us. They wore nondescript clothes, but I guessed these were Saral men. Someone had betrayed us. I grabbed my spear and tossed it at one of the men. It hit him in the stomach and unhorsed him. I heard Shiv groan and fall to the ground with an arrow in his leg. The rest of the men tried to form a circle around Prince Jay. He raised his sword above his head and fought them off valiantly. Kapil already hurt from the arrow, tried to break that circle. I attempted to do the same, but a horse hoof kicked my head, knocking me to the ground, unconscious.

"When I woke, I saw Shiv trying to revive Kapil. With dread, I moved around and searched the dead men. I came across the body of Vasu with a spear plunged through his heart. Prince Jay, however, had vanished. Help soon arrived, and General Devan ordered the new men to search the area. We examined every inch in vain. The General asked me to ride ahead to give you this news. He should be here in two days."

Minister Kripa, father of Vasu, gave an audible gulp at the news of his son's death. My father clenched his fists. "You failed your duties as Jay's guard. Head back to Saral and mount a hunt for him, while keeping the news from spreading as much as possible."

"King Vikram," Balan said, his voice breaking, "you are correct. I failed the prince. Send another more capable man to head the search. I wanted to see you and give you the message before fulfilling my vow."

It happened too fast. He took his dagger out, and I screamed, "Stop him!"

Rish ran to him but failed to prevent the horror. Balan plunged the dagger into his heart and whispered, "Goddess Durga," and collapsed.

Chaos ensued. I ordered one of the guards to fetch the royal Physician, Shukla. Mano and Rish rushed to Balan's aid. They ordered some men to carry Balan to his chamber. Kripa left with them, cursing the gods for taking away his son.

In the midst of the turmoil, I clung to meager hope. Jay could be alive. They just had not found him yet.

And Balan, what had he done? Chief Mano himself appointed Balan as the chief guard for Jay. A great warrior, level-headed and devoted. Considering their youth, I had hoped Balan would serve Jay for many years. Now, he had sacrificed himself. My sorrow tried to overwhelm me like floodwater overwhelming a dam. Father resumed speaking to Chief Kasu, so I left for my chambers, staggering through the corridors, to gather my thoughts.

Once there, I remembered a trip I took with Balan. A year ago, Jay sneaked a horse for me, and we rode to the rivers with Kapil and Balan. Balan came to the city from Biha, joined the city guards at a young age, and rose in ranks. We set out early in the day and passed by the river. Jay knew I could handle a horse well, so he took off with Kapil. Balan kept pace with me, keeping a watchful eye on my mount, ready to come to my aid, as if fearing I would be unhorsed any time. I laughed at him for that, and he turned a deep red. I scolded myself mentally for taunting him.

It had been a hot day with no clouds in the sky, and we stopped near an old banyan tree to wait for Jay to come back. Balan dismounted first and knelt next to my horse to let me climb down on his back. We sought shelter under the tree. It had several roots, reaching from the branches to the ground, looking like an insect with many limbs. Walking behind Balan, I watched as he carefully held the roots aside to clear my path. We soon reached the massive trunk in the middle. Four men could stand holding hands around it and still not cover the trunk completely.

As I sat on one of the many roots under the tree, he stood next to me, alert and awkward. I had asked him a few questions, and he responded haltingly. I remembered asking him how he liked living in the city. He said, where he grew up, royalty appeared even rarer than snow. Still getting used to us, he asked my forgiveness if he had committed any transgressions. A grown man, who could have lifted me with one hand, and with enough bravery to fight for Malla, had remained timid in front of me. People in and around Akash saw the royal family frequently. I had wondered what the subjects in the remote corners of Malla thought about those who ruled or if they even cared.

Jay and Kapil came back shortly. On seeing them, I stood and started walking. Balan joined me and dropped to his knee near the horse, to help me climb on. Before I could, Jay came closer, jumped off his horse, and lifted me onto mine. For a boy of fifteen, Jay had tremendous strength. When we got back to the palace that day, our stepmother talked to me about the perils of horse riding and painted a grave picture of what a fall from the horse could do to my life. Her words were proven right by my father, still recovering from his fall.

As time went, Balan grew in confidence. When Chief Guard Mano wanted to appoint him the head of Jay's guards, I agreed wholeheartedly. Now, in the short span of a year, we lost him. And Jay. I forced myself not to think about my brother, though everything in Akash reminded me of him.

The next day, Rish escorted me to Balan's chamber. My brother would have visited his wounded guard, and I felt compelled to visit in his absence. As head of Jay's guards, he had his own room. It was small and sparsely furnished. In the middle stood a bed, and a trunk for his belongings was placed at its foot. By the door, a desk held the only lamp in the room.

Balan lay on his bed, unconscious, and the Physician did not expect him to live long. In the dim light, I could see the blood-stained bandages covering his chest. Rish pulled up the only chair next to Balan's bed, and I sat down regarding the young man who gave up his life because he failed at his duty.

"Balan, you served Jay well," I whispered, not sure if he could hear me. A lump gathered in my throat, and I exhaled slowly, winding the end of my sari around my finger.

I heard a sudden rustle and turned to see Rish kneeling. With eyebrows drawn together, he gasped, "Meera, I cannot bear to see you in pain."

Had he called me by my name before? I could only recall him using the term *Princess*. His hair fell over his eyes, and I involuntarily reached out and pushed it aside.

His lips parted, and I snatched my arm back and let it drop. He caught it and covered it with his other. His rough hands felt warm, and he held mine gently, like flower petals. Warmth spread slowly in my stomach. The kingdom stood on the brink of being thrown into turmoil with Jay's disappearance, and I foolishly longed to kiss Rish's worry lines on his forehead away.

He continued, "I have been of no comfort to you these past few days. Tell me what to do."

Hold me in your arms, I thought. I mumbled, "Nothing. There is nothing anyone can do unless you can find Jay."

His eyes brightened, and he said, "I can help search for Prince Jay. I know Saral well. Allow me to go find your brother."

I did not want him to leave me, but I nodded. Rish fought in Saral before his father's death. He was of more use heading the search than remaining here in the palace.

Balan moaned, and Rish let go of me before leaving the room.

4

Search Underway

Balan passed away that night. I wished for Jay to conquer the world, and he needed loyal friends, willing to lay their lives on the line for him. Balan's death deprived Jay of a trustworthy guard.

The next day we gathered once again in the small throne room, this time waiting for General Devan to arrive. No sign of Balan's blood remained. I sighed silently at the life lost.

The General, our Southern Commander and Chief of Biha, strode in. A tall strong man, he appeared to have aged years in days. Deep lines were etched onto Devan's face and there was more grey than black in his hair.

Father asked, "Do we have everybody gathered? Where is Minister Kripa?"

Chief Guard Mano stepped up and answered, "My Majesty, General Devan brought Vasu's remains to Akash, and Kripa is mourning the loss of his son, and making arrangements to cremate him."

My father appeared troubled and asked the General, "Tell me you have updated knowledge about what happened in Saral."

The General started his story with sagging shoulders and a distant voice. "Our nightmare began when Prince Jay left for Maram. When the news reached me, I worried about his safety. I questioned Somu, his servant, about his whereabouts. He said the Prince headed to Maram in disguise to join the Buddha festival celebrations. I sent the Prince's three other personal guards, along with my men, to search for them. We found Balan and Kapil alive, Shiv wounded, and Vasu killed, along with several Saral men, but no sign of the Prince."

The General paused here and looked around the room. All eyes gazed back at him. Tightening his grip on sword hilt and jutting his chin, he continued in an urgent tone, "I don't know why Balan took only Kapil along, leaving his other three guards behind. I questioned Somu again about the Prince, even threatening him with whipping, but to no avail. He held that the Saral men must have captured Jay and to allow him to find out more. Not trusting anyone at that point, I threw Somu in the dungeon."

The General's actions troubled me. As his servant, Somu had taken care of Jay since birth. His story matched Balan's. Instead of helping search for my brother, he languished in a dungeon. I clenched my fist, and my fingernails dug into my palm.

General Devan sighed deeply. "I instructed Lieutenant General Satya, my second in command, along with Prince Jay's other guards, Kapil, Karan, Dev, and Giri, to continue the search. I then returned to Akash to give you the news in person. A wounded Prince Jay could have been taken by the Saral, so I instructed my men to watch for that."

Most of what the General said we already learned from Balan. But his last words brought some hope as well. If Saral men captured Jay, he would be too valuable a prisoner to be harmed. Father kept silent for some time, his head bowed.

Worry tore my heart, but I'd run out of tears. I thought about my mother. Few days before she died, she allowed me to touch her bulging stomach. As I grinned in delight when I felt the new baby kick, she rubbed my cheek and asked me to look after Jay. She wanted me to keep an eye on him while she cared for the baby. Then both she and the baby died.

I had not kept my promise to her. I had not taken care of my little brother. I still remembered the five-year-old boy who came to my room on the night our mother passed away and sat next to me on my bed. I had tears flowing down my face, and he started crying as well. I pulled him into a hug and told him I would keep him safe. I had failed.

The general opened his mouth as if to say something, then shut it. Seeing him hesitate, the king prompted, "Is there something else on your mind, General?"

"My Majesty, Prince Jay's servant Somu is from Saral, and my men spotted him talking to Saral men in the Lukla villages a fortnight ago. I had told the prince at that time, but he dismissed my warning. I worry that his trust was misplaced, and Somu colluded with the enemy."

My father seemed lost in thought for some time and then looked at the General. "Somu served as a loyal servant of," he paused and added in a whisper, "Kayal." My mother loomed large over us, even in death.

He continued in a normal voice, "I cannot imagine he would betray her son. This gives me hope. Somu knows the area well and has people there. If anybody can find Jay, it would be him."

"I hope that turns out to be true, my Majesty," said the General with a small shake of his head.

My father then looked up at the General, his eyebrows drawn together. "Balan thought he had failed the prince and because of that took his own life. I don't believe Jay is dead. Your actions speak volumes about your loyalty. I trust your words in most matters, but I have to overrule you on Somu. Send word to release him."

General Devan inclined his head in acquiescence.

Chief Kasu cleared his throat. "King Vikram, we have two young men who were at the Prince's side when he disappeared, Kapil Biha and Shiv Thari. I would throw them both in a Saral dungeon till we find out who betrayed the prince."

Mano Biha tensed and snarled, "Kapil is my son and he is one of Prince Jay's personal guards. He swore an oath to protect him."

Kasu sneered and snapped back, "A duty he failed."

First Somu, now Kapil. Kapil, Vasu, and Jay grew up together like brothers. This would not do. We could not turn against each other. I desperately hoped father would put an end to this.

General Devan touched his brother's shoulder. "Mano, Chief Kasu's question is a serious one and requires a similar response. Shiv Thari spent a long time away from the prince and is ambitious. With an older brother who would inherit Thari, he tried to forge his own path in the world. But he spent time with the Prince in Malla and never left his side in Saral.

"Kapil grew up with Prince Jay and has been loyal to him. Prince Jay trusted him to make him his guard. Kapil could have been enticed with promises of wealth from Prince Nakul, but Kapil knows he has a better future in Malla with Jay. And I had seen Prince Jay in close quarters in Lukla. After a few days with the prince, most men would have willingly followed him to their death. I cannot believe a few weeks with the Saral would change Kapil. I can send word for my men to keep an eye on both of them. They were both wounded and need time to recover anyway."

The king nodded. "Vindhya, Thari, and Biha are the pillars holding up Malla, and I don't want us to question the loyalty of our sons to the crown. If new information arises, we will deal with it accordingly. Consider this settled for now. In the meantime, I have asked Bhoj Thari to come to Akash. Let us discuss what to do next."

Vindhya, Thari, and Biha were the three regions that came under Malla rule. They used Malla coins and served in the Malla military with the king as the Supreme Commander. The chiefs of these houses served on the king's council and held important military and government roles. According to the customs, Malla chiefs sent their sons to be fostered with Jay, our future king. It allowed friendship to blossom between him and the men who would one day help him rule. These boys grew up and learned to fight together. Would one of them betray him?

General Devan sighed. "One more matter to discuss, my Majesty. My nephew Kapil told me that Kripa's son, Vasu, apparently wanted to marry my daughter, Riya. I cannot fathom how he thought himself a fit consort for the daughter of the Biha chief and General of the Southern command. This boy set to prove his worthiness by joining the Prince.

Instead of displaying his battle prowess, he ended up being killed by Surya's men. I judged him to be a coward, and cowards are easy to entice with promises of wealth. He might be our spy."

My father shook his head. "That boy is dead, and Kripa is already mourning the loss of his son. Let us not add to that wound."

Chief Kasu cleared his throat and spoke. "King Vikram, Surya instigated this conflict. As king of Saral, he will not rest till he is victorious over us or dies trying. He recently married a young girl to win the support and wealth of her father. A longer conflict will empty our coffers. You won half of his kingdom, including the Capital Lukla, after a very hard-fought battle. We should mount a larger army with an experienced commander and find Surya, Queen Anju, and Prince Nakul in the Saral caves and wipe them out. Then we should crown you as the King of the Saral kingdom as well and put an end to all this fighting."

My father said, "Uncle Kasu, you speak as a warrior befitting of all your brave deeds and conquests. And we may need to kill Surya to end this war. But I don't want to prolong the bloodshed by killing Prince Nakul, and killing women is not an act I would condone. Also, if Jay is their captive, this action may put his life in jeopardy."

Others agreed. My heart pounded against my chest at the thought of Jay's life in peril.

Chief Kasu Vindhya said, "King Vikram, this is difficult to say and discuss, but we need to prepare the kingdom for any eventuality. In case Prince Jay is not found, or gods forbid dead, you need to decide on who your heir would be."

Anger flashed through my father's face briefly as he replied in controlled tones, "I refuse to abandon hope that my son is still alive."

Minister Kripa responded in a thoughtful tone, "There is wisdom in what Chief Kasu is stating, my Majesty." His face appeared tired and tight.

The minister had walked in just a few moments ago. My father looked at him and said sadly, "Our sons have left their old fathers to grieve for them." Then he continued to answer Chief Kasu. "You forget I have another child."

Chief Kasu contemplated me briefly before stating, "Beloved though the princess may be, women cannot rule, my Majesty."

I felt helpless and powerless. I opened my mouth to release the breath that seemed caught in my throat, and my gaze fell on Rish. He glimpsed at me discreetly. The feelings in his eyes helped me think clearly. I am the only daughter of King Vikram. I am not powerless.

"Her sons could," my father continued, challenging the council. "If it comes to that, I will adopt my grandsons to rule the land after me."

All eyes fell on me, and I bowed my head to avoid their gaze. Chief Kasu turned towards the king. "Meera is a beloved princess of the land, and there is precedent for crowning a son of the princess."

General Devan added, "Having traveled all over this kingdom, I know the love the people of this land have for Princess Meera. Any son of hers would be accepted as the king."

I understood now how a blessing can turn to a curse. I imagined a swift wedding, and shortly thereafter a baby snatched from my arms and fostered in Malla to be raised as king. Jay's life would be in even more danger if my future husband thought he could control Malla through his heirs.

Women usually kept quiet at these council meetings, unless the king posed a question to them. Since these men were discussing my future, I could no longer stay silent.

I took a deep breath and whispered, "Father, please allow me to say a few words."

He gazed at me tenderly. "Tell us what is on your mind, my child."

I studied the men in the room and stated in low, but sturdy tones, "I understand why such matters have to be discussed and settled. Considering I am not married yet, this talk of my sons is premature. We all pray my father will be our king for many years to come. And I hope and pray Jay is alive. Let us do everything to find him."

I heard the queen's sari rustle, but I kept my eyes on my father.

My father nodded. "Let us discuss succession later when Bhoj is present. Devan, tell me what arrangements you have made to search for Jay."

General Devan replied, "My king, I left over twenty of my men most familiar with the area along with four of Prince Jay's guards to continue the search. Satya is also aiding the search from Theni, and he has the entire army at his command. I planned to send Balan back to lead the search, but did not think he would take his own life."

I asked, "General Devan, the remaining guards of Jay are young. What will they do when they hear the news about Balan?"

My stepmother cleared her throat, signaling her displeasure that I'd voiced a question, but I did not care. My future depended on finding Jay. And, we could not afford to lose more men loyal to him.

General Devan scratched his chin. "My lady, the boys stayed true to Prince Jay and Balan. They all swore to protect the prince with their life. They might also think that they failed in their duty and that taking their lives is the right course of action."

My father responded, "I cannot have more young men die. With Balan's passing, we need to choose somebody to head the guards, keeping them in line and focused. Kapil would be ideal, but he needs time to recover. Mano, what are your thoughts?"

Before Mano could respond, Rish chimed in, "My king, if I may?"

My father surveyed him in surprise. "State what is on your mind."

I held my breath as my eyes darted between the two men. Rish and I agreed to ask my father's permission for him to aid the search. I assumed we would do it in private, not in front of all the Malla elders.

Rish stepped forward, bowed to the king, said in a clear voice, "My Majesty, I served in Saral under General Devan, and I know the area well. Please allow me to head the search for Prince Jay."

General Devan asserted, "Rish commanded a small group of men in the Lukla battle and proved himself as a worthy warrior. He is more experienced than Jay's guards and is a reliable young man."

My heart pounded so loudly I wondered if the others could hear it.

"Yes, and his father, my chief guard, died protecting me in Saral," my father added thoughtfully, his eyes looking far away. "We tried to capture King Surya. With a small troop, we went in search of him. We found him holed up in a house with many women and children. I asked our soldiers not to harm any women and children, even though the Saral men did not hesitate to shoot arrows at us and did not care if they killed innocent people as well."

He paused and turned to General Biha, "Devan, you fought with me that day."

"Yes, my Majesty, and I witnessed the courage of you and your men. You fought bravely, but the Saral were intent on destroying us. One arrow shot your horse in the eye, and the horse ran, dropping you on the ground. In the chaos that ensued, you would have been killed in the stampede, if not for the valor of Veera."

The king regarded Rish, "Your father rescued me and rode to safety, even though he was mortally wounded. He showed immense loyalty and bravery and died saving my life. Many years ago, when he married, I declared that I would relieve him of his guard duties and move him to other posts in the army. Veera declined and continued to be my guard. Men like that are born once in a lifetime."

I had heard this story before and still felt moved by Veera Vindhya's bravery. When father came back to Akash to recover from his wounds, I went to the Vindhya palace to convey the crown's gratitude and my sympathies for the loss of Veera. Each of the three houses had their own palace in Akash. Rish had traveled to the capital with his mother to take his father's remains home, and he received me that day. Instead of the boy, I met several years ago, a battle-honed man, who had won praise for his fighting prowess, stood before me. He took me to his mother and sat next to her, showing her kindness and attention in her grief.

After a few weeks in Vindhya, instead of heading back to Saral, Rish came to the capital to train our men. Jay left for Saral shortly after, to finish what father had started, and Rish's company kept me sane in the ensuing months. My feelings for him had grown since then, and a part of me hoped that father would view him favorably if he rescued Jay. And grant my wish to marry him.

Chief Kasu cleared his throat as if he meant to say something and brought me back to the present.

My father turned to Rish. "I think you would be the ideal person to head to Saral, lead the search, and give hope to Jay's guards."

My father surveyed the room, and General Devan and Chief Guard Mano nodded. Chief Kasu looked around and reluctantly agreed as well.

Rish bowed to the king with his hands clasped together and said, "I am honored, my King. I will lead the search effort to find the prince and protect and defend him with my life or die trying."

My father added, "Rish, you will depart tomorrow. Take some men who came with the General to guide you. Search the surrounding villages. Listen to what the Saral men are *not* saying. Find my son."

Rish glanced in my direction briefly and bowed again to the king, "Yes, my Majesty."

I exhaled slowly. While I dreaded losing his company, I prayed he would find my brother. Back in my chambers, I sent him a message through Kantha, to attend me later that evening.

Night had fallen, and the moon appeared to float on the pond. Scents from jasmine blooms filled the air with an intoxicating fragrance. I sat on a bench facing the pond. Rish stood next to the bench. The moonlight cast his face in radiant light, and his hair fell on his forehead. I had a sudden urge to touch his hair again. He looked at me then, and I drowned in his eyes. For a moment, neither of us moved.

I stood up slowly and beheld him, trying to memorize every detail of his face. Involuntarily I took a step towards him, and the next moment his arms wrapped around my waist, and he pressed his lips against mine. I plunged my hands into his hair and returned his kiss passionately. We kissed with a sense of urgency, my mind split, between wanting it never to end and warning me to stop.

Chief Guard Mano of Biha had men all over the city, including this palace. And my father would be kept abreast of happenings. Kissing a young Vindhya man was foolish on my part. There were already tensions between the three major territories of Malla, especially with the Vindhya family playing such a prominent role. Biha and Thari would not be happy if they learned their princess showed partiality to a Vindhya man. I could not add fuel to this fire.

He let go of me suddenly, and I stepped away.

"This cannot get out," I whispered breathlessly.

"I would not be the one to reveal it, my lady. I could be beheaded if it did come out," he said grimly. I looked at the young man standing in front of me. My gaze lowered to his lips, and warmth rushed to my cheeks from the remembered kiss. I took a deep breath and raised my eyes to his. A hundred questions appeared in his that he could not ask, and I could not answer.

Quieting my heart, I tried to focus on the urgent matter at hand.

"Rish, I do believe Jay is alive. Find my brother and bring him back."

"My lady, you have my word that I will move mountains to find him. I will not come back empty-handed," he said earnestly.

He continued, "Meera", saying my name as if tasting nectar. "I don't claim to be worthy of you."

My heart leaped to my throat, and I gazed into his eyes. He quivered, "My beloved Meera, these past few days, I have been going insane with my desire to hold and comfort you."

I beamed, as he reached out to hold my hand. "If I rescue Prince Jay and help him defeat Surya, I hope to seek King Vikram's consent for your hands." The warmth from his fingers spread to mine, and a tiny glow radiated from my heart.

I reluctantly pulled my hand out of his clasp and removed a gold ring with a tiger carved on it from my finger. Handing the ring to him with trembling hands, I said, "Here is a token of my love for you. Come back to me victorious."

The next day, I walked to the Queen's chambers. She had organized a small gathering to bid Rish farewell, and I planned to arrive there with her. I reached her chambers earlier than I anticipated, still reliving my conversation with Rish last night. I heard voices inside and paused momentarily at the door.

"Riya Biha is being groomed by Princess Meera to marry her brother. Ask Cousin Mani to send Sudha to the capital to spend some time with the princess," said Rish.

Queen Charu replied, "I have been thinking about it. Why don't you stop at Vindhya palace on the way to Saral and convey the message yourself? You haven't seen your mother in a while."

I did not hear Rish's reply. After a pause, the queen continued, "I heard Princess Meera has grown fond of you. Your mission to head the search is ingenious."

I heard Rish smirk, and my heart sank into my stomach. My stepmother crowed, "Jay worships his sister. Once you marry Meera, we can control him and the kingdom. Vindhya glory would be restored."

With my heart pounding, I waited for his response. "Cousin Charu, please do not build castles out of thin air. I have just earned Meera's trust. There are many other obstacles in my path, and I need to overcome them one by one."

"Yes, the king would not easily agree to a union with a man with no titles."

Wanting to hear no more, I left. I had been a fool to trust a Vindhya man. I acted like any other young girl, forgetting I was a princess and a pawn in the royal game of chess. It shamed me to realize how easily he earned my trust and manipulated me with his charm.

I stood in the balcony later and watched him ride away on his horse, with the wind blowing his hair. Rage filled my stomach like a smoldering fire, at Rish, at me, and the gods for playing with my life. I would not let anyone use me to manipulate Jay and this kingdom, even men who have professed their love for me.

5

Princess in Saral

Blackness pressed all around me. I knew I had to fight it, but I had no strength left. I let it take over my senses and fell into a deep slumber. I heard someone calling my name, "Prince Jay," and I woke up in deep water, struggling to breathe. I tried to swim to the surface, but rocks tied to my legs pulled me down. I tossed and turned in the endless water and gave up when my limbs could no longer move. Blackness took over again.

My eyes opened, and I saw a beautiful *Apsara* pouring some nectar down my throat. I must have died and gone to heaven. I tried to move my lips to thank the mythical nymph, but no sounds came out. Instead, the pain came from nowhere. This must be hell, and I was being burned alive. Before I could scream, blackness took over again.

I tried to open my eyes, but why did it feel like my lashes were stuck together? I felt soft hands wipe my warm forehead with a wet cloth. Then I heard singing in a low voice. I had heard the song before. It calmed me, and I drifted back to sleep.

I heard voices talking in a whisper, and I could barely make out words.

"How is he doing?" asked a male voice.

"He is better. His fever is down. He should gain consciousness soon," answered a female voice.

"We cannot keep his presence secret for long. There are already—"

They moved away, and I could no longer hear them. My eyes opened a slit, and light flooded in. I shut them, unable to bear the brightness. I needed to remember something important, but sleep overtook me.

Gentle hands held me and fed me a warm liquid. Milk and honey with herbs. The drink soothed my parched throat. As I took a breath, I could smell coconut and jasmine. My eyes opened a touch, and I saw a young girl about my age. Her long hair hung in a braid over her shoulder and touched my chest. I opened my eyes wider and gazed at her face. She could very well be a heavenly *Apsara*. Perhaps I had died after all.

Her eyes lit upon seeing me awake, and her face broke into a slow smile. She laid my head down and stood.

A slender girl with muscles in her arms that spoke of hard work. She wore a simple sari, in the color of the sky after sunset, deep blue and not yet black, with a parting in the middle of her legs. As I gazed into her eyes, wondering if I had met her before, her voice startled me.

"Prince Jay, I have been nursing you to health for the past several days. You are quite the fighter."

Memories flooded back into my mind. Jay, my given name. I remembered a festival I attended with my friends. Elephants, why did I think of them? I tried to sit up, but excruciating pain rushed through my back, abdomen, and legs.

The girl hurried to my side, but she appeared shy about touching me.

"Jay, you were hurt in the scuffle, and your body needs time to heal."

I laid back on the bed with my eyes closed, waiting for the pain to subside. She handed me the cup with the rest of the milk. I grasped the beverage in my hands and raised my head slowly. I took a small sip and stared at her.

"Who are you? Where am I?"

"You will know shortly." She left the room. Worry nagged me. Where was I? What had happened to my men?

I drank some more of the milk and looked around. The bare room only held the bed, a bench, and two chairs. No art or other decorations adorned the walls. Light filtered in through a foot-wide window that ran along the top of the wall on one side. I saw just one door leading out of the room and heard footsteps approaching from outside it.

As I wondered whether to pretend to be asleep, the girl entered with a man I had met before. At the festival, I had kept my head low, hoping to mimic the demeanor of a servant, when my eyes caught those of a man across the street. Tall, with a turban wrapped around his head and a thick beard on his face, he'd stared back at me.

As the procession ended, darkness descended on us, and I could not spot him across the street. Just then, Shiv moved in front of me as the same man walked up to us. He stopped in the shadows and said, "I am the son of the village elder. I have not seen you in Maram before." He had three men behind him, and their postures reminded me of guards.

About to respond, I realized I played a part. I kept my eyes downcast and looked at Balan. I could see Balan studying them before he replied, "My brother and I were just passing through this area. We heard many wonderful things about the festival and came to watch it."

Even as Balan spoke, I could feel the man's eyes on me. He then said cheerfully, "This festival means a lot to Maram, and we were glad we could run it this year. There is still a war going on in Saral, so travel safely."

With that, he and his men parted, and we made our way back to the palace along with the dispersing crowd.

The same man now entered without his beard or turban. His eyes gave him away. They appeared to penetrate my thoughts, and he smirked, "Cousin Jay, we meet again after our chance encounter in Maram. I have been eager to see you since I heard you arrived in Saral. I still underestimated you when I sent only a dozen men to capture you. I heard you almost single-handedly defeated them all. You are a beardless boy, but fight like a man."

Next to him, I did look like a child. As a man in his early twenties, he knew how to insult an opponent while appearing to compliment them. Let him continue to underestimate me. I was my father's son and the son of his forefathers. Did we both play a part that day, with him as the son of the chief and me as the servant? If he had recognized me, then that would explain the attack that night.

Having called me *cousin*, I knew who he must be. "Prince Nakul, I wish I could have made your acquaintance in a different place and time, on a battlefield with our swords drawn." And if all I had heard of him was true, son and heir of King Surya, he would be a worthy opponent to vanquish and conquer Saral.

He smiled, and his mouth curled up just like Meera's before he said, "Your wish may yet come true. I found you at the footsteps of death. My sister nursed you back to health and saved you from the clutches of Yama."

The girl boasted, "Yama is not a forgiving god and does not like to be cheated. He probably claimed a different victim."

Standing side by side, I could see the similarities between them. She must be his sister, Princess Aranya. She looked more beautiful than any girl I had seen. One would almost be tempted to become ill, just so she would care for him.

I shook my head to clear such thoughts and then grimaced in pain. The pain cleared my head, and I focused on Prince Nakul.

I remembered the fight, my men falling one by one, leaving me alone and surrounded by half a dozen men. Did Kapil, Balan, and Shiv die? I recalled Vasu lying on the ground, looking at me with his eyes open. Why had he not come to my aid? Which of my friends betrayed me? The hurt from this thought overwhelmed my physical pain. I must have lost the fight, and instead of killing me, Prince Nakul captured and brought me here. What happened to General Devan and my guards? Were they still searching for me? These thoughts flashed through my mind in the blink of an eye.

The room felt hot, and sweat trickled down my neck. "How long have I been unconscious?" I asked Nakul. I had a thousand other questions on my tongue, and I struggled to project a calm demeanor.

"Less than a fortnight," he responded.

The news of my disappearance had probably reached my father and sister. They must be in agony. I'd never felt so powerless. I clenched my fists. I perceived no immediate danger to my life, but I did not know what King Surya had in mind for me.

"Prince Nakul and Princess Aranya, I am grateful for your efforts to restore my health. I would like to return to Theni immediately."

He sneered. "Prince Jay, you are our prisoner. You would do well to remember that." With quick steps, he left, his sister trailing behind.

Soon, I heard more footsteps. A guard peeked in before shutting the door to my room, leaving me alone.

In no capacity to fight my way out, I had to wait and see what happened. I felt like prey caught in a net, dreading the arrival of the hunter.

Later in the day, a physician came in with two men.

"What happened to me?" I asked. Ignoring my question, he removed my old bandages and cleaned my abdomen wounds. Pain overwhelmed me, and I bit my lips to prevent a scream from escaping.

A slow rage built in me and the agony did not help. I took a deep breath to stay calm. As a captive, it would not help me to antagonize him.

He applied a fresh herb mixture and rewrapped them as the men held me.

Wiping his hands, he said disinterestedly, "You were stabbed in your stomach. You had lost blood and were brought to me late. But you are a fighter and are healing well." He left the room. The two men remained, cleaning me with warm water before changing my clothes.

Princess Aranya did not appear again. Instead, one of the men brought me watered-down porridge. I managed to sit up in bed and feed myself.

Sleep eluded me that night. As I stayed awake, a figure entered the room. I shut my eyes and lay still. A hand touched my forehead, and I grasped it, opening my eyes. My eyes fell on the princess.

"Aranya," I whispered, letting go of her hand. She looked like a deer ready to bolt at the sight of a tiger.

I need to befriend her to escape this place, so I continued whispering, "Please don't leave. The porridge I ate earlier was tasteless, and I remember you feeding me milk that tasted like nectar. Even some water would do."

She brought a cup to my lips, and I drank thirstily. "Water has never tasted sweeter. I did not thank you properly for saving my life."

She shook her head, "You did not thank me at all."

She seemed a nice girl, and I needed allies more than ever. Before I left Akash, my father took me aside and said if I captured or killed Surya, my marriage to Aranya would bring peace to the two kingdoms. He wanted me to avoid harming her or Prince Nakul. As the crown prince, marriage always seemed a duty for me to fulfill. I'd never given much thought to the girl I would marry. Until now.

"Let me rectify that mistake. My immense gratitude to you. I have been reckless with my life before, embarking on dangerous adventures with little regard for my safety. Now that you have saved me, my life has become all the more precious. And I would never have seen you if I had died earlier."

With her hands on her hips, she chided me, "There is a story about a different Malla Prince, who stole a Saral girl away. This Saral girl will not be so easy to sway."

"I am glad you know my parents' story. You are wrong, though, in how it unfolded. My father, the Malla prince at the time, had never met such a beauty till he set eyes on the Saral girl. Even the Malla crown could not keep him away. He risked his life to claim her as his wife," I said, gazing into her eyes. In the moonlight, they shone brightly.

She smiled at my story. The sleeping guard in the doorway murmured, and she said, "I need to leave."

I suddenly longed for her to stay.

"You could tell me a story about your people."

"They are your people, too," she teased.

I agreed, "My mother hailed from Saral, and I have seen very little of it." I had been stuck in castles and forts and now in this prison.

She whispered, "If the stars align, I can show you this beautiful land." She paused. "I will do my best to return tomorrow with a story to tell." Then she left, leaving behind a trail of flowery scent.

The day passed slowly. I had no company except for the guard outside, who ignored me. A month back, I wished for some solitude from my constant company. I had it now, along with some pain. Life delivered what you ask for in unexpected ways.

A boy came in to give me my food but refused to answer my questions. He may have been deaf. My father employed a deaf oarsman so he could have private conversations on his boat.

Once alone again, I slowly put my feet on the floor and tried to get up. The room spun, and I almost collapsed. I held on to the bedpost for a while till the spinning stopped. Then I took my first step, and I almost keeled over in pain. Kapil would have mocked me for my weakness. He pushed me to fight harder, run farther, and climb higher. We grew up as brothers. Did he betray me? I cursed under my breath at the festering doubts.

I gritted my teeth and took the next steps. The ten feet to the water basin took all my strength, and I ran out of breath, but a slow smile spread on my face. Yes, I smiled at walking, but yesterday I stayed on my back, unable to move. I walked around slowly for some more time and then went back to my bed.

Alone in the room, with just my thoughts, I became despondent, and time passed very slowly. When dusk turned to night, I longed for the company of Aranya, the only friendly face in this forsaken place. But she never came, and I drifted off to sleep.

The next day, the physician came in again and inspected my wounds.

"You are healing well. Soon, some scars are all you will have to remind you of the injury," he said as he applied new herb paste on them.

"Can I move around?" I asked, to hear my voice, as much as to learn his answer.

"As long as you don't lift anything heavy, I don't see why not," he answered and departed soon after. "But be careful as too much movement may cause the wound to reopen."

Being young had its uses. You might get into more fights, but also healed faster from the injuries. The same two men from before came in. As they helped me change, one of them leaned in.

Did he whisper "Somu" or did I imagine it? Somu, my loyal servant, hailed from Saral. He'd come to Malla with my mother, Kayal, and remained there ever since. If anyone could get a message to me, it would be him. Before I could react, the guards finished and started to leave.

"My basin water needs to be changed," I shouted before they left.

The man who had leaned in came back, took the basin, and left. I stood up and walked slowly to the basin pedestal, grimacing in pain with each step. I held the pedestal tightly till the pain abated. I felt a tiny grain better than yesterday. Wiping the sweat off my forehead, I waited for him with my heart pounding.

He returned with fresh water and set the basin down. With his back to the guard, he whispered, "My lord, Somu is looking for a way to get you out. Meanwhile, he wanted you to get better, so you can be ready to depart when the time is right." Then he left, leaving me alone.

Relief filled me at his words, and I walked back slowly to the bed. Somu knew I lived. As time passed, my thoughts turned darker. Could this be a ploy by the Saral? To what end? I was already their captive.

Either way, I needed to get better. I took a few more turns around the room, willing my body to heal.

Sleep eluded me, and I heard the guard outside snore lightly. So much for my bravery. Even my captors did not fear my escape. Why would they? I had no strength to wield a weapon, let alone fight an opponent. And I did not carry my sword. My great-grandfather's sword. Before my departure to Saral, my father had handed me a newly polished sword, which shone brightly in the sunlight. The pommel had an ornate tiger carved on it.

He said, "Son, this is the sword made for your great-grandfather, and he won many victories with it. I would like to you to wield it. May it serve you as well as it did the great King Jay."

I'd taken the gift from him reverently and held it in my hands. I could imagine my great-grandfather fighting with this magnificent weapon. I looked at my father and said quietly, "I hope I can do you and our ancestors proud."

I'd failed to rise to this honor. Instead of capturing new cities, I let myself be captured, and the sword stripped from my person.

As I lay awake, the Princess walked in. My gaze followed her as she glanced at me and then went to sit down on the bench near the wall.

The bench had room for two, and her eyes beckoned me. With assured steps, I approached her and settled down, not worrying about the propriety of it. Her earrings were simple and made of gold with one stone set on it. It shone in the moonlight and cast a web of light on her face. I lowered my glance, and it fell on her breasts, rising and falling with her breath. Something stirred in me, and I averted my eyes. I needed to gain her trust, not be captivated by her. She twirled the ends of her hair in her fingers.

Why was she here, alone, in the middle of the night? "What do you plan to do with me, Aranya?"

"Your fate lies with my father, King Surya," she responded.

"With a daughter like you, he must be a noble and generous man."

"He is to his people. For his enemies, he is the incarnation of the death god."

"Then, I do not wish to be his enemy. We can become family, if he agrees to this Malla prince marrying a Saral princess," I replied softly.

Her lips curled like she was about to smile. She took a deep breath and said, "My father is still seeking revenge for the other Malla prince who stole a Saral girl."

I studied her lips. They were small and inviting. "Is there a way to pacify him?"

She mocked me. "There is. My father wanted a Malla princess to wed a Saral prince. Your father said no to a match between Princess Meera and Prince Nakul."

I sighed. "I don't claim to understand the workings of a ruler's mind. My father has been hesitant to part with Meera whether the suitor is Prince Nakul or Prince Amar."

"Prince Amar may be back as a suitor. We received news that his wife died in childbirth," she said.

King Verma of Padi sought Meera's hand before for his son Amar and would do so again. If they thought I was missing or worse, dead, my father would have to agree to the match. A sense of urgency came over me, and I felt weak and helpless once again.

I cajoled, "You saved my life. Now you and I can save our kingdoms from this war. Our union would bring peace to our people."

"Is that the only reason you would seek my hands?" she whispered.

I hesitated to reply. She tended to me herself while I laid unconscious. She could easily have had her servants do the work. And she sought my company tonight. I decided to be truthful.

"Many a girl has vied for my affections. Almost all of them had no idea what it is to be a Queen. A King has to place his Kingdom above all else, to be a good ruler. That means he would demand sacrifices from his family. I can see you are accustomed to such sacrifices with the ongoing war depriving you of the comforts of palace life. You are also independent-minded because you snuck into my room in the middle of the night. I assume you chose the guard yourself to allow such excursions. Such a sharp and independent mind would be an invaluable asset to me."

I raised my hand and held her chin lightly and turned her towards me. "Given time, I am sure we could grow fond of each other."

Her eyes caused a riot of emotions in me, and I lowered mine and landed on her lips. Instinctively, I leaned in and kissed her. The assault on my body threatened to overpower me when she weakly pushed against my chest. That brought me to my senses and I broke apart gasping for breath. She seemed in no better state than me. I have kissed a few girls before, but I did not remember these overwhelming sensations.

Before I could say anything, Aranya fled the room. I went to my bed, reliving the moment. Here I hoped to win an ally, and I was enchanted by her. That would not do. I needed to escape this place and come the time; I might have to do deeds without regard for her life. Even as I had that thought, my mind and body protested. I tried to quench the protests. In my sleep that night, dreams alternated between kissing a beautiful maiden and drowning in water.

I woke up and started my day with some sun salutations. I ignored the pain spreading through my stomach. Then I closed my eyes and allowed the rays to warm my eyelids. Refreshed, I started doing some of my sword training with no sword in my hand. When I heard movement outside, I stopped and lay on my bed.

The servant walked in with my morning meal. He deposited it on the table and started to leave when I said, "Can you bring me some books?" He left without acknowledging me.

I ate my food and ambled around the room. When no books were brought, I gave up hope. But a book of poems arrived with my mid-day meal. Saral poems on ordinary men and women. I sat on the chair and slowly started to read. A poem where the man describes his love for the girl he left behind on travels brought the image of Aranya to my mind. I shut the book and set it aside.

There were no sightings of the Princess in the next few days, but my body journeyed on the road to recovery. I walked more easily. I grew impatient for news from the outside world, and a glimmer of hope arrived that day. The man who whispered Somu's name to me before came in with my meals that day, and he whispered, "Tomorrow," as he left.

Tomorrow, I thought, *will put an end to this.* How would Somu craft my escape? In the evening, I contemplated various plans and how I could aid without a sword. Suddenly, Princess Aranya walked in, her eyes darting around the room, and shut the door. She held my sword and some clothes and appeared greatly disturbed.

"Jay," she whispered, "you need to leave now. I will help you escape." Then she handed me my sword, a coin bag, and the clothes. "Change into these."

I stared at her confused, and said, "Wait. Why are you allowing me to leave?"

She continued to hand me the clothes, and I grabbed her waist, forcing her to face me.

"Aranya, what is going on?" I whispered.

She gazed at me and said haltingly, "My father plans to kill you as revenge for what your father did. He will be here tomorrow and then—"

She paused and glanced at me and held out the clothes.

I considered her and could tell she spoke the truth. "Turn around," I said and changed into the guard's clothes. There was a false beard in her bundle, and I tried tying it around my head.

"Come and help me," I called out, and she cautiously peeked at me. Seeing me fully clothed and struggling with the beard brought a smile to her face. She came forward and helped me tie on the beard and wrap the turban on my head. I took the sword and regarded her.

"Follow me like a Saral soldier," she said and walked ahead. I followed a step behind, trying to act like a guard. As she opened the door and headed out, my eyes glanced around nervously. She quickened her pace, and I followed suit. Then she started talking, "I want you to head to my father and tell him we are ready." I only half-listened while keeping an eye for suspicious activity.

We arrived at a makeshift stable, and I wondered what to do next. Would I, pretending to be a soldier, grab a horse myself? Aranya had already thought of it and said, "Here is your horse, ready for your journey." She headed towards a horse, and I followed suit.

"Come with me," I whispered. She had tears in her eyes and shook her head.

I mounted and hesitated for the blink of an eye. Then I reached down and grabbed her waist. I hoisted her up in front of me and took off with the horse. Two men watching us in the stables raised an alarm, and I could hear men following me. Aranya gazed at me intently. I hoped she could not sense the confusion in me. I knew not whether I brought her as my bride, or as my hostage. The horse neared a forest, and as I pulled the reins to guide the beast to the road, she whispered, "In here," and pointed to a copse of trees.

She directed me deeper into the forest along a dirt path. The sun set when we lost the men in pursuit and I slowed the horse. The ride had tired me and we had to find a place for the night.

"There is a small cave not far from here," Aranya suggested.

"Would your brother look for you there?" I asked.

"Yes, but he is away. His letter to me earlier today divulged my father's intentions. But others might know of my fondness for this hide-out. There is a temple further along and would be closed for the night. We can find shelter there."

6

Flood Waters

Akash bustled as usual: temple bells tolled, bullock carts arrived with goods, horses cantered carrying men, and swords clanged on the training yard. The familiar sounds filled me with a yearning for my life a few months ago. Singing and dancing with my friends and worried about what to wear to a feast. I rarely ventured out the last few days, my mind swirling in turmoil. Thinking alternatively about Jay and Rish, I despaired. Should I go to father with what I'd learned? Going to father would mean talking about my naivete. I found the thought unpleasant and decided against it.

I sat by a window, overlooking the palace gardens, not taking in the view. I considered myself clever and well versed in palace intrigue. Rish had broken my confidence to pieces, like an elephant crushing a coconut with its foot. He'd schemed with my stepmother to marry me, and I had entrusted him with finding Jay. Oh, Mother! What have I done?

I rose to my feet and paced around the room. I locked my feelings for Jay and Rish in a small corner of my mind and thought dispassionately. Without Jay, my father would be inclined to marry me to a prince, to protect the kingdom. If Rish wanted to marry me, his best hope lay in finding Jay and claiming glory. Not that I would be inclined to accept his hands. I sighed. These thoughts did little to soothe me.

With Rish gone, the castle felt like a golden cage. Though it seemed he had no genuine affection for me, the man had his uses. With him at my side, I could move freely around the capital. In his absence, I found my movements curbed. My stepmother did not approve of my trips outside the city walls. I could have gone to my father to get permission, but Jay's disappearance and the kingdom's future lay heavily on his head, and I did not want to bother him with my minor grievances.

My father worried me. News of Jay had caused a setback in his health. His beard grew greyer than before. My stepmother, always the dutiful Queen, seemed outwardly devoted to him. What plots hatched in her mind? She would only be queen as long as father lived, so I could not imagine her harming him. Since I'd overheard her with Rish, every shadow, breath, and whisper arose my suspicion. My neck and shoulders ached in pain.

"My lady, you have not touched your food," lamented Kantha, bringing me back to the present. I suddenly realized the ridiculousness of my self-pity. My eight-year-old self would be ashamed. The smell of rain wafted in, and I blurted, "Warm-up my food. I will come back and eat."

I went to the court physician, told him to check on my father, and report back to me. The man had served him loyally for years. On my way back to my room, I decided I would try to get a message to Kapil to keep an eye on Rish. I returned to find Kantha waiting with some of my favorite dishes. Eggplant stew, bitter gourd cooked in jaggery, and a steaming bowl of sesame and coconut rice tempted me.

"I worried about you, my lady," Kantha searched my face. "You have not seemed like yourself for the past few days." I stepped forward and embraced her.

"I needed time to reflect." And mourn.

I decided to spend more time with my father, eating some meals with him. This seemed to cheer him up, and I could find out the goings-on in the kingdom through our conversations. I went with him on short walks in his garden to help him get some fresh air. Today, after we walked, we sat on a bench and admired the peacocks. Father had white peacocks in his garden. His mother, Queen Mother Priya, brought the parents of the current pride from Padi.

"Sing me a song, child," Father asked. I sang a song about a Malla king who wanted peace on his land and still had to take up his sword to achieve that peace. My father's eyes lingered on my face as I finished singing and said, "You look like my mother, but you sing like yours."

Then, the conversation turned to marriage. "Meera, if your mother still lived, you would have been married before your eighteenth birthday. With her gone, I did not want to deprive Jay of your company. He would be seventeen and a grown man soon. Malla needs strong allies, and both you and your brother's marriages can provide us that. I hoped to marry you to the Prince of Padi and your brother to the Princess of Saral. Things have not worked out that way, and now we are at war with Saral." My father paused in his thoughts. Emotions welled up in my throat, and I swallowed them. Futile to think of my plans to marry Rish.

He continued, "The three chiefs have asked me to consider marrying Jay to one girl from each of their households. Vindhya, Biha, and Thari are the foundation of the Malla kingdom, and this would strengthen our kingdom. I held out hope that he could marry King Surya's daughter first to avoid bloodshed, but we cannot put off Jay's marriage for long." He paused and rubbed his eyes. I could tell Jay's disappearance weighed heavily on him, especially while speaking of future plans.

"When he comes back from Saral, I will have to arrange this wedding. You, my child, I cannot bear to part. Once, King Verma and I had discussed marriage between you and his son Amar. But Amar is married now, and I don't want to condemn you to a second wife role, with little chance of you or your offspring sitting on the throne. Also, over the years, I have heard things about Amar that give me cause for concern. Verma's second son, Atul, is your age or younger, I don't remember now. But with an older brother —," he paused here in thought. "Chief Bhoj's son, Giri, is a good boy and though beneath you in rank, would be an able partner for your brother in governance. And most importantly, you could continue to live in Akash. We will find suitable alliances for both of you and have the weddings when Jay comes back from Lukla."

Giri Thari, a young man about my age, served in the Northern command with his uncle, General Karan Thari. I'd met him on a few occasions when he and his younger brother, Shiv, trained with Jay here in Akash. They were always deferential to me. Giri appeared to be a quiet man. He looked rather plain, but princesses did not marry for looks. I remembered watching Rish train the new recruits, his bare chest glistening with sweat. I shook my head. Why does my foolish heart keep thinking about a man who betrayed me?

"Why does King Surya refuse his daughter's hand to Jay?" I asked. I also thought it strange that my father did not mention Prince Nakul as a match for me. Maybe, he did not want to ally that closely with Saral, if Jay married the princess. Or was he trying to ally with both Saral and Padi?

"There is a reason in his mind." My father sighed. "It is a long story, my child. I will tell it to you one day soon."

With my brother gone and my father sick, I decided to take a more active interest in governance. Chief Kasu thought I meddled too much in the affairs of the state. Why was it strange for a princess to care for her kingdom? Even if I had to marry and go live elsewhere, wouldn't I be expected to take an interest in my husband's affairs?

My stepmother seemed to expect me to spend my day with my companions. It would serve the Vindhya interests for me to while away my time. In the past, my companions loved to do each other's hair and face and get dressed in splendid outfits. With most young men gone from the city, this activity lost its luster. When Rish lived in the city, I joined them in trying out the latest hairstyles. I did not occupy all my time in matters of the kingdom. I continued singing with my friends, especially some of the beautiful folk songs on the Malla kingdom. The songs about my great-grandfather Jay and his conquests filled me with pride, and I wanted to help my brother build such a kingdom. He had the capacity to rise to the occasion.

One day, father shared some worrisome tidings from Padi about

Prince Amar itching to conquer Malla. King Verma ruled Padi, the mountainous region located north of Malla. During my great-grandfather's reign, Padi had signed a peace treaty with Malla. When Jay left for Saral a few months back, Prince Amar reportedly urged his father to mount an attack. King Verma resisted because he saw no quick path to victory. King Verma had married the Sunda princess, an alliance made during the last battle, that my grandfather and uncle fought in. Padi and Malla had combined forces to defeat Sunda then, and the Sunda King would ally with his sister and nephews to defeat Malla now. What would happen if the word of Jay's disappearance reaches Padi? Would Amar try again to attack us?

I decided to visit the houses where the families of the soldiers in the Southern and Northern post lived. The women whose husbands or sons had gone to Saral with Jay appeared eager for news, and I shared what I knew, keeping back Jay's disappearance. They, in turn, informed me about the latest tidings from their husbands or sons. I asked if I could help these men or their families. Father had always stressed the importance of taking care of the men who serve you. The women worried about the approaching winter in the Northern post. I assured them all the necessary precautions against the cold would be taken by General Karan Thari.

One of the girls brought her newborn to me. The baby appeared weak and sick and had stopped nursing. I promised I would send a physician.

After the visit, I saw the Court Physician to inquire after father's health. He had a kind face and smiled at me. "The king's physical wounds are healing slowly. The welfare of this nation is on his shoulders, and the strain of it is why he is not making a fast recovery. Don't worry, my lady. He is a fighter and will overcome this." I could not sit on the throne, but I could share some of his burdens. I would help him govern where I could.

Then I told the Physician about the baby. He said he would send one of his students. I visited the Minister afterward to pass on the other requests of the families.

The outing lifted my bleak mood. People needed occasional help from their government, and I could do my small part, even if it is just sending for a few physicians.

The rains pounded Akash in the next few days. The well-built city had good drainage, and the water receded in a day or two after the rains. But some of the neighboring villages on the river bed were not so fortunate. The river overflowed and flooded them. Messengers arrived carrying news of destroyed homes, ruined crops, and lost lives.

The king called for a council meeting and invited me to join. Chief Kasu Vindhya, Chief Guard Mano Biha, General Devan Biha, and Minister Kripa were gathered in the small throne room. Father asked Chief Kasu what measures he'd taken to help.

"My king, I have released grains from our granary to feed the villagers for a week. Besides, we are sending clothes and supplies. The carts will leave Akash tomorrow along with Chief Mano's men."

I fought the urge to roll my eyes. Knowing Chief Kasu, he probably released old grains that would have gone bad, if not used soon, and clothes that would otherwise be discarded.

"What from you, Mano?" my father asked.

Chief Mano responded, "I am sending ten elephants to help with the rescue efforts and clean up uprooted trees. Twenty medics will also accompany the carts to treat the wounded. Also, 200 men will go with them to aid in the rescue effort and keep the peace."

My father nodded in approval.

Chief Kasu added, "These villages are in Thari lands, so I would like to send a letter to Chief Bhoj Thari to ask him to provide additional grains and supplies this year to replenish our reserves."

Men like Chief Kasu had their virtue in helping run a kingdom smoothly and making tough decisions. In times of crisis, when you needed to show compassion to the people's suffering, the same virtue turned into a handicap.

My father frowned. "Chambal River has played havoc along Thari. Bhoj has his hands full dealing with damage to his people, and crops. Now is not the time to demand more from him. Biha and Vindhya are unaffected by the floods, so ask them to provide the additional grains we need."

Chief Kasu did not look happy, but he did not disagree with his king. Left to himself, he would have done the minimum needed and left before people were back on their feet, not realizing the shortsighted nature of his decision.

Minister Kripa asked, "Who should we send to oversee the efforts, my Majesty?"

I thought about my desire to share my father's burden. I hesitated briefly and then said softly, "Father?"

He turned and looked at me kindly. "Yes, Meera."

I cleared my throat and spoke louder. "Father, traditionally someone from the royal family, has gone to inspect the damages and offer support to the people. You and mother are indisposed and Jay..." I could not say aloud that our enemies captured my brother or worse. "Jay is in Saral. Please allow me to go to the villages."

My stepmother looked like she would say something. She would not approve of me getting involved in visiting flooded villages or any other matter of the state. Previously, I would have naively fallen for her narrative that a woman's role revolved around her family, but since I caught her plotting with Rish, I had changed my mind. She wanted to reduce my influence, and I would not play along. With Jay missing, I needed to be his and father's eyes and ears.

My father said, "I wish I could go myself. With that not possible, sending you will be the next best thing." With his consent, I looked forward to leaving the capital for a few days, where every sight and sound would not remind me of the missing men in my life.

The next day, I got ready early in the morning. I went to my father's chambers to bid him and my mother farewell. After obtaining their blessings, I went outside and found Riya Biha. I decided last night to take Riya along with me. I had neglected her, in the past few days, with other pressing matters on my mind. I hoped to rekindle our friendship during this journey. With the roadways still flooded, I chose to ride in my palanquin on top of an elephant.

Our procession started soon with the men on horses in front, followed by our elephant. Behind us rode the supply carts with more guards in the rear. My maid Kantha rode in one of the supply carts. I pulled open the curtains to watch the scenery, and as we left the city, water greeted us everywhere. It covered the low-lying areas, and uprooted trees littered the roads. We progressed slowly, and I hoped we could reach the small palace on the outskirts of the flooded villages by nightfall. Riya, a normally cheerful girl, whispered, "My lady, is Prince Jay safe?"

Her father, General Devan, would have shared the news with her.

"I hope he is. There are eyes and ears everywhere. Let us keep this to ourselves."

After gaining some control of the turmoil in me, I smiled at her and said, "Jay did ask after you in his last letter to me." When I despaired, I would reread his letters. He described our mother's lands to me, and I could imagine the Chambal river flowing through Saral and the paddy fields on its banks. He did not *exactly* ask me about Riya in his letter. He wrote exasperatedly about her father talking about her.

She blushed and said, "Princess Meera, now you are teasing me. I spoke to my father last night. He showered the Prince with praise. Prince Jay had won him and his men over with his deeds."

That did not surprise me. Jay had this quality in him that made men and women alike want to follow him. The more time you spent with him, the more loyal you grew.

Riya appeared thoughtful and asked, "I wonder why women do not go with the men to fight wars? We can help treat the wounded and offer comfort."

I replied, "Because the men do not want us. They would be worried about our safety, and we would mostly get in the way. Women help in other ways, though. All the households of the soldiers in Saral, are run by women. They tend to the fields and shops and their children while the men are away."

She sighed and said, "Life would have been easier as a simple farm girl." It took me by surprise to see her echo some of Jay's thoughts.

When his newly appointed guards followed him around everywhere, day and night, he mused about the life of other sixteen-year-old boys, free to roam where they pleased. Does she wonder what her life would be like married to a king?

I said soothingly, "Farm girls have their challenges. Their life depends on Mother Nature and her fury. The girls in these flooded regions will have to worry about the lost crops and where they will get their grains for the year."

She smiled and said, "At least I don't have to worry about food."

"Or clothes," I added, and she laughed. For this short journey, she'd brought enough clothes to last a month.

"Princess Meera, when one is as beautiful as you are, there is no need to turn to clothes or jewels to enhance your looks. Even with my bright silk saris and delicate gold and diamond jewels, one boy in particular never took notice of me," she added wistfully.

"Jay respects and honors women. Once you are betrothed to him, I am sure he will shower you with attention," I said with as much conviction as I could muster. He would marry for duty. Would he also marry for love?

We plodded along uneventfully for the most part, though the flood slowed us down in places. Riya engaged my mind, not allowing it to race many miles, into lands best kept hidden. I treasured this beautiful girl's company, with her keen insight and cheery disposition. Even if my father did not agree to Jay marrying the daughters of the three chiefs, Riya rose above other women as a worthy consort for a king.

Along the way, we talked about our life in Akash. Our conversation kept me from delving deep into my own chaotic emotions for Rish. We reached the small palace by nightfall.

As the elephant came to a stop, I resisted the temptation to slide down the back, like I had done as a child with my father on hand to catch me. With my luck, I would end up sprawled on the ground. I imagined the shock on the men's face, and this thought brought a smile to my lips. Instead, I waited for the guards to bring my stool, and I dismounted regally.

The small palace contained only ten rooms. Adjacent to it stood a temple. Both these structures were made out of granite and had survived the torrential rains. The temple sheltered the people who'd lost their homes or could not get to their homes due to the flood.

In the courtyard, the men had set up stoves to cook a stew of rice, lentils, and vegetables, and the aroma of pungent chilies and peppers wafted up. Darkness settled around us, impeding a meeting with the villagers, so I headed to the room assigned to me to get some rest. With only ten rooms, I asked Riya to share mine. Kantha came in and helped me clean up.

"Princess Meera and Riya, would you like to join the men below for your evening meal? If not, I can fetch your food and bring it here."

Riya said, "Being on top of the elephant all day has made me lose my appetite. I am just going to lie down."

I could stay in the room, but I'd traveled all this way to comfort the villagers affected and offer them aid. Ignoring my tired body, I uttered, "Kantha, tell the men I will join them."

Soon, one of Mano's men, Guna, came to escort me. He bowed and said, "My lady, I am delighted you can join us." As I followed him, I saw a line of people waiting in the courtyard.

"Guna," I spoke, and he stopped. "I want to say a few words to the folks."

"My lady, allow me to get additional guards," he said, but I did not wait for him. These were simply people affected by the flood, and I did not need guards holding them back. I walked down the steps and arrived at the courtyard. When the villagers saw me, a murmur went through the crowd. Some said my name.

I arrived at where they stood and said, "Your king is concerned about the floods and the toll it has taken on you. He sent me here to offer what support I can. I will meet with you in the morning to hear your concerns."

I heard a chorus of "Victory to King Vikram and Long Live Princess Meera" and I walked back up. Guna strode by my side, alert, with his hand on his sword. He escorted me to a terrace where men gathered around a fire. A half-moon shone up in the sky, and its light reflected in the water around us. The pillar nearby had a flaming torch mounted on it, and its light cast eerie shadows on the terrace. The men grew quieter as I came near, and Guna led me to a seat. I sat and looked around. Most of them were young, about the same age as Jay, when he left for Saral.

Guna sat beside me. "I hope you traveled here in comfort," he said.

"Yes, I love riding on an elephant. Being up so high, you can almost imagine you are flying," I said. He smiled. Servants arrived then and served us the stew. The meal appeared simple, but the men around me ate with a ravenous appetite.

Soon the conversations started again. One boy mustered courage and asked, "Princess Meera, we heard the news about Prince Jay. We are all at the ready to head south and join the search. We would move mountains to find him and bring him back." Others nodded in agreement, and I panicked that these men knew of Jay's disappearance. I could sense a hunger in them that food could not satisfy. Young men and their desire for glory on a battlefield have led to many wars. But Jay's search needed stealth. If Mano's men knew about his disappearance, soon it would spread far and wide. I despaired thinking about how Padi and Prince Amar would react.

Taking a deep breath to hide my anguish, I said, "Our king will be happy to hear about your loyalty to the Prince. General Devan has made all the arrangements, and the king has sent additional men from Akash. Our place is now in the capital, protecting her and the king. Let us make sure we keep the story about Jay to ourselves."

Rish had warned me it would be difficult to keep the lid on information about Jay. Accounts of his disappearance would cause pain to our allies and elation among our enemies.

As the conversation turned to other subjects, I brought my attention back to the flood and said to Guna, "Tomorrow morning, I would like to meet with the villagers. Can you make arrangements for that?"

"I will, my lady."

"Where are the wounded being treated?"

"In the temple courtyard, my lady. With only one doctor to help us, many have gone untreated. With the physicians we brought from Akash, there should be enough to treat all the sick and injured."

A cool breeze blew in the terrace. I tried to wrap the sari around me to keep me warm, but the cold penetrated it. I pictured Rish's hands wrapped around my body and my body drawing warmth from his chest. A shudder went through me again, but not from the cold. I cursed my weak and treacherous body.

After the meal, I headed back to my room. Riya slept through the noise I made getting ready for bed. That night I dreamt of flying across the skies on an elephant. Rish sat on the elephant, and I sat behind him. He turned and smiled at me and asked me to hold on tight to him. Then he flew the beast over Akash, and I looked down on the city. Suddenly, I lost my balance and fell from the elephant. Rish tried to grab my hands, but he missed. As I tumbled, I woke up in a sweat. My gaze fell on Kantha, braiding Riya's hair.

When she saw me, she said. "Princess Meera, Guna is ready and waiting to take you to see the flood victims." I nodded and started getting ready. Once she finished with Riya, Kantha helped me put my hair up. I wore an unadorned sari in the color blue found in peacock feathers. After a simple meal of fruits and milk, we went out. Gesturing with his hands, Guna talked to some men as we approached him. When they saw me, they bowed.

"My lady, I can have the men bring the palanquin for you," he said.

The temple stood about 200 yards away, and I would have preferred to walk. But the path lay strewn with water puddles, and I could not arrive in a mud-stricken sari. I agreed, and the palanquin arrived. After Riya and I climbed up, four men carried us on their shoulders. Guna rode on his horse in front, and other guards followed.

Riya leaned in and whispered, "My lady, all these puddles remind me of my childhood in Biha. After the rains, my brothers and I would run around to find the deepest pool of rainwater and then jump in and splash water all over our clothes." She grinned. "Would the guards be shocked if we jumped into the big puddle of water there?"

I replied, "If we were not among people who had lost all their possessions, the puddle would have tempted me as well."

"You are right, my lady. Thoughtless of me. I forgot my duty."

I touched her arm, comforting her. "Never apologize for thoughts of joy, Riya. They allow us to enjoy life. Simply keep in mind your surroundings before you act."

As we approached the gate, I could see the temple bustling with activity. Men had setup large stoves and cooked sweet millet porridge. Older children helped take care of the younger ones. In one of the long halls, I saw physicians tending to the sick and injured. Women wove roofs from fallen coconut and palm leaves. Once the floodwater receded, these thatched leaves would be used to rebuild the homes.

The men came to a stop inside the temple and lowered the palanquin. As I got out, a crowd of women gathered around me. Some had suckling babies on their arms.

One woman grabbed my hand, and I saw the guards moving as if to remove her. I shook my head at the guards and studied this woman. She seemed young and had a small child holding on to her legs. She peered up at me with tear-stricken eyes and pleaded, "Princess Meera, the flood came suddenly. I heard a roar, and then the water flooded our house. I grabbed my son, and my husband tried to help my father—" She sobbed and added through tears, "But we could not save him, and my husband broke his leg trying. We lost all our belongings and our crops. Please, you have to help us."

I patted her hand and said reassuringly, "The king is concerned for your wellbeing. We will provide the help you need to rebuild your lives." Nothing, however, would bring her father back. I thought about losing my father, and the idea felt like fingernails digging into my heart. I needed to steel my emotions before I heard more stories. Otherwise, I would be the one in need of comfort.

Other women spoke to me, and I listened patiently, offering them hope. They did not lack courage and just needed some help getting back on their feet.

Guna spoke to a group of orphaned boys over the age of twelve. "You can come to Akash with me and join the city guard. You will be clothed and fed and trained to protect our city." The boys looked at Guna in wonder with his splendid clothes and weapons and vigorously nodded. All of them would want to join him, but I needed to make sure only those with no younger siblings to take care of, joined the city guards. If they had siblings, the village elders would need them to take care of their families.

My mind jumped to my younger brother. That first year after my mother died, I told him to be brave and not cry when in front of others. He asked innocently what to do if he missed mother. I directed him to hold my hand when that happened. Whenever we gathered in the throne room, he held my hand tightly, not letting go. A lump formed in my throat, and I moved away.

Riya went to where the little children played. She gathered them around her and took them into the courtyard. I could hear her tell them a story, and they listened with rapt attention. I smiled, thinking of how she would be with her own children someday.

Soldiers unloaded the supplies we received from the city yesterday and stored them in one of the temple rooms. I could see two men make note of the new provisions as others placed them in the room.

I walked among the sick and injured and listened to their stories and offered what little comfort I could. Just seeing me appeared to give people hope. Most suffered minor injuries and broken bones. I watched the physicians instruct their students on how to help. The injuries would mend, and broken bones would heal in a few months, but how long before their lives returned to normal? It would be days before the floodwaters receded and many moon months before homes could be rebuilt.

In a partitioned corner, I could hear a pregnant woman screaming from her labor pains. A midwife and some older women were on hand to help her. Life did go on amidst this disaster.

As I wandered on, a group of men approached me. I stopped, and suddenly they surrounded me. Trying to stay calm, I asked, "How can I help you?"

Stepping closer, one man whispered, "Where is Prince Jay?"

My eyes darted among them, and I found no weapons on their person. The smell from their unwashed bodies attacked my nostrils.

Just then, the soldiers brought in two newly rescued children. Breathing deeply, I shouted, "He is in Saral, fighting for King Vikram."

On hearing me, one of the soldiers observed us. He quickly yelled at his men and strode towards us, drawing his sword. "Step away from the princess," he ordered. Before long, others joined him and dispersed the men. Guna spotted us and ran towards me. "I apologize for letting you out of my sight, my lady."

I took him aside and warned him. "Ask your men to stop talking about Prince Jay. Do you understand?"

He swallowed and nodded. It was no use. Once it got out, news of this nature was like spilled flour. It would get everywhere and be nearly impossible to put back in the bag.

Soon the temple bells rang, and the priest performed a *pooja*. Devotees gathered around to seek the Almighty's blessing. Then volunteers served food in the courtyard. Men, women, and children lined up to get their meals, and Riya and I headed back.

Outside, soldiers set off on boats to navigate the river and look for stranded survivors. People had been found floating in the river or holding on to treetops or grounded on rooftops. We only had another day to rescue them before they drowned or died of hunger or other causes. The additional soldiers from Akash helped with the efforts.

The palanquin halted in the palace courtyard and lowered to the ground. I got out and headed back to my room. After freshening up, Riya and I took our meals with the city guards and physicians who had come from Akash.

Afterward, I held court for merchants in the neighboring villages. They had brought in additional grains and clothes. One of the men who appeared to be their leader stepped forward and said, "Princess Meera, I welcome your presence in Thari. Please accept these gifts from me and my fellow merchants."

His servant brought in jewels and silk saris and laid them at my feet. I glanced at them briefly and turned back to him. "I accept these gifts on behalf of the king. I also appreciate all the additional supplies you brought here to help the flood victims."

"Princess Meera, we also have come to pledge additional support for the dam King Vikram and Chief Bhoj Thari are building across the Chambal River. Once the dam is built, we can prevent floods such as these. We would like to meet the king in person and pledge our support to him."

We discussed some more things, and the men left after I promised to get them an audience with the king.

That night some of the villagers performed a dance show in the courtyard for the visiting court members. With no stage or elaborate costumes, the children and adults still made the story come alive with their singing and dancing. I laughed and enjoyed the performance.

In the end, one of the older women asked, "Princess Meera, we have heard so much about your beautiful voice. Can you please sing a song for us?"

I looked at Riya and asked her to join me. We sang a song about a girl pining for her lover who had gone to the fight in a war. Riya appeared moved by the song and performed with real emotion. My thoughts turned cynical. Why do poets write only about love when it came to girls? They heaped praise on boys for valor on the battlefield or perseverance in building everlasting monuments. The girls merely longed for the men, contributing nothing else except for their devotion. Perhaps, I did not want to be tied down by love.

The next day, I asked Kantha to inform Guna that I wanted to see the dam being built across Chambal. There were no rainclouds in sight, so it would be safe to visit. I asked him to bring me a horse to ride. I hoped news of my riding a horse wouldn't reach my stepmother's ears. Riya wanted to visit the temple again and spend time with the children, so I allowed her to stay behind.

We left soon with a few guards on horses and a horse cart that pulled, among other things, a small boat. In case the roads flooded and we could not ride back, the small boat could be used. It fit only two people, so the rest of the men would have to float on the wood from the cart.

The sun blazed almost overhead when we reached the area. Instead of the calm river that feeds the earth, she appeared ferocious, tossing and turning mighty trees in her path. I could see other trees uprooted on the shore from the recent flooding. The river flowed wide here, and you could barely see the other side. Men in charge of the dam waited for me along the shore, and we stopped our horses nearby. One of the guards held his hands out for me to step on, and I dismounted.

The man in charge came up to me, bowed, and said, "Princess Meera, I am Veeranam, and I am in charge of the dam construction. We are honored to have you visit the Chambal river dam." The construction of the dam had stopped due to the rains, but I could see tens of stone pillars laid on the river. He walked with me to the site and stated, "These pillars will go across the river and reach the other shore. Once the dam is built, we can reduce the Chambal river floods. There will also be storage tanks on both sides of the river that will be used to irrigate the fields in Thari."

"When will the work resume?" I asked.

"In a fortnight, my lady, when the floodwaters recede," he replied.

I had watched masons repair the temple stonework in Akash. The sounds of chisel and hammer joined with the prayers and temple bells, created a mosaic of music, like the sweet and sour dish made of raw mango and brown sugar that I was fond of. Today, I heard the roar of waves crashing against the stone. Keen to learn more about how they carved these pillars to withstand the flood, I asked several more questions and came away impressed by how much effort went into finding the right rocks. Work for this began two years back and would be a source of pride for the Malla kingdom once completed.

After answering my questions patiently, Veeranam said, "Princess Meera, I have a simple meal prepared for your visit. I hope you can join us."

I said I would be delighted. His men laid a carpet on the floor, and Veeranam asked me to sit. As I sat, Guna and Veeranam continued standing, and I invited them to join me on the carpet. One of the men served us coconut rice on a banana leaf. As we ate, Veeranam recounted stories of the dam. My father had visited when the construction began with a *pooja* to Lord Ganesha, the remover of obstacles.

Delicately, Veeranam said, "Princess Meera, with the fighting in Saral, we have not received all the gold we asked for the construction. Winter will be soon upon us, and it will be difficult to get the rocks from Padi in winter. Please convey my wishes to the king to procure an audience with him soon."

I agreed to talk with my father.

As we got ready to depart, I told Guna, "I would like to visit the Kulam temple on the way." The priest at the temple had helped me in the past, and I needed his help again. As we neared the old temple situated a few miles away, I dismounted from my horse. Guna already walked beside me. Normally one could go on foot to the temple, but the river had flooded the area. We could only reach the place by boat. I approached him and asked, "Can you row?"

What a foolish question to ask a city guard, I thought. He replied patiently, "I grew up in the Vindhya lands where there are countless rivers, my lady. I can keep a boat afloat in these waters."

"Good. I already know your prowess with the sword. Let us go."

He hesitated for a second and then went to talk to the men. He said something to them and watched as they unloaded the boat. Two men carried it on their heads and slowly set it on the water. Guna held the vessel with one hand while I climbed in, unsteadily. It had been a while since I traveled on a boat. Rish rowed me last time. I quickly dismissed the memory.

Once I sat, he propelled us towards the temple. Debris floated in the water, and Guna navigated deftly. My mind jumped back to the vision of Rish rowing and his bare chest moving in harmony with the oars. Color crept up my face, and I turned away from Guna to look at the crows flying in the sky above. I usually traveled with female companions or Jay or Rish. Today, even among some of the king's loyal soldiers, I felt lonely.

We arrived at the temple shores, and Guna nimbly guided the boat to the shore and jumped out. As I started in the direction of the temple, he shouted, "Princess Meera, please wait." He caught up with me.

"Allow me to make sure it is safe."

With that, he took out his sword and surveyed the shore. We saw another boat a few yards from us. I assumed it belonged to the priest. But Guna took no chance and went to check it. I looked toward the temple carved on the side of a small hill. Recent rains had washed away the usually sandy path, leaving it strewn with gravel and pebbles.

Having completed his inspection, Guna walked towards the temple, and I followed him, my footsteps crunching the gravel. He moved slowly, so I could keep up with him, alert and ready to spring like a tiger. The priest rushed outside to greet us as we approached.

"Princess Meera, what an honor! I would have prepared a special *pooja* if I had known you were coming. With the flooding, I was not expecting anybody today. I only have some banana for an offering today."

"I wanted to worship in peace," I said, going inside the small temple with him. He belonged to a small group of people who served as my eyes and ears in this kingdom. And I came here for more than prayer. Guna tried to follow me inside and I turned back towards him, "Keep a watch outside, Guna. I won't be long."

God Vishnu, in this temple, reclined on his snake bed. I closed my eyes and prayed to the Lord to keep my brother safe. I thought of him being held in chains, or worse, and I prayed for Rish to find him and bring him back. Rish's face with long hair that fell on his forehead came into my mind. Taking a deep breath, I prayed for strength to no longer care for him and opened my eyes. The priest gave me the banana and walked around the temple with me.

"Do you have any news from the north?" I asked.

"Yes, Princess Meera. Some traders came in yesterday morning to the village. I heard from them that Princess Sapna died during childbirth."

I stopped and turned to look at the priest, my fingers clenched in front. *Prince Amar's new wife, dead?* I thought. "And the baby?"

He shook his head slowly, his mouth drawn into a thin line, "Dead as well. King Verma reluctantly consented to Prince Amar's marriage to Sapna. She suffered from poor health and could never leave the palace."

I felt like a noose tightened around my neck and involuntarily raised my hands to my throat. Jay's disappearance, Rish's betrayal, and now this.

With effort, I resumed walking, and the priest continued alongside. "Prince Amar grew restless before with being cooped up in Padi. When he heard Prince Jay left for Lukla, he raised a storm about attacking Malla, and only relented to stay with the pending birth of his child. Now, after a brief mourning period, he is bound to ask his father for permission to set sails to the islands and beyond. There were rumors he thinks Malla is prime for capture as well, but King Verma prefers a union of a different kind," said the priest, looking at me meaningfully.

When the news emerged that Sapna carried Prince Amar's child, rumor had it that her wealthy father forced the marriage. Amar never let his marriage stop him from enjoying the company of other women. He did not prescribe to my father's view on how to treat the people of captured lands. He acted ruthlessly and laid waste to both the land and its people. If I could stop such a fate to Malla by agreeing to marry him, what was my duty? Would I be considered selfish if I put myself before my people and realm?

I turned away. These were idle speculations on my part. Malla could defend itself and did not need her princess to be the sacrificial goat. Yet. A part of me knew Jay would not force such a choice upon me. But with him missing, the choice would be mine. What a frightening decision to make.

Setting these thoughts aside, I came to the real reason for my visit. I took a letter from my sari folds and handed it to the priest. "Can you make sure this gets in the hands of Kapil Biha?"

"With the utmost care."

My letter read simply, "When it comes to Jay's rescue, trust only those who have earned it."

I worried about the Vindhya plotting. Kapil grew up with Jay, and I hoped I could trust him.

I thanked the priest and walked outside. The sun hid behind a cloud, and a chilly wind blew across the water. Wrapping my sari around my shoulders to keep me from shivering, I signaled to Guna that we should head back.

That night I could not sleep and went to my balcony. The moon bathed the river below in its light, and I could see white swans in the water. I suddenly wished I could talk to my mother. My memories of her were of a woman deeply in love with my father. Did she love him in the beginning, or did she have no choice when the king himself expressed an interest in her? At least with royal men, once they wed the first woman for strategic reasons, they could marry others. I would only get to wed one man for life. If it happened to be somebody like Amar, I would still be the queen of Padi, which is an honor that others would give their life for. But the prospect made me shudder.

A different face appeared in my mind, that of a man who had kissed me fiercely under the moonlight, and I felt anger stir inside me. Rish's love for me turned out to be an act to gain control of the kingdom. Like a fool, I'd allowed my heart to rule my head.

7

Royal Companions

After a few wrong turns, Aranya and I found the temple in a small clearing in the woods. The small temple, made of sandstone, stood nestled among tall peepal trees and would have been hard to stumble upon. With the recent fighting in Saral, the path lay hidden among the overgrown brush, and the building itself had fallen into despair.

In the moonlight, I brought the horse to a halt in front of the structure. Though I wanted to jump off the animal in front of this girl, considering the injuries I'd sustained, I slid off slowly instead and approached the gate. She had seen me delirious with fever, and I still made a mark on her. It would be foolish on my part to try to show off, and end up sprawled on the ground.

A huge lock secured the door. As I searched for an opening, Aranya called out to me in a loud whisper. She pointed to a branch that spilled over the wall, from a tree inside the courtyard. I understood her intentions and nodded. She guided the horse there and climbed from its back on to the wall nimbly and then on to the branch and disappeared from my view.

In a few moments, I heard my name again and proceeded around the temple. Aranya stood by an open side door with a smile on her face.

Apart from a few scratches on her arms, she appeared fine. I led the animal through the door and tied it to the tree. It started grazing on the grass, and I looked around. Spider webs covered the small court-yard. My eyes rested on the tree Aranya had climbed. The main trunk branched at ten feet above the ground, and she must have jumped from that distance. Her actions, from nursing me back to health, to helping me escape, and her resourcefulness and fearlessness impressed me.

Aranya locked the side door and came and stood next to me.

"We can sleep in the main sanctum," she said in a low voice, pointing to the master structure. The inner shrine only held room for the idol. The main sanctum extended a few feet beyond held up by four carved pillars.

During peaceful times, there must have been a priest who took care of the temple. Now grit and insect webs covered the vacant place. Only some dried flowers adorned the Muruga idol in the inner shrine. I re-membered the beautiful temples in Akash and the idols covered in silk and gold. The unadorned god here appeared serene and peaceful. Aranya searched and found a small cupboard with the priest's supplies. She grabbed a broom from it.

"Can you please fetch us some water?" she asked while she started sweeping the floor. I picked a pot and watched her for a few moments before going to the back. As a princess on the run, she would have had to pick up a few skills that were not normally taught to her. It wouldn't surprise me if she knew how to sew and cook as well.

A draw well stood among neem trees. Using the clay pot and coir rope I found nearby, I drew some water from the well. I dunked my face in the cold and refreshing liquid. I cleaned myself and refilled the pot. When I came back, she had swept the floors clean. Aranya found some old saris, that previously adorned the idol and had now been put away, and spread them out in two corners for us to sleep. She opened the bag she had given me and brought out some small bananas.

"Let us save two for tomorrow," I said. She put two aside and glanced at the remaining three hungrily. She then handed me two bananas and kept one for herself. I grinned and handed her a banana back.

"I have been on a sick man's diet lately."

She smirked at that and ate the bananas.

"Would King Surya have really killed me and destroyed any chance of peace?" I asked.

She gazed at me with pained eyes and nodded slowly. "My father has been consumed by hatred for a while now. Nakul waited to tell my father about your capture, fearing his actions. His fears came true when father ordered my brother to bring you to him. He planned a public beheading."

"And now I have put your life in harm's way," I muttered.

"You tied my fate to yours when you—" she halted and whispered, "kissed me."

A foolish boy's action to win the affections of a girl. A prince's marriage decision lies with the king. I would have to face the consequences later. Bringing my attention back, I said, "We must leave before first light. Let us get some rest for now. I will take the first watch."

She bundled up one end of a sari as a pillow, curled up, and went to sleep.

I walked around, vigilant, and Somu invaded my thoughts. He'd had a plan to rescue me, but the king's decision to kill me had foiled that plan. Somu would most likely still search for me, once he heard I escaped the camp. So how to find him?

I remembered a game I played with him as a boy. He would leave clues for me that would lead to a surprise at the end. Each clue consisted of a triangle with stones in the middle, and the number of stones in the middle would count up from one. The number of clues he left me matched my age.

I strode outside the temple and found a tree near the wall. A gap existed on the ground between two of the roots. I made a triangle with some sticks and placed a small stone inside. If Somu came this way, he would know I'd passed through. Then I patrolled the wall slowly, staying alert for any noises. All the animals and birds remained quiet, and I went back in.

Aranya slept, her chest rising and falling slowly. A warmth spread through me as I leaned against a pillar and watched her. I liked her without a doubt. I had been able to be myself with her, a rarity for a prince. But I realized I needed to harden my heart before any deeper feelings took root. I had to face her brother and father in battle, to fight and defeat them, to reclaim these lands for Malla. Love was for poetry books, and there was no place for it in a prince's life. Not if he wanted to become a king.

I woke up with a start when someone shook me. Aranya stood in front of me. I wiped the sleep from my eyes and sat up. She'd dressed in a man's *dhoti* and looked like a young boy. She tried unsuccessfully to tie a turban around her head to hide her lustrous locks. I stood up and said, "Let me help you."

She allowed me, and I tied the turban around her head, tucking in her hair. It felt soft and smooth under my fingertips. I stood back to inspect her. She turned around and said, "What do you think?"

The men would be seeking a princess, and though she still appeared too beautiful in my eyes, she could pass for a boy from a distance.

"I hope no one comes close to inspect," I beamed.

I went to the well to wash.

When I returned, she had cleaned up the area and packed our meager belongings. Then she inspected me and said, "Your skin is lighter than the men of Saral. That won't do." She scanned around, and her eyes rested on the black soot from the temple lamps. I followed her gaze and went near the lamp. I touched the soot and rubbed some on my cheeks.

I must have looked quite a sight because she burst out laughing. She found a cloth in our sack. She dipped it into some water and came towards me, slowly spreading the soot on my face. I stood still, gazing at her.

"It is not a sign of good breeding to stare at young women, Prince Jay," she said mischievously.

"Only the ones that saved my life," I said and lifted her chin. She looked into my eyes, and I leaned in to kiss her. She stepped back and pleaded, "Jay, we need the blessing of at least one king."

I sighed and then nodded my agreement and said, "I will keep my gaze averted. Finish your work."

We prepared to leave.

"Take the horse out," I said to her. "I will lock the door from inside and climb up the tree. It is safer to leave it as we found it."

"I have heard the Prince has great respect for his sister."

I studied her, puzzled. She continued, "Princess Meera would have told the Prince not to be foolish and risk injuring yourself again."

I felt frustrated with my injuries and being unable to take care of us. She saw the frustration on my face and came to stand next to me and held my hands. Then anger flared up in me. Does she have to see me in all my weaknesses? I removed her hand and approached the tree.

"I am not good with a sword, but I can climb a tree," she said softly. I held the tree trunk. I had strength in my arms to hold on to the trunk, but did I have strength in my recently mended body to climb? She was right. It would be foolish if I fell and reopened my wounds again. The thought made me unhappy.

I took a deep breath, and I said, "I will save my chivalry for another time then," and strode out with the horse. While I waited on the other side, she scaled the wall and perched on it with her feet dangling.

I gaped. "What do you do in your spare time?"

She giggled. "I climb hills and caves. And elephants."

We soon set off on the back of the horse. As we rode, I said, "Aranya, we cannot ride into the village. We will have to make the journey on foot. They will expect us to be mounted."

She leaned in closer and said, "At the edge of the forest, we can set her free." She sat behind me with her arms around my waist. I realized I enjoyed the ride despite the dangers facing us. I did not know of any young lady who could survive this journey, traveling with a broken young man with no shelter or food. Instead of being fearful, she seemed resilient and resourceful.

We soon reached the edge and got off the horse. Aranya led her back into the forest and whispered in her ears and set her free. She galloped back the way we came.

"Ready?" she asked.

"Not quite. I cannot carry my sword like this," I said, pondering what to do with it.

"We can collect some firewood and bundle it up, hiding the sword in it," Aranya said. I beheld her admiringly, and she blushed.

We set to work. As we collected the wood, I left a triangle clue for Somu with two stones in it. Soon we collected enough wood, and I had a bundle on my head. With that, we walked side by side into the village. This area remained under Saral, but a skirmish had taken place nearby between Saral and Malla men. I could see the ravages of the battle in the mostly deserted location. People had fled to the coast held by Saral or to the area under Malla control. The few left were old men and women, orphaned young children, men with missing body parts, and stray dogs.

A young child of about four years peeked hungrily from behind a wall. A boy or girl, I could not tell from this distance.

Malla men had rebuilt the areas around Lukla under King Vikram's orders. Here I saw the effects of the war. Father had spoken to me a few times about how the war affected the lives of ordinary men and women.

"Use spies, diplomats, and marriage alliances to win the fight without waging a war," he'd taught me. "A good king also needs to know when to spill blood," he had said, and Saral counted as one such occasion.

Alongside me, I saw Aranya scan the desolate village. Her eyes rested on the child. She took one of our remaining bananas and held it out. The child came to us slowly, took the banana, and scurried away. As he started to peel the skin, two older boys came from nowhere and snatched it away. Aranya turned to shout at them, but I held her hands and shook my head. We could not attract attention. The child wailed and ran after them. I led her along and could see her blinking tears away.

As we left the village, we came across unplowed fields overgrown with weeds. The able-bodied men had left these villages to fight, and some had perished in the war or fled it. With none to farm, the lands were at the mercy of nature.

We saw dust clouds in the distance, followed by faint hoof sounds. Our disguise might not hold in front of many men, so I looked around. Then I touched Aranya lightly on the shoulders and said, "Let us hide behind those overgrown bushes till we can ascertain the identities of the men."

She followed me, and I dropped my bundle and crouched behind the shrubs, with my hands on the handle of my sword. Aranya kneeled next to me and parted the branches to see the road.

The horses came in sight, but there were no flags bearing fish or tiger emblems. Nothing unusual about it in this part of Saral. With neither Saral or Malla in firm control of these lands, men preferred to travel incognito. As the horses came closer, I could discern two men in the middle, a young man with royal bearings and an older man. I recognized Prince Nakul in the younger man. My eyes rested on his companion. A head shorter than the prince, the passing years had left a mark on his body. Unlike the Prince's lean athletic build, this man's ample waist, visible even from this distance, showed someone who either overindulged in food, neglected his training, or both.

Aranya stared at him intently and then whispered, "Father—"

King Surya rode with his son. The furious look on his face, combined with their sense of urgency, told me that they knew the Princess left with me, either by force or willingly. I glanced at Aranya, and her face expressed a tumult of emotions. She had only to stand up and walk to them, and she would be beyond me in moments. United with her father, who opposed our union. Who wanted to behead me.

Instead, she turned her back to them and put her head between her knees and sobbed silently. At that moment, she bound our future together irrevocably. I put my arms around her, and she laid her head on my shoulders. I rested my chin on her hair and stayed that way till the sound of the hooves receded.

Strange emotions filled me. When I'd tried to befriend her in captivity, I looked only for a means to escape my prison. Just now, when Aranya choose me instead of her father, she entrusted her life and honor in my hands. She slowly peered at me with tear-filled eyes. I kissed her forehead and then her lips. She did not push me away this time. As I tasted her salty lips mingled with tears, I briefly forgot my fears and trials. Acute desire coursed through my body. Aranya weakly pushed against my chest, and my body urged me to ignore her. But my mind's screams to stop got louder, and I slowly pulled away from her.

With my hands still around her, I said, "My servant Somu planned to rescue me in your camp. I have left clues for him to find us. With your father back here, our time is short. I need to go find the Malla men. Then we will be together."

"Marry me," she whispered. I wondered if I had heard her correctly. "Marry me and make me your wife. No one can separate us then," she said, gazing at me intently.

I remembered my parents' wedding happening in secrecy. No, that was not how I wanted to wed her. I cupped her face in my hands. "I am the Prince of Malla, and you are the Princess of Saral. Our wedding should mark the end of the enmity between the two kingdoms and be celebrated by the people. My father has wanted this union and would not be against it. Do not despair now. Let us reach safety first. Then within a fortnight, we can reach Akash. With my father's blessings, we can wed."

My father loved my mother, and as a boy, I dreamed of finding a girl of my heart, instead of marrying to strengthen our kingdom. Now older, I realized love alone was not enough. My father still had to marry Charu Vindhya to keep an ally in the fold. I knew I was falling in love with Aranya. Would I have the strength to do what was right for Malla, even if it meant hurting her? I imagined facing her father on a battlefield, with my arrow notched and pointed at his chest.

The men rode past us, and I stood extending my hand to Aranya. She took it and rose. As she spent a few moments to retie the turban around her head, I scouted the place. We resumed our journey and spent the rest of the day uneventfully.

By nightfall, we reached an inn.

Aranya whispered to me, "We are poor merchants, trying to reach the city. We cannot take a room for ourselves. We will have to sleep in the hall with others."

I agreed and opened the coin bag. Inside I saw copper coins. "I don't know the values of these coins," I said sheepishly. I'd brought gold with me to Saral and had handled silver on occasion, but nothing I'd buy would only be worth copper.

"Good that I have been on the run this past year, hiding from your men," she said without ill-will and took the bag. I let her do the talking at the inn. I could never pass for a poor Saral boy if I uttered more than a few words. These southern lands had a distinct tongue that I had not mastered. She called me her cousin and bargained with the innkeeper, and I surveyed the inn. There were only three or four others in the hall, so it should not be difficult for us to find a corner to spend the night. I observed the men closely, and none had the bearing of a fighter.

After a simple meal of rice porridge, we lay side by side on a thread-bare mat. The night fell, and the room remained dark except for one dim lantern that cast dark shadows and smoke. Through the open windows, a slight breeze wafted in, along with the hoot of the nighttime owls. A mouse ran on our mat, and Aranya sat up straight, clutching my upper arm.

"It is only a mouse," I whispered. She slowly laid back, her fingers still digging into my arms. I smiled to myself in the darkness. She moved closer to me, her body almost touching mine. I resisted the urge to wrap my arms around her. I could feel her breath slowly settle into a rhythm.

I dreamt of her vividly that night, and in the morning light, I flushed at the recollection. I looked around for the girl in my dreams. She conversed with the innkeeper, allowing me time to compose myself.

8

Queen Mother

News of Prince Amar's wife dying added to my despair, with Akash offering no diversion from my dark thoughts. Kantha tried to engage me in a conversation while I readied to meet with my grandmother, and I paid only half attention.

She muttered, "Padma said the Queen talked about her cousin this morning."

Kantha, a loyal servant, kept me abreast of the palace gossip. She had eyes and ears among the other maids and with the servants in the kitchen.

A current of sadness had touched her early in her life. Widowed at fifteen and childless, like a pumpkin flower that wilted on its stalk, she never bloomed. Her father had readied to send her off to live the rest of her life among Buddhist monks. My mother hired her instead to watch over her five-year-old daughter. She'd stayed with me ever since, and the thin girl transformed into a plump woman.

I have read about women remarrying in distant lands. If that custom existed here, she would have made a good mother. In my days of sorrow, when I lost my own, she kept me fed, bathed, and cared for.

"Which cousin?" I asked, knowing full well the answer.

"Rish Vindhya, Princess Meera. Padma could not hear everything clearly, but she heard your name along with his."

I wondered what they were talking about. How deep did this young man's betrayal run? Beholden to his family, what if all his actions had been aimed to gain my trust and then betray me? Though I wished that thought would have a sobering effect on me, my heart still sang a different tune. A tiny grain of desire lay nestled inside me, hoping that he did care for me, in his twisted way. Kantha finished styling my hair, and I straightened my shoulders, ready to meet my grandmother.

I lived in the main palace along with the king and the queen within the city. My grandmother's palace adjoined ours. I strolled along the private path connecting the two buildings with one of the city guards. Sunlight poured in through the windows situated at the top of the wall. At night, servants lit the flaming torches placed on the wall.

I reached her chambers and strode in. Her floors were covered with woolen carpets from Padi, cotton rugs made here in Malla, woven jute mats from Saral, and silk rugs from Sunda and beyond. The different materials, colors, and textured floor coverings were arranged to create a pleasing pattern.

My grandmother sat in her seat, the curtains half drawn. She liked to keep the room in semi-darkness as the bright light hurt her eyes. She noticed me as I came near. I touched her feet to seek her blessings, and she said, "May God Shiva bless you with the finest husband."

"Grandmother," I complained.

"Come and sit beside me, so I can see your face," she said. I took a seat next to her and held her hands.

Many considered my grandmother a northern beauty with her light brown skin. She still looked beautiful today with her grey hair swept up in a bun, and a sari in the color of dark betel leaves, with gold threading along the border.

"Meera, my child, you are glowing today," she said, gazing at me. I smiled at her. I hid my sorrows well then. She asked after Jay and I gave her the latest news. "I still think he should have been married to one of the chief's daughters before he went to Lukla. I told so to your father as well. Young men have their heads filled with battlefield glory. They are trained all their youth to fight, and that is what they want to do. And you. By your age, I had already married your grandfather Karan and had a suckling baby in my hands. Instead of thinking about your marriage, your father went chasing Surya in Saral. Now he is ailing, and I have to go see him in his chambers in my old age."

I protested, "Grandmother, father is improving and working hard to gain his strength back, if for no reason but to visit you. And he has talked to the chiefs. They want Jay to marry one girl each from Vindhya, Biha, and Thari, to unify the kingdom. Father has agreed to it. Sudha Vindhya and Riya Biha are in Akash now. I will bring them to visit you soon. Tanisi Thari is still a child of eleven, so we would have to wait a few years before that marriage can occur."

She peered at me. "How about you, my child? Has your father found a suitable husband for you? I am sure the queen is whispering in your father's ears about the possibility of Rish Vindhya as a match." I could hear my heart pounding as I listened to my grandmother. "I hope your father has more sense than that. Yes, the boy's father died protecting his life, but many more have died for this king and kingdom. Make him a commander to show him gratitude. I was born to a king, married a king, and I hope to die as the mother of a king. That is how it should be for you. You are born to a king and will one day be sister to a king. You should marry a king. And raise your son to be king."

Raise my son to be king. I had never thought about my children before. Jay's first-born son will inherit the Malla kingdom. My son can only aspire to his father's throne. An image floated in my mind of a young man being crowned and his mother watching with pride.

She fretted, "Four years back, Verma sought your hand for his son Amar. Your father is extremely fond of you. He did not want you to marry and leave Akash. I told him he cannot keep you by his side forever. But he said Jay needed you as well and asked Verma to wait for a few years. Amar then got a child in Sapna and had to marry her."

My grandmother watched me, and I glanced at her. "Is what I heard about Sapna true?" she asked.

I affirmed. "Princess Sapna died in childbirth."

She said, "My nephew Verma wanted to strengthen the alliance between our kingdoms. Your marriage to Prince Amar would do that. And I, a Padi Princess crowned Queen of Malla, would like to see you, a Malla princess, be crowned Queen of Padi."

I hesitated. "Grandmother, I've heard disturbing rumors about Prince Amar."

"Meera, all men have their vices. Your grandfather and your father are no exceptions." I stared at her. She continued, "Verma is no fool. He knows you have powerful allies in your father and brother. He will make sure Amar understands that and curtails his behavior."

This morning I had woken with a cry in my heart, and now it had grown into a lament.

"Grandmother, tell me about your marriage to King Karan."

"As the youngest child of King Rudra and the only girl, I ruled the palace. My father loved to read and write poems, and he would share those with my brothers and I. One autumn, I woke up as a young girl in Nanga, unaware of the coming dangers. With the approaching winter, my family prepared to move to Daya.

"I loved Nanga at that time of the year. Birds and animals stored food for the winter or headed to warmer climates, just like humans. A calmness settled in the air. A mist would cover the castle in the mornings. Most trees were barren, and the fields were harvested, and the hay would lie in piles. Before winter approached, we had an unwelcome visitor. King Jay laid siege to the city." King Jay, my great-grandfather, worshipped as a hero and legend in Malla had brought Padi and Saral under Malla rule. He was the last King of Magadha. I hoped my brother, named after him, would one day rule the same lands.

"He attacked us at the right time. With the move to Daya in winter, we did not have a stockpile of food. King Jay had blocked the aqueducts delivering water into the city, and the situation grew dire, then grim. My father decided to surrender. King Jay, a wise man, let my father rule Padi and signed a peace treaty with him over our shared waters. My father agreed to pay trade taxes to Malla. King Jay asked for my hand for his son to seal the pact. My father agreed."

I gasped. "Did you see Grandfather Karan before your marriage?"

Grandmother shook her head. "I had just turned twelve, and your grandfather celebrated his fourteenth birthday a few moon months before. Our wishes and thoughts did not matter. The kings made the decisions. Our marriage took place in Daya, and I laid my eyes on your grandfather for the first time then. My father sent me to Malla with my guards and maids. Fear wrecked me about leaving my father and brothers and coming to live in this strange land. I cried in my pillow so that nobody would know." I squeezed her hand lightly, feeling sorry for the child who traveled far from home, and she glanced at me.

Her eyes drifted to the floor as she quavered, "Your grandfather Karan, a boy still, accustomed to getting his way, hit me a few times in the early days of our marriage when I refused to obey him. In a strange land, with no friends, I remained quiet. One day, he pushed me, and I fell and bruised my chin."

I groaned in horror. She did not hear me and continued, "We ate with his father that day. King Jay observed my face and his son. Karan kept his eyes on his food. He turned to Karan and asked who'd bruised his wife and future queen and the mother of his children. He chided him for not protecting me. He admonished him to punish whoever did this to me and make sure this never happened again. The hitting then stopped. We even grew fond of each other. Kings and Queens are considered gods in our land. I considered only King Jay truly worthy of worship," finished my grandmother.

"King Jay fought Padi," I blurted, surprised to hear my grandmother's praise.

"He performed his duty as a king. He cared about his people and fought for them. The waters from Padi allowed Malla farmers to grow their crops. And he acted as a kind father to me and helped me learn the ways of Malla."

A strange notion occurred to me. I had thought only of Malla all my life. As a queen of Padi, with children in line for the throne of Padi, would Padi take the place of Malla in my heart? Or would it be tugged in two directions?

"Grandmother, you were a Padi princess and a Malla queen. Did you have to choose between the two lands?"

She peered at me and stated, "That is why the kings marry their girls to strengthen alliances. You will do everything in your power to stop both kingdoms from going to war. Vikram or Jay would not provoke a war if you are Queen of Padi. A wife has more powers than a daughter or sister. Use those powers, and Amar will heed you as well."

I wrapped my sari end around my fingers and listened as she continued, "My brother and I hoped our kids would marry one day, my daughter marrying his son Verma or his daughter marrying Rudra. But we both had only sons. As time goes on, the land of your son and grandson takes the place of the land of your father in your heart," she added somberly.

If I had to choose between my children and Malla, I knew who I would pick. That left me feeling unsettled.

9

Arrival of the Guard

At the Saral inn, I headed through a narrow hallway to get to the back, and a man approached the other way. I paused to let him through, and as he came near, he stared at me. Recognition flashed on both our faces at once. Though dressed in the clothes of a traveler, I identified my guard Dev instantly. Before I could warn him not to make my presence known, others entered the passage, and we became separated.

I could not wait in the passage any longer without arousing suspicion, so I continued to the backyard. There I did my morning duties while my mind raced. My trials galloped towards an end. As I pondered where to meet with Dev, he came to stand next to me. He drew water from the well, and in the noise of the pulley whispered in a low voice, "There is an abandoned granary a mile from the inn, my l—," he paused, gathering himself, "If you could meet me there?" He glanced at me briefly, and in that instant, I could see the well of emotions playing on his face. I would have embraced him, but instead, I nodded once.

After he left, I went to find Aranya. She stood in the main room with two lotus leaf plates carrying day-old rice with some yogurt and a pickle on top. I took the plate she extended. As we ate, I leaned in and whispered, "I met one of my guards in the inn. He will wait for us at an abandoned granary a mile from here." My excitement at the news, visible in my face, soon reflected in hers.

We finished our morning meal, gathered our meager belongings, and proceeded to the building. As we approached the granary, I slowed, my ears perked. Aranya startled at a sudden owl hoot, and I grinned, pulling her along, "Come on. That is the sign from Dev."

I strode into the granary with Aranya and saw Dev standing inside, alert with his drawn sword. He waited for me to close the door and then stepped in front and bowed. "Prince Jay. You are still alive." His voice quivered. I let go of Aranya and embraced him. We pulled apart with tears glistening in both our eyes.

He studied Aranya, and I said, "Dev, this is Princess Aranya of Saral. Aranya, one of my guards, Dev." Still dressed as a boy, she removed her turban to allow her hair to flow down. He kept whatever thoughts he had about seeing the princess with me to himself and bowed to her. I examined the small room, devoid of any furnishings. Dev pointed me to a window and said, "From this window, I can watch the roads while we talk."

"What happened after the Saral captured me?" I inquired, standing in the middle of the room to avoid being seen.

"Kapil and Shiv were injured in the fight but will recover. My lord, we found Vasu dead at the site," he said, watching me. It took a few moments for the words to sink in. Vasu, my childhood friend, the son of my father's minister Kripa, dead? Vasu, Kapil, and I grew up together. I remembered us training together under the watchful eyes of Chief Guard Mano Biha. Vasu never took to fighting. I had asked him to join me on the journey south without a thought to his safety. During our travels, I would question him about the place we passed by or a temple we could see in the distance, and he regaled us with the stories of bravery, deception, and conquests. Those stories of my ancestors rejuvenated me and put me in a better mood. Vasu entertained us with stories, and I'd failed to protect him. "What happened—" I started but could not finish my sentence.

"We don't know. General Devan and Commander Balan left for the capital and took his body with them. He asked Karan, Giri, and I to continue the search under Lt. Gen. Satya," he said, understanding my unfinished question. I nodded absently, staring outside the window.

"My lord, General Devan threw Somu in the dungeons because he refused to answer any questions about your whereabouts;"

"Somu? Has the General gone mad?" I replied angrily, coming out of my despondent thoughts. Somu had been looking after me since my childhood, and I would never question his devotion.

Remembering the man who whispered Somu's name to me while I endured my captivity, I added, "A man approached me during my imprisonment and said Somu planned a rescue effort."

He nodded. "We used the castle in Theni as our headquarters, and Somu asked for Kapil one day. Kapil went to talk to him and then called a meeting of your guards. Somu wanted to send a message to his sister, Thangam."

On hearing Thangam's name, Aranya started but did not say anything. Dev continued, "Before the General left, he cautioned us that Somu might have changed sides, but I could never believe it. We've known Somu over the last year and decided amongst ourselves to use his help in finding you. This led to the news that you were alive and held captive by the Saral. That account filled us with immense hope. Then Rish Vindhya arrived from Akash and ordered us to release Somu from captivity." He paused here and eyed me. "Prince Jay, Rish came bearing other news from the capital. Our Commander Balan, took his own life in Akash because he thought he failed in his duty to protect you."

"Balan?" I moaned, trying to make sense of it. He stayed quiet, giving me time to process more bad news. Aranya, who'd listened intently so far, looked questioningly at me. I sighed and bleated, "Balan headed my guards."

I had been crown prince for a few moon months, had lost a childhood friend, and now my head guard had killed himself. If I continued this way, by the time I was the King, there would be no men left to fight with me.

"What news do you have of the king and my sister?" I asked urgently.

"They are well, given the circumstances. The news of your disappearance has started spreading beyond the capital. Prince Atul of Padi is in Akash, seeking Princess Meera's hands for his brother, Prince Amar."

Amar was unprincipled, and the thought of Meera marrying him left a distaste in my mouth. I had to get to safety and send a message to my father. "Tell me how you came to be at the inn."

Dev said, "Somu did not know your exact location, but he suspected it. We agreed your rescue should be done in stealth and worked out the details. Somu planned three escape routes, and Rish ordered Karan, Giri and I to head south of Pullikadu in disguise, to those places. Meanwhile, Rish got the men ready in Theni. We selected this granary as one of the places where Somu would bring you."

"I could not wait for Somu's plan to commence. King Surya decided to come back and serve his justice."

Dev glanced at Aranya and back at me and asked, "Where is Somu, my lord?"

"I haven't seen him since the assault in Maram. Whatever he set in motion, the honor of rescuing me belongs to Princess Aranya. King Surya rode on his way to execute me, and she learned of his plans and helped me escape," I said, slowly reaching out to hold her hands. The gesture did not escape Dev, and he observed us incredulously.

Aranya spoke now. "By now, my father will have mounted a search party. I'm sure his men found our abandoned horse. They will know we could not have gotten far."

"Tell me your plan," I said.

"My lord, I have a horse in the back, and a boat hid along the river bank. You and I would have left on the horse at nightfall to reach that spot along the river. Then, we would have taken the boat to Theni Palace. However, with a third person, the plan will have to change."

Aranya and I could take the horse and leave, but I hesitated to leave Dev behind. I remembered a time when I dreamt of being alone in the world. The constant companions around me stifled me. Before my time in captivity.

Dev said, "Prince Jay, I don't like the thought of staying behind, but there seems no other option. I will tell you where to find the boat. You and the princess can leave at nightfall. I will stay for some time to make sure no one pursues and then find my way to Theni."

I glanced at Aranya, and she inclined her head in agreement.

Once we settled our plan, Dev said, "My lord, you have to travel at night. Please get some rest, while I stay on guard."

I laughed. "Rest? All I have been doing the past few days was either lying in bed or escaping captivity. I have not had a chance to train. Come wrestle with me."

His face lit up and said, "I will go easy on you, my lord."

Aranya kept one eye on the road and one on us. I circled slowly, watching Dev's actions and making mostly defensive moves. Dev started with simple strikes, trying to gauge how far he could push me.

"Come, Dev. Have you lost your abilities with no Prince to guard?" I taunted him.

I worked up a sweat and started to make offensive moves on my own. Dev still fought with restraint, and when I attacked him, he hesitated for the blink of an eye, and I used it to push him to the floor and sat on his chest. For a man just pushed down, he had a huge smile on his face.

I stood up and reached out my hand to pull him up.

"True to your words, you went easy on me," I said. I rubbed my stomach, aware of the pain of stretching a freshly healed scar. I could fight if I needed to, but I would not last long.

"Initially, yes. But the last few moments, you were the Prince I knew. You were two steps ahead of me, keeping me guessing what your next move would be. For weeks, we worried we had lost you, my lord. Even with Rish's encouraging words, desperation set in. Just seeing you would lift the men's spirits."

We ate a simple midday meal of coconuts, bananas, and roasted peanuts. Aranya laid down to rest, and I spoke with Dev while he kept guard. He filled me in with other news, and then I told him about my captivity.

We heard horses in a distance, and I woke up Aranya.

"My lord," Dev said, "I will stay here on the watch. Please head to the back and stay mounted on the horse. If you hear the hoot of the owl, it is safe to come back. If you hear a peacock scream, please escape with the princess."

If I aspired to rule one day, the time had come for me to act like a king. "No, Dev. Two swords are better than one. I will stay here with you."

Dev opened his mouth to say something, but my glance quieted him. I looked at Aranya as she pulled a small dagger from her waist. We gazed at each other, and I gestured for her to stay behind us.

The men on horses approached on a slow trot. In the middle, Somu lay across one of the beasts on his stomach, his hands tied. My heart pounded as I tightened my grip on the sword and stood alert.

The men around him were strangers to me, but Aranya regarded them intently, signs of recognition on her face.

"Where is the cowardly prince of yours?" one of them asked.

"Not far from here," croaked Somu. The horses flew past us.

Aranya relaxed as the sound receded, but Dev and I stayed alert for a little longer. I made a decision then.

"Dev, if we are caught, I am in no position to fight a dozen men. We will leave together at nightfall on foot, and we can steal an extra horse along the way."

Dev inclined his head in agreement. Aranya looked at us and said, "I will keep watch. You both should get some rest."

In the bright daylight, sleep would elude me. But I stretched myself on the ground. Dev ignored Aranya's call for rest and kept his watch.

I shut my eyes, and my thoughts turned to Balan. A few moon months ago, Mano appointed Balan as my head guard. He had served me well, and now I had lost a loyal friend. Balan killed himself, Kapil wounded fighting for me, Vasu dead by my enemy's hands, and Somu captured. I seemed to be a dangerous person to be acquainted with.

I turned to sleep on my side and slowly drifted off. Knives plunged into my heart, and I turned with shock to observe Balan, Kapil, and Vasu wielding them. "No," I shouted, waking up.

Dev heard me, and his footsteps halted. I opened my eyes and spotted him. He approached, and I stood up slowly. Still a prince, I could not let him see my turmoil.

Aranya slept a few feet away, and I glanced at her face. Her hair fell across her forehead, and her long lashes fluttered in her sleep. Following my eyes, Dev said, "I requested the princess to lie down." Resisting the urge to touch her face, I walked to the front.

"Dev, get some rest. I need you alert tonight." He heard the command in my voice and did not resist. He found a corner and laid down.

I looked out the window, watching the sun sink. Nightfall approached, and I woke up the princess and my guard. We ate a quick meal and readied ourselves. Dev retrieved the horse, and we exited the building in the back.

A sliver of a moon dimly lighted our way, while countless stars sparkled in the night sky. We moved as quietly as we could, alert for any sound. A few times, we hid behind trees and bushes when we heard noises, but our journey proceeded without interruptions. In one of the villages, Dev sneaked in and found a horse. Then the three of us mounted, Aranya and I on one and Dev on the other, and rode towards the river. About a mile from the river, Dev signaled us to halt, and I reined in the horse.

"My lord, it is best if we left the horses here and covered the rest of the way on foot."

I agreed. We dismounted and removed all our belongings. Dev led the horses into the trees and tied them, away from the eyes of the travelers on the road. Then we set out to find the boat. He had hidden it under some bushes, but in the dark, one shrub looked like the other. A snake slithered away from one of the bushes when Dev used his spear to part them. After a while, Aranya called to us, "Here."

Dev rushed towards her, while I scanned the area, alert for any attack. She had found the boat, and he helped her turn it around and take it to the water. I assisted Aranya into the boat and got in after her. Dev boarded last and grabbed the oars and started rowing silently.

"My lord, arrows from the riverside can still reach us. It would be safer if you and the princess crouched down."

I muttered underneath my breath for being foolish enough to be captured in enemy territory but saw the sense in his words. Aranya and I hunkered down, away from any wandering eyes. Dev came over and covered us with old sheets from his pack, hiding us completely. There were a few holes in the sheet, and I could see out through them. When the moon rose overhead, we heard some horses on the shore.

"Stop," yelled a voice, and Dev obliged, angling the boat away from the shore.

"Who are you and where are you headed in the dark?" questioned the voice.

"I am Vela, a boatman, my master," responded Dev, using a Saral street dialect. "Going to Theni to bring a groom and his family to my village. The bride's father, Karuppa, he hired me," he continued.

He waited patiently, as the men on horse viewed the boat. Aranya and I held our breath, though it would be hard to detect such tiny movements in the dark.

"Did you see anybody else on your way?"

"Just the fishermen and tradesmen, but I see them daily, my master," responded Dev in a humble voice.

One of the men waved the boat off, and Dev rowed away slowly. I could hear Aranya's heart beating loudly in the quiet, and I reached over and put my arms around her. She rested her head on my shoulders and gazed into my eyes. Her lips glistened, inviting me, and I leaned in and kissed her gently. As we pulled apart, a slow grin spread on her face, and she settled comfortably in the crook of my arm and circled my waist with her arm. A matching smile spread on my face as I rested my hand on her back.

10

Matter of the Heart

Sudha of Vindhya, my stepmother's niece, arrived in Akash and came to visit me. She walked in with her cousin Riya and bowed. My mind raced to compare the girls vying for Jay's hands in marriage. Taller of the two, Riya had Malla blood in her. With her sari draped to accentuate her wide hips and straight hair braided with flowers, she appeared like a dancer carved on the palace pillars. Sudha, slender and delicate, her curly hair put up with wisps of hair framing her forehead, still looked like a child. The Queen sent for her niece, at the urging of Rish, when he witnessed how fond I had become of Riya. I tried to forget Rish's hand in this and my gullibility.

I asked them to sit beside me. These two girls being cousins may be helpful if Jay had to marry them both. The girls knew each other, and Sudha's mother came from the Biha territory and married into Vindhya. Hopefully, this would strengthen their family ties and allow these powerful families to work in unison for the welfare of the kingdom, instead of clamoring for power.

"Uncle Rish called Prince Jay one of the finest sword fighters he had ever met," Sudha said. At the mention of Rish's name, my heart fluttered. I cursed my mind for continuing to care for a man who betrayed my trust. In my sleep, he tormented me with his passionate kisses, and in my waking hours, many sights and sounds of Akash brought him into my memory. The small part of me still capable of thinking rationally thought Rish had done his duty to his house well, in trying to strengthen its alliance to the royal family through marriage.

"Tell us more about your brother, my lady," Sudha asked.

"What do you want to know?"

"Anything."

"Everything," chimed in Riya.

"My father had no male heirs for a long time. Soon after I turned three, my mother gave birth to a baby boy. When my father came to see the baby, Jay cried at the top of his lungs. The Physician said he would grow to be strong. My father's joy knew no bounds. He handed out silk and gold coins celebrating his birth," I recounted.

I remembered my mother telling me how my father's eyes welled up with tears of joy when he held Jay. My mother also allowed me to hold him and said that when he heard my voice, he would calm down.

"As he grew older, he turned the entire palace into his playground and put everybody from the king to the guards under his spell." I smiled as I recalled the stories. "As a young boy, he loved to hide in the palace halls." We usually found him quickly, and I remembered his laughter rang with childish delight on such occasions.

"One day, four-year-old Jay ran away, and we did not find him in his usual haunts. My mother became worried and urged my father to help search for him. Father left for an important council meeting that day, soothing mother's fears. While several servants and guards searched our living quarters, my father found him sleeping on the throne when he walked in for his council meeting." Instead of asking a guard to carry him back, my father brought him himself. I remembered mother bursting into cries of joy on seeing him and father placing Jay on her lap gently as if he held the most delicate thing in the land.

Riya and Sudha listened with rapt attention. "I teased him about being fond of the throne ever since," I said, smiling at them. I wished we could find him as easily now.

"As a young boy of ten, he loved to ride. He had a horse that he grew very fond of and would take her out every day."

"I remember that horse," Riya interrupted me. "I visited Akash with my parents, and Prince Jay took me to the stables one day to feed her. She stood taller than both of us, and her coat shone in the sun."

"Riya, let the princess tell her story," Sudha scolded her cousin.

"My story adds to hers," Riya said, winding her long braid in her hand.

"I forgot you visited us in Akash then, Riya. What fun you and I had, going into the palace gardens and picking ripe mangoes to eat."

Riya broke into laughter, "My stomach ached, and our faces and clothes were covered in sticky juice."

"Princess Meera, what happened to the horse?" asked Sudha impatiently.

Suppressing my urge to laugh with Riya, I continued. "One day, he took her to the river and jumped across the water in various parts. The horse slipped on the rocks and hurt her legs. Jay held on to her back and rode her back to the palace slowly. Chief Guard Mano said we had to put the beast to sleep, and father agreed. Jay seemed heartbroken.

"The next day, when the guards came for the horse, they found Jay sleeping next to it. He told the guards he would keep her company till the end. My father and I reached the stables. He told Jay to come to him. He asked him if he wanted to stay and watch. Jay nodded, his face solemn. Father and Jay watched as one of the men beheaded the horse with a single blow from an ax." I paused. I had turned my head away that day, unable to view the act. Jay had tears streaming down his face, and blood splattered on his clothes and body. Father put his arms around Jay's shoulders and held him for a few moments.

"Jay learned an important lesson that day. He'd been careless with his horse and decided to face the consequences himself. One of you might one day become the queen of this great land. Being the queen means putting the land, your king, and your offspring ahead of your own needs. Jay would expect this of his future queen."

I studied the girls. Riya would be a loyal wife, but could she be a partner to the king and help him rule? Sudha remained a mystery to me. If Jay ended up marrying one or more of these girls, would Sudha be fine if her son was not the next in line to the throne? She glanced at me, and I could see confusion in her eyes.

They were both young and had years to learn about life as a Queen. No need for me to terrify them yet. "For the most part, being the queen is an honor and privilege. Merchants all over want to clothe you in their saris and jewels, which is an added benefit," I said, and they both laughed with me.

"I am going to the Nataraja temple with the queen. Why don't both of you join me?"

After they left to get dressed, my thoughts stayed in the past.

As he grew older, I realized Jay had also stopped naming his horses and rotated around five or six of them, never becoming close to one. Worried about him, I asked him why. He looked me in the eye and said, "I will be king one day. I cannot allow myself to get hurt by a mere horse."

Concerned he was going to shut out people as well, I said, "Jay, horses are one thing. You cannot avoid being hurt by people, though."

"Some people are worth getting hurt for," he said, giving me a quick hug before running away.

When we arrived, heavy crowds thronged to the temple. Dancers would perform today in honor of the Lord of Dance, Nataraja. I wondered how many had come to see the god and how many the queen and the princess.

After the prayers, my stepmother, Riya, Sudha, and I sat on the carpet in the main hall. Soon the performers appeared in their splendid costumes. The first part of the dance depicted Shiva meeting Parvati and his wedding to her. The women moved to the accompaniment of singers and instrumental music. They led through a slow and gentle sequence, with melodious music associated with the creation of the universe.

When Parvati placed her flower garland around Shiva's neck, I glanced at the queen. She had waited with a garland of her own for my uncle Rudra, only for it wilt and never reach its owner. She blinked a few times as she watched the artists. After their performance, they came and bowed to the queen and me. The queen handed out their rewards.

The next set of performers depicted the cosmic dance of Nataraja, a fast-paced piece portraying the destruction of the universe. The music burst forth and the performers spun around the room with great energy. The bleak scene matched my mood. It culminated in a crescendo of music and dancers leaping into the sky. I recognized one of them. Afterward, I found one of my trusted men and whispered to him, "I would like to talk to the dancer, Madhavi, the one in the peacock green sari. She has just come back from Padi." He turned to spot her and inclined his head in understanding.

That evening I stood in the gardens, waiting for Madhavi. The sky turned dark blue, and the sun itself appeared a ball of fire, painting the clouds red and orange. I heard footsteps and turned. The guard walked in with Madhavi, and I dismissed him with a nod.

Madhavi glided towards me in a gorgeous black and red sari. I said, "I am looking forward to hearing all about the songs you have collected on this trip."

"My princess, as you requested last year, I started compiling songs from the various cities I performed. This time, I came across three spellbinding poems. A young boy at one of the temples in Padi sang them set to his tune, and it melted my heart. I learned them from him."

I gestured her to join me and started walking.

"You should come and teach the songs to me soon. Also, I will ask one of our poets to write them down as you sing them." We came to a secluded spot with no one within earshot. I sat at a nearby bench and gestured for Madhavi to join me.

"I'd like to know about your travels," I whispered. "Did you meet the royal family while you visited Nanga?"

"Yes. Princess Sapna had requested us to dance at the palace temple. She rewarded us generously afterward. We then left and traveled all over Padi and performed at various temples. We returned to Nanga to do our final show before returning to Akash. We soon heard that Princess

Sapna died in childbirth. A couple of days later, Prince Amar came to our quarters, drunk. We knew of his infamous reputation with women, and he started groping the girls and asked them to dance in front of him."

I gasped in shock, and my shoulders tensed. With trembling lips, she continued, "We pleaded with him that we only danced in front of Lord Shiva and tried to get him to leave. Luckily, before things got out of hand, Prince Atul came in and took his brother back to the palace. He apologized to us before he left and came in the next day to ensure our safe passage to Akash.

"All over Padi, people suffer from anxiety and general unease. Rumors have spread that the King would set aside Amar and crown Atul instead. With the death of Princess Sapna, though, the King hopes for a royal alliance that will win over his people. Even before the cremation of the princess, people talked about Princess Meera of Malla and her virtues and how she could turn the prince around."

Could a woman change a grown man? I also knew very little about Padi and its people. I panicked and turned to Madhavi.

"Madhavi, tell me about Padi and its people."

"My lady, Padi, like Malla, comes from old customs and traditions. Everywhere we went, people showed us kindness and generosity. In winter, snow falls on the ground, unlike here in Malla, so the clothing and food are more adapted for colder weather." As Madhavi continued, I realized I knew most of what she narrated, and I relaxed. My grandfather Karan had married a Padi princess, and my grandmother had told me many stories about her land. King Jay had captured Padi, and he let King Rudra rule the land while paying homage to the Malla kingdom. Lack of knowledge of the history and culture of Padi would not rank among my hurdles to overcome.

"Arts and culture have not flourished as much as they have in Malla. We are hoping one Malla princess might change that when she becomes queen," she concluded.

I thanked Madhavi and took a gold coin from my purse to hand to her. She refused and said, "I am honored to be of service to you, my lady.

I have not forgotten all the help you gave my family." When her father fell ill, I'd arranged for the royal Physician to treat him.

"Come back soon and teach us your songs, Madhavi," I said, and she bowed to me and left.

I twisted my sari end. The more I learned about Prince Amar, the more I despised him. He reminded me of a cobra, with its head raised to strike. No, not a cobra. They left people alone, usually. He sounded like a hyena, feasting on the dead. Fear burned my stomach. The vision my grandmother painted for me appeared in my eyes, of being crowned queen, of raising a son to be king one day. Now was not the time to give in to fear.

11

Marriage Proposal

I walked past the table with the tiger carvings in the large formal room father used to meet with his council and entered his smaller sitting room. Portraits of the past kings adorned the walls. Father sat under his portrait painted a few years after his coronation. The painting depicted a tall young man, with piercing eyes full of life. There appeared only skin and bone on his face now. He was reading a letter and looked up when I came in. I embraced him tightly, and he kissed my forehead. As I stepped back, he gazed at me thoughtfully.

"Meera, I received this letter from King Verma seeking your hand for his son, Prince Amar. Let us go and visit my mother. I will tell you the details there."

I expected this, and though it seemed better than a call for war, my heart plunged into despair. This may not be a war with men proving their fighting prowess. Still, it remained a battle, a test of my wit, grit, and strength.

I held out my hands. He grasped them, and we set out. A morning chill lingered. Winter would soon be upon us. We would get a respite from the heat and the rains for a few months.

I held his hands, and he strolled with his back held straight. I wor-

ried that the long walk would tire him. Eyes and ears observed everything in the palace, and a king could not show any weakness. I did not
talk to him, so he could preserve his breath. As we entered the passage
connecting the two palaces, he momentarily tightened his grip on my
hands and slowed. His eyebrows were lowered, and his lips were drawn
in pain, but he hid it quickly. He resumed walking, and I held on to him
tightly.

When we reached my grandmother's chambers, she watched her second son as the door closed behind us. I let go of my father, and he approached his mother. She raised her right hand as if to support him. She
must have held his hands as a young boy, helping him learn to walk. Today, he ignored her outstretched hand and moved on his own. When he
got closer, he touched her feet. My grandmother embraced her son with
tears in her eyes. Then, she guided him to a seat and sat down next to
him.

"I feared you would no longer be able to walk to my chambers," said
my grandmother in a broken voice. Since father's injury in the Lukla
battle, he had not left his palace, before today. Initially confined to his
chambers, his health improved gradually for him to hold court in the
small throne room. In recent days, I have accompanied him on short
walks in his garden. Amidst all the other dark tidings, his ability to
cover the distance to my grandmother's palace filled me with happiness.

My father stroked her hands gently and said, "Mother, just the
thought of you having to visit me gave me the strength."

"I prayed to Lord Krishna to take my life and give it to you, my son. I
did not want to face the prospect of losing you, as I lost your father and
brother those years back. Now I face the danger of losing my grandson."

My father patted her hands and said, "Mother, you were a queen of
Malla. You cannot despair. If something happened to me, Meera would
still need you to comfort and guide her."

My grandmother gazed at him and said, "Son, there is nothing crueler for a mother than to lose her children. I bore it once for your sake. I
am too old and weak to bear it again. And it is not a pain I want you to
face. Let the lord take me away when my son is flourishing as the king."

They talked some more while I wandered around the room, gazing at a beautiful painting of a snow-covered Nali mountain. I might be the queen of that land. The thought caused my stomach to tighten.

"I received a letter concerning Meera," said my father. I strode back to them at the sound of my name, and my father continued, "Wasting no time, my cousin Verma has requested her hand in marriage to his son, Amar. His second son, Atul, journeys to Malla to seal this."

My grandmother seemed happy at the news. She said, "I may not live to see Meera crowned the Queen of Padi, but I want to see her married. Vikram, you should agree to this marriage. This alliance of my birth house with Malla will help you in your fight with Saral."

My father appeared thoughtful and said, "Yes, this alliance would strengthen our ties. I understand why Verma is sending his second son, Atul, to win us over. He has grown into a capable young man, respected among the Padi court elders. If he'd been the eldest, I would say yes to Meera's marriage to him. But I have heard things about Amar that—"

My grandmother interrupted him, "As a princess of Malla and your only daughter, the military might of Malla would defend Meera. Amar and Verma know that and would treat her with respect. In your fondness for this girl, don't ruin her life. At nineteen, she should have already born offspring who would be future kings and queens. Instead, you treat her like a child. I have seen how well she protected Jay from her stepmother Charu with her astuteness. As a wife, she would have Amar singing her tune in no time."

After my mother's death, I did try to smooth things between my stepmother and us. I thought I grew adept at navigating the royal plots. Rish's scheme had shattered that illusion. My marriage to Amar and thoughts about my life after worried me. My son would be heir to the Padi throne. My grandmother thought this would strengthen ties between Malla and Padi. Padi had its schemers and plotters. Their own Vindhya, hungry for power. Suddenly, I felt trapped in a bees hive, with thousands of them stinging me.

My father glanced at me and said more to himself, "I have to accept this offer if I don't want to start a war."

With Jay missing, we could not afford to fight a battle with Padi as well. I took a deep breath.

"Father, my grandmother is right. Do not worry about me. I am a princess and your daughter. But a girl's place and future rest with her husband. I am ready to start that phase of my life." I smiled bravely while I said this.

He sighed. "I will send a reply back to King Verma that Malla will be ready to welcome Prince Atul."

12

Prince Again

I woke up with a start when the heat stifled me. I slowly came to my senses and realized we were still on the boat. I looked through the holes in the cloth, covering Aranya and I. Dev had steered us off the main river and currently rowed down a canal.

Aranya stirred slowly in my arms, and I instinctively pulled her closer. She radiated some of the heat trapped inside our sheet. The rest came from the sun, slowly rising out of its slumber.

Aranya's eyes fluttered open like butterflies, and I fought the temptation to kiss them. She sensed my gaze on her and glanced at me. Her lips curled up. The light filtering in, cast a web of light on her face. I stared, mesmerized by her beauty.

She lay half on top of me, having spent the night with her head on my chest. She sensed how close we were and tried to slide away, but the little boat did not have much room, and I kept my arms around her waist. She gazed into my eyes then and relaxed in my arms. I sensed the boat turn and peeked once again through the holes.

"Dev," I whispered from underneath the sheets.

He stopped rowing and came towards me. He bent down as if rummaging for something and whispered, "We will be at the palace canal soon, my lord. You can come out when you are ready."

He went back to rowing, and I slowly moved my legs to get feeling back in them. I mouthed the word "ready" at Aranya, and she nodded, straightening her clothes. I slowly pulled the sheet off us and sat straight up. I could see men in the distance, but could not make out faces yet. I grabbed the hilt of my sword and waited for us to approach closer.

I could hear men call the boat to a halt, and Dev stopped. I heard murmurs, and someone waved at us, and Dev began rowing again.

Theni palace, built of limestone, gleamed in the sunlight. The Malla army had captured it a few months ago in a fierce battle. Men along the canal stared at me, wondering, whispering. My eyes traveled, coming to rest on the palace entry by the waterway. More men stood there, Rish Vindhya among them. I regarded him, and as the boat came closer, recognition flickered on his face. He stepped forward on the dock, a riot of emotions passing across on his face.

His glance fell on Aranya, and I followed his gaze. She had put her hair up and still wore a man's clothes. That did not deter from her charm. She sat away from me, with her back straight, viewing the men onshore. I caught her eyes. Her face betrayed no emotions and conveyed a calm strength. Raised to be a queen, I trusted she knew how to act.

I turned back to scan the men, more of whom had gathered by the dock. I searched for Karan and Giri, but then I remembered Dev's words. Like him, they'd traveled to different locations, to await my rescue. Kapil and Shiv were not among the men either. I longed to see Kapil, to make sure he had healed from his injury. I missed him during my time in captivity.

The boat reached the dock, and Dev threw a rope from the craft and tied the other end inside. One of the men grabbed the opposite end and secured it to a pole. I stood, and Aranya did the same. I jumped off the boat on to the dock. With all the men watching, I hesitated whether to help Aranya. She decided for me by holding out her hands. I took them and helped her onto the dock.

The men approached and bowed to me, Rish at the front.

"Rise," I commanded. "Princess Aranya is my guest. Please find her a comfortable room and make sure her requests are met." Veer, one of the young men in General Devan's command, jumped and answered, "Yes, my lord."

I turned to Aranya. "Princess," I said. She inclined her head at me with a twinkle in her eyes and followed Veer.

"Rish, lead me to my room."

"Yes, my lord."

"Who is in charge here?"

"Lt. Gen. Satya, the General's second in command."

I did not see him by the water. "We can go talk to him after I hear your story."

I arrived in the room, and a servant greeted me. I took the wet cloth he handed and cleaned myself. I longed for a warm bath to wash off the grime, but that had to wait. Shedding my worn clothes, I changed into the fresh ones he laid out for me. That simple act made me feel like a prince again. Dismissing him, I sat down behind my desk and regarded Rish.

"Tell me everything that happened since I disappeared."

Briefly, he narrated the story, ending with Balan's death and being sent to Saral to find me. As he spoke, a plan formed in my head.

A knock sounded on the door, interrupting us, and Rish opened it. Kapil entered, shutting the door behind him. "My lord," Kapil quavered and bowed to me, and I embraced my oldest friend, each living through our shared memories. I had many things to talk to him about, but those matters would have to wait for when we were alone. "Prince Jay, as your guard, I failed to protect you."

"Kapil, I hold you blameless in this. I proposed that foolish trip to the festival, and you cautioned against it."

He had a determined look in his eyes, "Prince Jay, with Balan dead, we need a new commander and a new member for the guard."

"Do you have anyone in mind for my guard?"

"There is a young man called Veer, who is devoted to you. I have watched him in training. He is fearless."

"I know him, and I agree he will make a good addition to my guards."

"I will bring him soon and have him swear his oath to protect you."

He paused and studied me intently. "There is something else you need to know. That day, Saral men knew where to find us and knew how many traveled with you. Only Somu and the men with you on that day knew of the plan, so all of us should be suspect."

I had thought about this myself but shoved it into the back of my mind, worrying about escaping captivity first. But now, I had to face the reality that one of my close friends had betrayed me.

Rish cleared his throat and said, "If I may, my lord." I nodded, and he continued, "When I arrived here, I investigated this matter. Five men could have betrayed you, Somu, your servant, Balan and Kapil Biha, members of your guards, Vasu, a childhood friend, and Shiv Thari, a nobleman of House Thari."

I listened without interrupting while my mind raced through these men to see if any could have betrayed their oath to me. Somu raised me from childhood and appeared devoted and loyal to me. But he came from Saral, and his sister, Thangam, had raised Prince Nakul.

And what about Kapil, who stood before me? Or Balan, now dead? Had he taken his life as a traitor, too afraid to face punishment should he be found out? What about Vasu?

I shook my head briefly, trying to clear these thoughts. This wouldn't do. Suspicion, once rooted, would take over my mind. Next thing, I would be suspecting my sister Meera of conspiring against me. I needed to listen to what Rish had learned first, then punish the traitor, whoever it may be.

Rish continued, "King Vikram did not believe Somu would betray you, and after speaking to him and several others, I arrived at the same conclusion. He seemed distraught at your capture and provided valuable information that led to your escape. General Devan had thrown him in the dungeon before he departed for Akash, and I set him free after ascertaining his innocence. He left the castle with a few men to help you."

I added, "Somu is a Saral captive now. I don't doubt his loyalty to me. But since I escaped with Princess Aranya, he will be tortured for information. He would die rather than betray me, but I don't want to lose a faithful servant. We have to find him and set him free."

Both men nodded.

Rish said, "Balan sacrificed himself because he did not protect you. This happened right in front of my eyes, and his actions were not that of a spy."

I stared into the distance, thinking of the young man who had been my shadow for months now. He'd done his duty well but had not learned how to say no to his Prince. To protect me from my own mistakes.

"I looked into Kapil's actions during the fight and in the days preceding and following it, and I have reached the conclusion he is loyal to you, my lord."

I glanced at Kapil and remembered him and I playing with wooden swords as little boys. "That is a relief. Nobody covers my back better in a fight than Kapil." Kapil's lips curled up a tiny grain.

Rish cleared his throat. "Shiv Thari spent time with you in Akash. I don't have anything concrete, but he had the opportunity to meet with Saral men when he searched for King Surya. The injury to his leg appears genuine, though."

Shiv, a fierce fighter, would rise in Malla ranks. Why would he turn against me and seek Nakul?

"That brings us to Vasu. He is dead, and I heard from Kapil that he quarreled with you about his cousin, Riya."

I remembered Vasu's eyes peering at me from the ground as I fought several Saral men at once. Vasu, Kapil, and I grew up together. Kapil excelled as a natural fighter and swordsman. Though strong and agile, he fought with his head as much as his body. Vasu would never win acclaim for his fighting prowess. His impatience and aggressiveness caused him to make many mistakes. Why had I brought him along on an expedition that required physical strength? Did his weaknesses drive him towards Nakul?

Vasu had taken a liking to Riya Biha, and I would tease him about it, not taking his feelings seriously. Once in Lukla, the General dropped a few hints that he hoped I would marry his daughter. Vasu heard these words, and once during a meal with me, he stormed out, saying as a Prince who always got what I wanted, I had no idea what someone like him endured. I wanted to yell back and say he had no idea what burden I carried. But something stopped me. What did life hold for him, a Minister's son, with just a few acres of land to his name and no great prowess at fighting? Though a good friend, I knew he could be irrational at times and not very thoughtful or methodical. Would I have appointed him as a Minister or other ranking official in my court? If I couldn't understand how my friends feel, how would I feel the pulse of the kingdom?

Coming back to the present, I rubbed my eyes, "What better way for Prince Nakul to defeat me than to sow doubt in my mind about my friends?"

I looked at the two men in front of me. "Shiv that day appeared unconscious like Kapil. I don't want to cast doubt on an innocent man and turn him against me. He hails from the Thari Noble house, whose support is important for all we do. Let us not endanger that." They both nodded.

I continued, trying to not let bitterness creep in. "My last conscious memory of the skirmish was Vasu staring at me from the ground while I fought several men at once. He did not come to my rescue." Saying this aloud deepened my sense of betrayal. Kapil gasped, his eyes mirroring some of my pain. I clenched my fist to control the anger and pain bubbling in my stomach. I had more important things to worry about. "Vasu is dead. Let us consider this closed unless new evidence surfaces."

I turned to Kapil. "I appoint you as the new Commander of my guards."

His eyes shone, and he stepped forward and bowed to me with his hands clasped together in front and said, "I hope to prove myself worthy of this honor, Prince Jay." He turned to Rish and said, "Uncle Rish, can you please have one of the men fetch Veer?"

Rish replied, "I will go myself and send both Dev and Veer. I need to find Lt. Gen. Satya as well."

When he left, Kapil turned to me, dropping my title and said, "Jay, you are not going to like this."

I knew this would happen. "Kapil—"

He interrupted me, "I had tremendous respect for Commander Balan, but he cowered in your presence and never said no to you putting yourself in harm's way. As the new commander of your guards, my first job is to protect you, even from your own ideas. I am going to have men shadow you day and night. Your disappearance for the past few weeks threw the country into turmoil. That cannot happen again."

I knew I had made the right decision then in promoting him. I raised my eyebrows and teased him. "You also swore to obey me."

He allowed himself a tiny smile, and I added, "Don't hinder my ability to rule, and you can have your way."

I asked him something that bothered me, "Why are you addressing Rish as Uncle? He is not that many years older than us."

"My aunt is married to his cousin," he said, shrugging his shoulders.

My stepmother and Rish shared a set of grandparents too. Royal families entwined many times through blood and marriage, and it hurt my head to think of the web of relationships. I usually just followed Meera's lead on this. Uncle Rish? That did not feel right. As the crown prince, I would address him by his name.

He then added, "I have a letter from Princess Meera, asking me not to trust anyone, till we determine the truth about your disappearance. The letter arrived after Rish, so I am keeping a watchful eye on him as well." I nodded, realizing this constituted my new reality.

Dev and Veer came in then, and Kapil informed Veer of our decision.

Veer then laid his sword at my feet and recited, "I pledge allegiance to Prince Jay and swear to obey his commands. I swear to protect Prince Jay with my life or die trying. I devote myself completely to this duty, this day and all days thereafter. I swear to take my own life if any harm comes to the prince during my watch."

Kapil turned to Dev. "Find some food to eat and get some rest. You will be on guard tonight. Till Karan and Giri are back, we have to forgo some sleep."

I let him finish arranging the guard duties and then sat down, penning a letter to my father. My brief message spoke of my safe return and hinted at my plan. Having escaped with Aranya, I needed to act now and could not wait for my father's words back. King Surya would not delay getting his daughter back. When I finished the letter, I said to Kapil, "Let us find Lt. Gen. Satya."

Kapil and Veer accompanied me to the hall where Lt. Gen. Satya stood talking to Rish. He acknowledged my entrance with a head nod when I entered. A man of medium height and build, his men respected and liked him.

He halted his conversation with Rish and approached me. "My lord, I could not believe our good fortune, when I heard of your return," he said, bowing.

"Satya, I need to send a message to my father. Find two of our best horsemen to take this letter. Then gather your men and wait in the great hall for me. They would have heard the rumors of my escape by now. I need to appear before them in person."

He found two men for me, and after handing the note off to the messengers with strict instructions to entrust it only to the King or Princess Meera, I went to the Great Hall with my guards and Rish.

I climbed up the raised platform with Kapil and Veer on either side and faced the group of men. The room erupted in cheers, and they all shouted, "Long Live Prince Jay." I waited for them to subside and surveyed their faces before I spoke. "Malla soldiers. Prince Nakul and his men captured me, but I escaped captivity with the help of Princess Aranya. She will stay here as our guest.

"My resolve to finish what my father started is stronger now than ever before. Let us capture Saral and bring her under Malla rule. The battles ahead may be long and arduous. Are you ready to fight with me? To bring glory to our kingdom?"

The room exploded again, and the men took up the chant, "Victory to Malla." I climbed down and whispered to Kapil, "I need to mingle and speak with them individually." He nodded and stayed close to me. I spent several moments within the crowd, talking to each one, hearing their concerns for me when I'd disappeared, their happiness in seeing me alive, and their eagerness to fight.

I have dreamt of traveling near and far to conquer lands and expand the Malla kingdom, like my namesake and hero King Jay, my great-grandfather. Under him, Malla ruled from the Puna Sea in the South to the Nali Mountains in the North and Sunda in the East. That would be a reality if we defeated Surya and annexed Saral to Malla.

When I left the great hall, I said to Veer. "Take me to Princess Aranya."

Veer marched to the other side of the castle, and Kapil and I followed. Soon he stood in front of her door and waited for us to reach him before he knocked. An old maid answered. Her eyes darted between us, with no recognition on her face. Kapil cleared his throat and announced, "Prince Jay here to see the Princess."

She bowed to all three of us and stammered, "Yes, my lord," and went in, leaving the door open. I raised my eyebrows at Kapil, and he shrugged, "We hired some local help."

Veer appeared ready to follow her, and I ordered, "Wait." A princess should be allowed to deny a visitor. Not that I expected anything other than a welcome.

Aranya herself appeared by the door.

"Welcome to my humble abode, my lord," she teased. As I entered behind her, I could see she had changed into a fresh sari in the color of a lotus flower. After seeing her in a man's clothes for many days, my eyes welcomed this sight.

"Princess Aranya, have you eaten your morning meal yet?" I inquired.

"No, my lord," she responded.

I turned to the maid and ordered, "Fetch our meals. I will partake mine with the Princess."

I turned to Kapil and said, "I would like to converse with the Princess alone."

He nodded and still came inside with Veer. Both of them walked around and searched the room. In a castle under Malla control, what were they expecting to find?

"No hidden men under her bed?" I snapped with a note of irritation.

"None behind the curtains either. I will stand guard outside, my lord," he said dispassionately and shut the door behind the maid. Faint color crept along my neck for my idiocy. Kapil performed his duty to protect me and Aranya, and I acted like an impatient five-year-old. Some five-year-olds had better sense than me.

Aranya touched my arm and brought me to the present.

I led her to a small table and pulled a chair for her to sit. She twirled the ends of her hair as she sat down. Her dark hair shone in the light like a polished black granite sculpture. I liked her hair in a braid, especially after being out of sight in a turban during our escape.

I took a seat beside her. "Aranya, these last few days, I have been thinking about this futile war we are waging. It needs to come to an end, and that can only happen if I capture King Surya and Prince Nakul."

She clasped her fingers on her lap and looked down.

I continued, "I promise to do my best to safeguard your father and brother's lives. But in war, there are no guarantees for any of us."

She sighed. "For the last several months, I have been hiding in one castle or another, traveling south, fleeing the invading Malla army. My father is consumed by revenge and lost any concern for our land and her people. Nakul has barely slept in months, keeping my father from pursuing his insane plans, recruiting men, strategizing with the elders. Each time I move, he accompanies me, and once I am safely behind palace walls, he leaves, and I don't see him for weeks."

There were worry lines on her forehead, and I wanted to kiss them away. I squeezed her hand instead.

"When you were brought to me unconscious and I cared for you, hope sprang in my heart. When I escaped with you, I chose life and a future. Future for me with you, a future for Saral, and my brother Nakul. Now you are giving me the same choices of death and despair."

I could not hold back any longer. I held her face in my hands and kissed the lines on her forehead. She leaned into me. "Jay."

"Aranya, you and I can leave Saral today and head to Malla. We can get married with my father's blessing and never think about Saral. Is that what you want to do? Will your father stop this war then?"

She bit her lip and shook her head slowly. "He would rather see me dead. Nakul would stop the fighting, though."

"Prince Nakul is not the King. I see no way out of this but to capture King Surya."

She looked at me then and said, "I cannot choose between your life and my brother's. He has been more a father to me than the king. I want no harm to come to you either. I have gone to a lot of trouble to keep that from happening."

The maid arrived with our food and set it out. We were quiet, immersed in our thoughts. She departed soon, shutting the door behind her.

"Would you agree for Nakul to be crowned the King?" she asked.

"The decision rests with my father, but I would make that request, and I see no reason for him to refuse it."

We ate quietly for some time. The warm rice porridge with coconut milk and palm sugar was the best meal I had in a long while.

"Take me with you when you leave."

"It is a war; I cannot protect you completely from danger."

"I can help you navigate the territory."

"We have spies with that knowledge."

"I know my father, so I can tell you how he would react, and I cannot stay here worrying about all of you."

A flash of irritation passed my face, and she caught it. "Princess Aranya," I said firmly, "I understand what you would like. I will give it due consideration and let you know my decision once I have met with my men."

"Am I your prisoner then?" she asked with a burst of anger.

Her anger softened me. I gazed into her eyes, "We are not married yet, so you have not pledged your love, loyalty, and obedience to me."

"You will not get *blind* obedience from me," she whispered.

I laughed and said, "I would expect no less. Disagree with me in private. Once I make my decision, pledge your support. I, in turn, will pledge my love, loyalty, and protection."

I stood up and walked to her side and leaned down to kiss her hair. "I will come back later to share the details of our plan with you."

13

Arrival of the Prince

Akash city woke up to a clear day to welcome Prince Atul. *I may be betrothed to his brother, Prince Amar before I see Rish again.* I put that thought aside. Why did this heart still pine for a man who probably had no love for me? Rish had sent a letter to the King when he arrived in Theni, describing the steps he'd taken to find Jay, but I had heard no news from him since.

Chief Kasu Vindhya and General Devan Biha mounted and left for the city gates to escort the prince.

Riya and I stood at the palace steps to welcome him. With one hand, I held a silver plate with an oil-filled lamp on it. My other hand shielded the lighted cotton wick from the wind. Soon the men rode in, with a young man in the middle. Riya, holding a basket of flowers, leaned into me and whispered, "He is young."

"He is older than Jay," I whispered back, observing the slender young man of medium height. "But not quite as old as I am."

He dismounted at the entry, smiled graciously at us, and bounded up the steps. Riya held a hand over her mouth and said in a voice only I could hear, "And fine-looking." I smiled back, not acknowledging her words. To me, his features appeared mundane, except for his slightly large nose.

Atul stopped two steps below me. I welcomed him to our city by waving the lamp around him to ward off the darkness. I then handed the plate to a maid and greeted him. He returned my greeting courteously and fell in step with me as Riya showered him with flowers.

I led him to the small throne room where my father, mother, and grandmother were seated.

He touched my parent's feet, following the traditional way of showing one's respect. My father blessed him and said, "I hope your arrival ushers in good times for Padi and Malla."

Prince Atul replied, "Uncle Vikram, I bring you the well wishes of my father and mother and all the people of Padi."

He then touched my grandmother's feet, as well. She said, "Last time I saw you, you were a child of five or six running around with a wooden sword in your hand. And now you are a grown man." As he raised, she continued. "You and your brother take after your mother, Princess Radha of Sunda. We have to find you a bride as well while you are here in Malla."

Atul smiled at this and said, "Great Aunt Priya, let us arrange one wedding at a time. I came here seeking Princess Meera's hand for my brother. My wedding can wait."

My grandmother retorted, "You young people have all the time in the world to wait. At my age, I want to see my grandchildren married off before I die. Jay," she choked on the word, and father cut her off gently.

"Mother, Jay will be here soon."

My stepmother turned to Atul and said, "Atul, we were sorry to hear about Princess Sapna. I hope Prince Amar and your parents are well."

"They are, my lady. Amar mourns the loss of his wife and baby. Though he grieves, he is still the crown prince of Padi, so my father wants to see him wedded again soon. He also desires to wed my cousin, Princess Mala, to Prince Jay. Here is his request."

He handed a letter to my father, who took it. He read the letter intently. His face a mask, he said, "Atul, you must be tired after your long journey. Get some rest now. We will speak of these matters soon." He smiled and added, "The queen and princess have arranged a feast in your honor tonight, including entertainment. I will see you then."

Guards escorted him to his chambers, and I retired to mine. As Kantha tidied up, Riya entered. The normally cheerful girl had a worried look on her face. She'd been with me this morning, helping me prepare for Atul's arrival. What caused this sudden change? When she saw me, a sob escaped her, and I immediately silenced her. I waited for Kantha to shut the door and then turned back to Riya. "What causes such sadness in you, my dear?"

"Princess Meera, seeing Prince Atul reminded me of Prince Jay..." she sobbed, unable to control herself. I put my arms around her and led her to a seat.

"My heart does not allow me to believe any harm has befallen him," I replied with as much courage as I could muster. "Riya, if you are going to marry a prince, you need to ensure no one ever sees you cry. Save the tears for your pillow and face the world with courage," I said, repeating my stepmother's advice to her.

She slowly wiped her tears. "I dreamt a silly girl's dream of marrying a prince and becoming a queen."

"It may yet come true, Riya. Clouds may hide the sun briefly, but the sun cannot be hidden for long."

She whimpered, "Unless a long night has fallen, and I perish before dawn."

"Such gloomy thoughts are not proper in one who is destined to be queen." Apt advice for me as well. The disappearance of Jay, betrayal of Rish, and my approaching marriage to Amar had left me feeling dejected. I had a guest to entertain. I needed to bury my sorrow.

"My lady, before now, with my parents and you taking care of me, I had no worries in the world. But now I feel my world has come crashing down around me. And my idle mind takes me to these dark and gloomy places with no way to escape."

"Find an occupation for your body and mind then. Pray for the lost or help with tonight's festivities," I told her gently. "Stay here as long as you need to gather your strength. Then go and put on some finery for the feast. The Riya that brought happiness into the lives of the children who lost their parents due to the floods is in there. Allow her to come out."

Over a hundred people gathered for the feast that night. Steam from the food and smells of peppers and other aromatic spices filled the hall. It befitted a king, but I had no appetite to taste the delicacies. My mind dwelled on Jay. I noted that my father barely touched his food, as well. Atul sat between the king and my grandmother. I saw him speaking to both and eating with the hearty appetite of a young man.

After the feast, we headed to the theatre, where an elaborate stage greeted us. Riya sat next to me. She had listened to me and dressed for the occasion. Though she appeared normal, a keen eye could see the pain in hers.

The artists in the play enacted the life of Rama and his marriage to Seetha. The queen probably thought it appropriate for the occasion. The elaborate costumes, mesmerizing music, and intricate movements captivated the audience. As the birth of Rama and his brothers were announced to the King of Ayodhya, the performers broke into a joyful dance. The birth of Jay had caused a similar celebration in Akash.

When Rama stood and walked towards the bow, which he had to string to prove his worth, the tempo of the music changed. When he broke the bow and won Seetha's hand, the music reached a crescendo. I let out an inaudible sigh. Next to me, Riya had tears flowing down her cheeks.

I leaned over and whispered, "Wipe your tears, Riya, before Atul thinks something is amiss." After the marriage, Seetha endured pain and suffering in her life. She'd lived in the forest with Rama before her husband exiled her to bring up her sons alone. The play today depicted the happier note of Rama and Seetha's wedding.

The next day, Chief Bhoj Thari arrived in Akash. My father wanted to meet with the three chiefs, so he asked me to escort Atul around Akash. I met him outside the king's palace. His face broke into a smile when he saw me. He had not inherited his mother's beauty, but when he smiled, his face lit up.

"My lady, in the daylight, you look even more beautiful if that is possible."

I laughed and said, "Atul, do Padi women fall for your flattery?"

He smiled and said, "Cousin Meera, you will be my Queen one day. So, I only speak the truth in your presence. You have more of Padi in you than me and my brothers."

We reached the stables, and I wondered how to travel. If I choose the palanquin or the elephant, I would be sitting alone, and Atul would be riding on his horse beside me. There would not be many opportunities to converse. We could take the chariot, but my eyes fell on the horses. I remembered riding with Rish, but I locked that thought away.

I turned to Atul and asked, "Do women in Padi ride horses?"

He seemed surprised by the question and nodded. "In Nanga and the surrounding areas, most women do. When there is snow on the ground, it is easier to ride a mule in the mountains around Nanga."

"Let us ride on horses to explore the city then."

I ordered one of the men to bring them. Soon, we rode towards the temple, with me pointing out the various buildings we passed to Atul and answering his questions.

We dismounted at the temple entrance, and I sauntered in with Atul. We stopped to admire the beautiful sculptures of dancers depicted throughout the temple walls. Atul showed a keen knowledge of history and arts.

"You seem to know a lot about our culture, Atul. You don't need a guide to tour this city."

He beamed. "My lady, I do love to read books, to the concern of my father. He worried I would never be a warrior if I buried my head in books all day. He ordered me to go train with my brothers. I have mastered sword fighting while staying true to my first love. The past events of our ancestors are fascinating. Gods played a more prominent and active role in their daily lives, appearing before them and granting them boons."

"I am glad the gods are currently staying out of our lives. It is one thing to be a pawn in a royal chess game, quite another to be a pawn in a god's hands." As I said it, I realized I'd revealed too much. This young man was easy to talk to, and I understood why his father had sent him to Akash. He regarded me thoughtfully. He seemed as if he wanted to say something but then changed his mind.

As we strolled through the temple courtyard, I asked him to tell me more about Padi. He obliged. "I love our capital, Nanga, in winter. The king and most of the royal household move to Daya, before the snowfalls. When the first snow arrives, it blankets the land white. It is quite a sight to peek out the palace and see the mountains covered in snow."

"Also, staying back in Nanga allows you to indulge in your reading," I teased.

He laughed. "Princess Meera, you are very perceptive. I hope my secret is safe with you. Yes, I love to read in winter, when the palace is empty, and the world outside stays quiet."

"The lakes in Daya are beautiful," he continued. "The valleys are filled with flowers when spring comes, and the distant snow-topped mountains glisten in the sun. It is a sight to make a poet of anyone. You will love both our cities," he said with a simple pleasure.

We sat on the steps to the temple pond. "Tell me about your brother, Prince Amar," I said.

He bragged, "Cousin Meera when you marry Amar, you will be marrying the most handsome man in Padi."

I taunted him. "In Malla, men are not valued for their beauty. They are valued for their strength of character and valor."

He boasted, "Amar is strong and fast, and I have never seen him lose a swordfight. He could beat me in a fight with one hand tied to his back."

He smiled and added in a softer voice, "He is a wild horse, though, that needs to be tamed, Cousin Meera. I saw the way you rode your horse. With your wit and beauty, I cannot see a better person to do just that."

He remained a dutiful brother, and I realized that would be as far as he would go to describe the flaws in his brother's character.

He studied me and said, "Uncle Vikram will insist Amar does not marry anyone else besides you, and my father will oblige."

He would oblige as long as I produced an heir for his son. Otherwise, I would be Queen in name only, like my stepmother, and Amar would marry other women.

"And you, Atul? Is there a girl waiting for you in Padi?"

He shook his head, and with a twinge of sadness, said, "As you stated before, we are pawns in royal games. One of the Padi chiefs has a daughter about my age and a large army to boast. My father would expect me to marry her or one of the other chief's daughters with the most wealth. Though they would do better to marry one of their own, a chief's son with lands, than a prince who would never be king."

He suddenly stopped as if he'd revealed something unpleasant and started apologizing, "Cousin Meera, Amar would be my king one day. I am bound in honor and duty to the king of Padi. I did not mean to—"

I cut him off. "No need to apologize. You would be a prince subjected to the whims of your father and then your brother."

"And serving them is my duty," he hurriedly added.

"I can see you do your duty admirably. You would advise your brother on things he does not want to hear about. You would fight his wars and heal his wounds."

As I said my words out loud, I wondered if Prince Amar could be the monster he is portrayed to be, with a brother like Atul?

I stood, and he followed. I enjoyed this young man's company, despite the worries gnawing at my chest. We then strode outside the temple, and I turned to him. "My grandmother is expecting us to share her mid-day meal. We should not keep her waiting."

He nodded and mounted his ride. Once back at the palace, we left our horses at the stables, and I told him I would meet him in the Queen mother's chambers shortly. As I turned to leave, he said, "Princess Meera, let me accompany you."

Surprised, I agreed, and he walked beside me. He lowered his voice and said, "Your eyes are filled with sorrow. I heard rumors about Prince Jay on the way to Akash. Since I have been here, I have heard he is missing."

It brought a lump into my throat, and I said more to myself, "I do not think any harm has come to him."

"I pray the same. I had heard many wonderful things about Prince Jay and eagerly awaited meeting him. Let me know if there is anything I can do to be of assistance to you."

We arrived in my corridor, and I turned to him. "I am grateful for your kind words. We will part here, Atul. I will see you soon," I said and headed into my rooms. I heard his footsteps receding as I entered. My maid Kantha helped me clean up the dirt from the ride. She combed my disheveled hair and rebraided it.

"Princess Meera, I know you are worried about Prince Jay. After your mother's death, you looked after him yourself. All that care you gave him will not be for naught. He is bound to be safe and will be found soon. Though some people act as if they wish otherwise."

Kantha would go to war to defend me. "Why, what happened?"

She snorted, "Padma, the Queen's servant, heard the Queen urging Sudha to forget Prince Jay. Padi has three princes, and the queen wants her niece married to one of them. She has set her sights on Prince Atul."

She will whisper in my father's ears when she thinks the time is right. Anger rose in my heart. While father and I are praying for Jay's safe return, she and others are scheming on what to do if he never comes back. Was I being naïve in refusing to acknowledge that possibility? An irrational part of me thought if I pictured him alive, he would be.

In Jay's absence, she will not be the only one plotting. King Verma will have designs on the Malla throne as well. Schemers and plotters will be waiting for the right opportunity to strike, like scavengers surrounding an elephant corpse.

I wanted to find out what happened in the council meeting earlier that day. Instead of looking forward to eating with grandmother, now

I wanted to skip the meal so I could go visit father. But Atul would be there, and my desires would have to wait.

I headed to my grandmother's chambers. My grandmother and Atul were conversing as I entered the hallway, and I could hear them.

"As a child, I would eagerly await the festival of Rama. The streets of Nanga would be lighted with thousands of lamps, and people would gather for the evening festivities. The giant straw statues of Rama and Ravana would fill me with delight, and I would watch as arrows flew between them. When the final fire-lit arrow found its mark and the Ravana statue went up in flames, I would cheer along with the crowds," my grandmother recalled, a wistfulness in her voice.

"Father wanted the entire kingdom to celebrate the birth of the new baby prince, and he ordered the festival to be grander than ever," said Atul. Then he stopped as if he remembered something, and I walked in. As he heard my footsteps, he stood up to greet me.

"Even a king has limited powers in the face of death," my grandmother said solemnly. "Your father probably mourned the loss, but a king cannot wait to act. He fulfilled his duty by sending you along to seek my granddaughter's hand in marriage. Even my beloved Padi may not be worthy of my beautiful and brave Meera."

I smiled at these words. My eyes met hers, and I knew she spoke as much about Jay's loss as about Sapna's. She hid her feelings about his disappearance as a true queen would.

Atul said sincerely, "I speak for my father when I say Padi will strive to be worthy of such a princess."

"I am an old woman, and I forget you young ones must be hungry. Let us sit at the table. Meera, call for our food."

Atul helped her to the table, and I summoned the servants.

Once the servants served our food and departed, grandmother turned to Atul and asked, "I've heard strange stories about Amar. If even half of them hold true, he disgraces the Padi name. Is he a worthy prince for Meera?"

Color crept along his face, and he stammered, "I would not lie to you. He is not worthy of her. But he will be our king one day and needs a strong and virtuous queen. There is no one better than Cousin Meera."

"Verma is a worse fool than I thought. Fathers can act like fools when it comes to their sons, but a king cannot. Amar is no longer a child to be coerced with punishment," stated my grandmother.

I had heard enough about Amar and wanted to hear no more. I steered the conversation to the festival of Rama, allowing myself to indulge in the beautiful descriptions given by Atul, and ignoring the dread in my stomach at what I knew must be done.

I must marry Amar.

14

Battle Plans

As I headed outside, I saw Kapil standing guard. I nodded at him, and we strode towards the council room. I sensed he had changed during our time here in Saral. He had lost his playfulness. Events in Saral had left a mark on him. I had changed, as well. I no longer dreamt of greatness and a place in legends either.

As soon as Lt. Satya and a few of his men saw me, they stood respectfully, waiting for me to come in. Another privilege of being the prince, ministers, and soldiers old enough to be your father and grandfather stood up when you entered a room. When my father fought in Lukla, I attended my first council meeting without him. After some time, tired of sitting, I stood and began pacing the room. Then I realized the entire room rose as well. The minister had smiled kindly at me and said we could have the meeting standing up if I preferred. I wanted to say, "Council members, I am only a boy. There is no need to show me such respect. Please take your seats." But I knew they respected my title, not me personally, and asking people to break tradition in my first meeting was not a good idea. So, I refrained from saying it aloud and sat for the rest of the meeting.

Today, I scanned their faces and spotted Shiv among them. When he saw me, his lips curled up. "Shiv," I called. He came closer and bowed to me. I embraced him. Shiv appeared leaner and more muscular and carried himself as a fighter.

Shiv had come to Akash almost four years ago. As two years his junior at the time, the fifteen-year-old boy impressed me during our training. He grew up with an older brother, so he had no qualms about beating me bloody in our fights.

Kapil's father, Mano Biha, trained us, and once he came across Shiv sitting on top of me, pounding my face, while I tried weakly to defend myself. He pulled Shiv away, yelling, "Boy, didn't anybody teach you how to behave towards the prince?" Chief Guard Mano then asked him to take his upper garment off and handed me a whip. I knew Chief Mano wanted me to whip him. Punish him for his offense. All my friends gathered around, and I stared at the whip and Shiv's bareback. I dropped the whip and jumped onto him instead, pushing him to the ground.

"Who asked you to fight back, Shiv?" I yelled while punching his face.

"You," he whimpered.

I stopped my blows. "Then why are you not?"

Shiv realized my intentions, and so did Chief Guard Mano. He recognized what I desired, though he wanted to ensure no harm came to me in the training yard. He warned all my friends, "You can fight with Prince Jay, as long as you cause him no permanent damage. If I see a scar on his face or a broken tooth, you will become tiger fodder."

Shiv broke me out of my musing by saying, "I thought I had lost you forever, my lord."

"It is not that easy to kill me," I said in a low voice.

Then I roared, "Men, the Saral war has lasted for too long, and the time has come to end it." A cheer went around the room, and I raised my hand to silence them.

"How many men do we have here in Theni?" I asked.

Satya answered, "We have 2,000 men, my lord. Another 1,000 are a day or two away. Most of our men are in Lukla, helping rebuild the fort and the surrounding villages. It has the best facilities to station our men."

Satya spread a map on the table. Lukla, the Saral Capital, situated north of Theni and closer to the Malla border, held a fort on top of a hill with excellent views north to Malla and south into Saral. Malla controlled the land between Lukla and Theni.

South of Theni lay the land still under King Surya's control. I could see on the map the river east of us, the mountains to our west, and the sea beyond the mountains.

Malla's standing army had three units. One stationed in the north under General Karan Thari, one in the south under General Devan Biha, and one in Akash. Each unit had an elephant corps of 500 elephants, two cavalry corps with 1,000 horses each, five infantry corps with 2,000 men each, and a medical corps with 200 doctors. We also had 200 naval ships with 100 men on each.

Of the southern unit under General Devan, about 5000 men, along with 100 elephants, and 500 horses were in Lukla, and the remaining were spread all over the territory we captured.

"Leaving forces to guard our captured cities, gather the rest of the men, horses, elephants, and supplies in three days. If he hasn't already, Surya will have soon heard of my escape. I have his daughter here with me. He will try to get her back. However, she desires to remain, and I have granted her asylum. Let us be on the offensive. Send our spies to find out Surya's location and what he plans."

"My lord, it is good to have you back," said Satya, and he dispatched some of his men who could speak like a Saral and were good with disguises for the search.

Then we discussed how to rout King Surya.

"Wherever he is hiding, we have to capture the City of Maram first," said Satya. "All the supplies to Surya come from there, and if we capture it, we will cut off his supply chain."

Saral men captured me in Maram. Heading back had a sense of destiny. We debated our strategy to attack Maram. The City was the gateway to where Surya hid. The road leading South had hills with a network of caves, with more than one entrance to them. Saral men guarded the caves.

"What are our options to capture the caves?"

Satya responded, "We can take 300 men and surround the hills. But we don't know how many men Surya has in the caves and we could suffer heavy casualties. The men would also be alerted to our presence and could escape."

Rish said, "We could take a small force and infiltrate the caves. This is riskier, and we may lose all our men, but we'd have a better chance of catching him."

One of Satya's men expanded on this. "If we split our forces into four and climb each side of the hills, I can lead the troops to one of the entrances. If we can climb on top of the cave at night and kill the men who guard the holes, we can breach the caves."

More opinions were offered, and I considered the options. All seemed like suicide missions with little chance of success. I picked the one which would have the least casualties. I glanced at Satya and asked," How many do you need for this stealth attack?" He responded that he needed forty, nine in each group with a leader. Men eager to prove themselves, came forward to join the fight.

Shiv stepped up and said, "Prince Jay, please allow me to join."

Rish concurred, "He can join the group heading east, my lord." A veteran of many battles and a trusted soldier led that group. I agreed, and men left to set that plan into action.

We turned to the second aspect of this strategy, capturing the Palace in the City. Satya said, "We estimate about 500 men guard this palace. Once the caves are captured, we can surround the palace and breach the walls."

"How many men should we take for this?"

"A thousand would overwhelm the Saral guards."

I nodded and said, "How do we get our soldiers in place without alerting the Saral men?"

We decided to send a force of about 500 to Pullikadu hills and another 500 to try to approach Kadal, Capital of Gomti. With these diversions, if we could keep Surya from guessing our true intent, we could attack Maram palace.

Lt. Gen. Satya added, "I will lead this mission."

Before I could say anything, Rish chimed in, "Lt. Gen., I will join your cause."

I didn't want the men to think I preferred to stay safe in palaces while I sent them into harm's way. I needed to lead for the men to follow. Otherwise, tales of my lack of courage would spread.

I said, "Satya, I will command the mission myself."

He looked at Kapil and me, and said, "Prince Jay, south of Pullikadu is still under Saral rule. You just escaped captivity, and this would put you in peril again. You are our Prince and heir to Malla. I promised your father I'd keep you safe."

"My men risked their lives for me. A king needs to lead from the front."

"Prince Jay, if you were married and had heirs to the throne, I would agree with you."

Yes, once I have sons of my own, I can be dispensed with. My worth depends on my ability to procreate. Sudden rage coursed through me, and I tried to control it. I chided myself for such unworthy thoughts. He spoke the truth. As the Malla heir, I had a solemn duty to ensure the continuation of that line. I'd put my kingdom in jeopardy by my capture. I led men on a fool's errand in disguise earlier. It would be safer for me to allow Satya to lead this battle. But my heart rejected this. I felt the need to reclaim my tarnished reputation by leading this battle.

I tightened my grip of the hilt and said, "I trust over a thousand Malla men can keep me safe. I have considered your advice and have decided to lead the attack. I cannot ask my men to do something I am not willing to do myself. I would be honored to fight beside you. Find a person to take your place in Theni in our absence. Let us discuss our strategy."

We set the plan in motion, and I left with Kapil to my room.

When we reached my room, he studied me and said, "Prince Jay, men who know you think you are brave and will be a just ruler. I am entrusted with protecting you and would do so in Gomti. You don't have to risk your life to demonstrate your battle credibility."

"What about the men who don't know me, Kapil? What will they believe? My actions will speak louder than any words."

Surya would not expect me to lead this attack myself. And I wanted to see this land of my mother's filled with rivers and coconut trees. A little voice in my head said that I'd let anger provoke me, but I suppressed that voice.

Kapil opened his mouth to say something and then shut it abruptly. He watched me, as I sat down to write some letters, and read messages sent in my absence. A servant fetched me my meal and left it at the table. I had a stack of correspondence to read, so the food went cold.

I looked up when I heard soldiers training in the yard and saw Veer standing guard in the room. Rubbing my sore neck, I went to a window to observe.

"Veer, is there a quiet place for me to train? I have not properly held a sword in ages."

"There is my lord. Do you want me to come and train with you?"

"Yes, let us go."

We spent an hour training, and I grew tired by the end of it. But I'd gained strength in my abdomen, and the ability to move swiftly. I reached my room and found a physician waiting for me. He inspected my stomach wound, now a puckered scar, and pronounced that it had mended.

"I am sure you are itching to get back to your training routine. I would advise you to start slowly," he said and departed. I noticed Dev standing on the balcony outside with a spear. I went out to talk to him. He pointed up when he saw me.

"There is something above us. I heard noises."

Feathers littered the floor. "Most likely birds, nesting above."

He followed my gaze, "I am going to climb and inspect. To make sure it is nothing else."

"Don't break your neck while doing it. Kapil needs you more than ever. With just the three of you to guard me, I think he has hardly slept since I arrived."

"I will be careful, my lord."

"Report any findings to me later. I must make an appearance."

I cleaned up and went to the training yard. Most men were excited about heading out, even if they did not know all the details of our plans. I talked to various soldiers, accepting their gratitude at my return. Then I met with Satya and others, getting an update. Our plan seemed as solid as we could make it.

When I arrived back in my room, I noticed Dev climbing down a pillar on the balcony. He jumped from a height of about eight feet and landed perfectly.

"What did you see on the roof?" I asked.

"A hawk's nest with two baby birds, Prince Jay. When our men secured the place, they must have left the nest alone."

It was nightfall when I sent for Aranya. I waited on a small terrace facing the river. She entered, escorted by Dev. Dev stayed back, giving us some privacy. She came to stand next to me and named the various mountains and temples we could see from here. In turn, I briefly told her about the plans we'd set in motion.

"Have you made your decision about me traveling with the army, my lord?" she asked. Her eyes appeared bright with hope, and I hated having to disappoint her.

I shook my head. "I have. We are not ready to face King Surya or Prince Nakul yet, so I need you to stay behind. There will be still several hundred men guarding this palace."

While I knew I'd made the right decision for her safety, I did not like rejecting her request. She nodded. I felt grateful when she did not push me. I could tell she understood the reason behind my decision, even if she did not like the outcome. She had the makings for a great queen.

As I laid down in bed that night, my sister's and father's faces floated in my head. Guilt at my decision to lead the battle consumed me. "Meera, I will return safely," I whispered into the darkness.

Over the next few days, I spoke with elders from nearby villages to check on their supplies, did daily rounds at the palace and spoke with several of the soldiers and men, and ramped up preparations for the upcoming battle. My favorite activity, though, was sparring.

The rooftop provided the seclusion I needed to gain my skills back. Unlike most of my friends, Rish had real battle experience and understood I needed to be ready. He typically had both him and Kapil fight me, and he wanted me to be able to ward them both off.

The first day, being high up on the top with the wind blowing fiercely, I could barely hold my sword, let alone fight them off. In the last few days, though, my footwork improved tremendously. Today I fought with a fierceness I did not know I possessed, and swords flew everywhere, and for the first time, I disarmed them both.

Rish eyed me curiously and said, "My lord, you will soon become one of the best sword fighters of Magadha." I suspected he said it just to please me. People often said things to my face just to get in my good court.

Kapil stood up from where he had fallen, and said, "You fought with tremendous strength and an inkling of brutality. I thought my head would be chopped off a few times."

I suppressed my grin and said, "Don't worry. If I am going to chop your head off, I will make a ceremony out of it."

Then Rish offered to take me to see some temples in the nearby villages. Rish, Kapil, and a few other guards came with me. Rish took us to a temple of Buddha. Beautiful sculptures of Buddha in various poses with his serene and peaceful face greeted us. Born a prince like me, he gave up his royal life to find answers to his subject's suffering. I stood in front of a life-sized statue of him, depicted standing on a lotus.

Rish came up to me and said, "I know Princess Meera is an admirer of art and sculpture, so I thought you would be interested in these as well." The way he said Meera's name caught my attention, and I glanced at him. Maybe I had an admirer of Meera beside me. Unlike a prince, a princess can only marry one man, so Rish's chances amounted to nothing. Besides, Atul had arrived in Akash, seeking her hand for Prince Amar.

"Yes, Meera loves sculptures. Apart from helping the poor and needy, she spends most of her money on restoring old castles, temples, and tombs," I replied. His uncle, Chief Kasu, disliked Meera spending the crown money for these, so she limited herself to the income from her lands.

That evening, I watched the sunset paint the river in a rainbow of red, orange, and blue from my balcony. I could see fishermen returning home on their boats. Coconut trees lined the shores. The first stars for the night appeared in the sky. I also saw rain clouds moving our way.

"It is going to rain soon, Dev. Come in when it does."

"Pardon me, Prince Jay. This castle has not been completely secured. There are forests behind us and too many spots for somebody to climb up undetected. I would miss any intruders if I came inside. A little rain will cause me no harm."

Kapil strode in, and I went back into the room. "We don't have enough men to guard you, my lord. I will have to stay in the room with you, while Dev remains outside."

Karan and Giri were on their way, so that left Kapil with just two guards for the present. I observed the dark shadows under Kapil's eyes. "We have a long day ahead of us. You need to get some sleep."

"Veer is sleeping now. He will wake up in four hours and relieve Dev."

I tossed a blanket and cushion at him. "Get some sleep. I am not sleepy now. I have to read some of my correspondences. I will wake you before I go to sleep."

"Prince Jay—"

"Don't argue with me, Kapil. You will be more useful tomorrow if you are awake."

Karan and Giri arrived in Theni the next day and with all five of my guards here and other plans complete, the time had come to depart.

15

Alliance Forged

After my meal with grandmother and Prince Atul, I departed for father's chambers. I wanted to find out what happened at the meeting of the three chiefs. I found my father seated, staring into space. As I entered, he glanced up and tried to smile, but he gave up midway and beckoned me to sit next to him.

When I sat, he held my chin with his hands and regarded me. "My child, what sorrow I have caused you," he said slowly.

"Father, I know of no such thing."

"You are a good daughter and have been more a mother to Jay," he said. Then he scanned the room and stated, "I need some fresh air. Let us go for a ride on the boat." There were eyes and ears everywhere, even in the king's chambers, and a boat ride meant he wanted to tell me something in confidence.

Our deaf oarsman brought the boat to the land and helped my father climb in. When he rowed away from the shore, father sighed and said, "Meera, Atul sent a messenger to Padi this morning. I let him go but asked our men to slow his passage. However, the news of Jay's disappearance will reach Verma soon. His choices are clear: conquer Malla through marriage or war. A war would devastate us. I can no longer refuse to give your hand to Amar. That marriage will take place soon. When you go back to Padi, I can send men to safeguard you, but not from Amar."

"Father, be not afraid for me." I was raised to do my duty for this kingdom, and I was not going to shy away from it. As a young motherless girl, I learned how to observe people and build my network of friends and alliances to stay informed. With Amar, it would be about building goodwill among his allies and friends. Whether that would be sufficient was a different story. Was this how soldiers felt before a battle, a hollow pit in their stomachs?

Father paused and observed me before narrating a strange story. "As a young boy, I would wander off alone, away from the palace guards. On one such occasion, as I rode my horse on the edges of the city, rain clouds gathered. I headed back to the city, but a downpour started before I reached the gates, and the road became too slick for me to continue riding. I found shelter in a wayside building.

"As I watched the rain, I sensed another person alongside me. When the next lightning struck, I saw a girl about my age in tattered clothes. She must have sought shelter there as well. Though I could not see her between lightning strikes, I felt her gaze upon me. Suddenly she touched my face, and before I could move, she spoke.

"*Crown, I see on your head.*"

"Her voice startled me, and as I opened my mouth to question her, I heard noises. I swiveled towards the sounds and saw lights approaching me, which grew into lanterns. Then I heard my name. The men carrying the lanterns wore city guard gear. I called out to them. As I spoke, the girl disappeared into the shadows. The men were pleased to see me and took me back on a covered chariot. Before I left with them, I searched for the girl, but she had vanished.

"In time, I forgot the girl and her words. When you were born, your mother and I took you to the Durga temple. There we offered food and clothes to the poor in honor of your birth. A woman in a torn sari approached us, her face dirty and hair in tangles. She bowed to your mother, and your mother bid her closer to receive a new sari. When she came near, she muttered, "*Crown I see on your head, like I said under the rains.*"

"Shocked into remembering her words, I realized they had come true, for as the second son, I should not have been king, yet I was. She saw you then, a baby in your mother's hands, and she whispered, "*Queen she will be one day, her name will be celebrated, near and far. Her son will rule the three kingdoms and beyond.*"

"Your mother thanked her for her blessings and gave her the sari. Her words stayed with me this time. We held a larger celebration for your brother, soon after his birth. I scanned the crowds, wondering if she'd have words for Jay as well, but the woman never came."

His tale left me speechless. Could the same words fill one with both joy and trepidation? Queen of Padi or Malla or both. My son, king of the three kingdoms. King of Magadha. I could almost see him, a brilliant gold crown on his hair, ruling justly. Then my thoughts turned to the father of my son and soured. I would be married to Prince Amar, a monster in the eyes of all who knew him. And what would happen to Jay, if my son was the ruler of the Magadha? I almost laughed out loud for believing the ravings of a madwoman.

"Father, this woman, in the presence of her king, said what she thought would please you," I said, reaching out to hold his hands. He sighed and stared at the distant trees.

I steered the conversation back to the council meeting.

"Tell me what happened in the council meeting, Father."

"Fools all of them." My father sounded exasperated. "Bhoj Thari wants your hand for his older son. I might have entertained that possibility some months back, when— Things have changed, and the vultures are circling over us.

"Devan is loyal now, but he is married to Princess Lata, my cousin. If I make the wrong move, he would be ready to pounce to capture the throne for his sons.

"In my youth, I acted foolishly. With an older brother, I was never raised to be the king or the father of queen and kings. Where I should have acted, I failed, and I have no leverage over Vindhya. Kasi Vindhya, my father-in-law, will act in the interests of his family. He asked my leave to dine Atul in his castle, and I granted him his wish. He would not forsake his desires for his granddaughter Sudha to wed Jay yet, but he is a man who likes to keep his doors open.

"Kripa stayed after the others left and forced me to think about determining the succession without the kingdom descending into chaos. My cousins, Princess Mohini and Princess Lata, both have sons. Princess Mohini is married to Padi Prince Rudra. If I die—" I tried to interrupt him, but he ignored me and continued, "and Jay is not found, we can have her son, Prince Naren, rule as the regent, till you bear sons. He is a Padi prince, and King Verma would ensure a successful transition to his grandchild."

All this talk of succession disturbed me greatly. "Father, my heart tells me Jay is alive. Rish and his guards will find him. Somu, who has been a faithful servant, is probably still in Saral."

"I agree, my child. Somu, if anybody, can find Jay. Devan thinks he has betrayed us to the Saral, but I think otherwise. My son is alive and can be crowned if I have the courage to do the right thing."

My father regarded me and said, "I should have done this a long while ago, but my heart failed me. If the news from Saral does not favor us, I will send men to kill King Surya. Yes, that is the only option. I will have to find a way to delay your wedding until then. Then, Prince Nakul can be crowned as King of Saral."

I did not follow him. Was he planning to wed me to Prince Nakul then?

"Father—" I said, but he interrupted me.

"Meera, the time has come for me to bare my secrets to you. Secrets a father should be ashamed to narrate to his child, but they cannot die with me."

Then he told me another tale: "I led a carefree life as a young boy. My father crowned Rudra as the crown prince. The same teachers taught us both, and your grandfather took every opportunity to involve us in ruling the kingdom. Still, I had more freedom than my brother. Sunda kingdom, across the Tunga Sea, started an open rebellion. My father and brother sailed the seas to stop the uprising. Padi and Malla enjoyed close ties, and Prince Verma joined them with the Padi army."

I had heard about the Sunda war in which King Verma, my grandfather, and uncle fought in.

Father continued, "While they fought, I squandered my time away in Malla. Saral crowned a new king, and I heard rumblings from there. Father won the war, and along with his victory message, he ordered me to go to Saral to meet the new king, Surya. Ostensibly, I would pay tribute to King Surya and extend Malla's hand in friendship, against a common enemy across the sea. My father also asked me to study King Surya and ascertain his willingness to continue our alliance.

"On the way to Saral, I recognized I would never learn the truth as a Prince of Malla. I needed to mingle with the people of the kingdom and would have to travel incognito. With a small group of men for protection, I landed in Gomti, disguised as a sailor. Part of my plan worked, and I learned many things I would not have otherwise."

Father paused here and gazed at the sky. After a few moments, I urged him to continue. With a faraway look in his eyes, he said, "At our stop in Kadal, I wandered the streets of the city, admiring the people and the buildings. Under the twilight sky, we strolled through the forest near the city, when a young girl on a horse rode past us. She appeared suddenly before me like a goddess. She slowed as she crossed us, and our eyes briefly met. Her face bewitched me, and her eyes haunted me. I was not naïve enough to think I would be allowed to marry a common girl, so I asked after her. I learned the girl, your mother Kayal, hailed from the Gomti house. Once I ascertained her noble birth, I set myself a new mission. In my youthful and brash ways, I sought her company in court. She refused my audience, but I persisted. My newly acquired patience paid off. Soon I had an opportunity to save her when her horse threw her. I revealed myself to her and declared my feelings."

As if picturing my mother in his head, he whispered, "I spent many a day, dreaming of her long curly hair, musical voice, and beautiful dark face in rapture. I never had to work harder at anything than to make your mother return my love. She slowly came around to accepting me.

She feared my affections were fleeting, but I proved to her otherwise. We said simple vows and lived as man and woman for a few blissful days. Soon after, word reached me that Father was on his way to Malla after securing a marriage alliance for Verma in Sunda. I had delayed meeting Surya for too long, so I promised Kayal I would be back for her after seeking my father's blessing. I gave her my ring and promised to return, as the prince this time."

My heart raced, and I suddenly knew where the story headed. With my eyes wide open, I listened with bated breath. "When I came back, fate had set a different path for me. I had to take on the reins of the kingdom when my father and brother perished at sea. And I married the girl promised to my brother. In a few months, Kayal sent a messenger to me. Somu came to me and said Kayal carried my child."

I gasped. My mother was pregnant before she had me?

"My world turned upside down again," he continued. "I left in disguise again to bring her to Malla. Time had passed since Somu left for Malla. Queen Lata came home to deliver her child, and she helped your mother hide her pregnancy from the world. Your mother gave birth to a baby boy. News of my ascendance to the throne reached her, along with my marriage to Charu. With no reason to expect my return, Kayal felt she had no choice but to give up the baby. Lata delivered a stillborn son and worried about not producing an heir. The two women hatched a scheme to claim my baby boy as Lata's son, to save Kayal from disgrace.

"Surya arrived in the city before me, and Lata handed the baby to him as his son. Surya claimed my son, Prince Nakul, as the Saral heir and Queen Lata died shortly after. When I arrived in Kadal, the woman who sent for me refused to leave the city and her son. I wanted to hold my son in my arms and proclaim him mine.

"Few days after my arrival, things took a turn. Baby Nakul grew attached to Kayal, and Surya wanted to marry her. With no wish to marry Surya, Kayal now agreed to leave the city with me. But in a sudden madness, I wanted my son raised as a Saral prince, not thinking things through. I assumed there would come a time when I could reveal the truth to him and claim him and Saral as mine. I told your mother that

King Surya would destroy us if we snatched his presumed son, so I asked her to leave him there. He would be safe, as the heir to the throne. Only four people knew the truth, his two parents, Somu, and his sister, Thangam. Thangam agreed to take good care of him and send us news of him and Kayal left heavy-hearted."

My father fretted, "My foolishness continues to haunt us. When Jay came along, I grasped my mistake. The world saw him as my firstborn, and I had to raise him as my heir. I realized I could never claim Nakul as my son and deprive Jay of what he thought of as his birthright. And afraid to destroy Nakul, I have been tempered in my fight against Saral. Meera, now you know my secrets. When there comes a time when Malla needs a king, you can reveal the truth to Nakul. Your mother left him a necklace, and both Kayal and I have penned him letters which are in my chambers."

A secret brother? My head spun after hearing the news, and I felt I needed many days to understand what he'd revealed to me. But I knew now why father never sought Nakul's hands for mine.

My father gestured towards the boatman, and he started rowing back. I tried to piece things together, and Father had a determined look on his face. I accompanied him to his chambers in silence then headed back to mine, my head whirling with thoughts.

Later that day, I strolled in the gardens, still sifting through my father's story, when Sudha came to see me. The girl still remained a mystery to me.

Sudha had attended the feast yesterday, but with my mind occupied elsewhere, I did not observe her then. Now, I gazed at her face to see if I could gauge her feelings. She appeared confused and conflicted. I asked her to sit next to me on the bench and said, "What brings you here, Sudha?"

She glanced at me and whispered, "Princess Meera, my Uncle Rish has gone to find and rescue Prince Jay. Do you think... hope your brother is alive?"

I watched her closely as she said this. She appeared downcast, but not devastated.

"Hope, yes, I hope my brother is alive, and your Uncle Rish can find him."

I held back my fears because I did not want to acknowledge them to myself, lest they become true. And now I had another brother in Saral. Sometimes, knowledge was burdensome.

"Prince Atul seems to be a gallant young man."

"Yes, Atul is chivalrous." I knew Mani Vindhya had arrived in town, ostensibly to discuss Jay's disappearance. He would not want to miss an opportunity to meet Atul, Prince of Padi. In the three kingdoms, princes were rarer than a white peacock. Still, leave it to a Vindhya to make sure no door was closed to benefit the Vindhya family.

"Have you met the Prince? I will be meeting him tomorrow and —" before I could finish, Sudha interrupted me with a blush creeping across her cheek.

"Grandfather has invited him for dinner tonight, my lady."

"Then you have to tell me all about it tomorrow," I said. The Vindhya wealth would be in full display at the dinner, no doubt.

The next day, I set out on an elephant to the Krishna temple built on the hilltop. I had asked Riya to accompany me, hoping to offer her comfort. Instead of her usual cheerfulness, I found a quiet, contemplative girl pondering her future. Atul met us promptly at the courtyard in the morning, and we started early. The rains had stopped, and green stalks of grains grew in the fields we passed. They would be ready for harvest in two moon months.

I remembered the last time I visited the temple with Rish Vindhya. Was I that carefree just a few fortnights back?

Riya interrupted my thoughts and said, "Princess Meera, my father wants to take me back to Biha. I miss my mother and my brothers, as well. It has been many months since I saw them. And the change of scenery would help me."

"Riya, you have been my constant companion. I hoped for that companionship to continue during these trying times as well."

"My lady, the thought of leaving you is what gives me pause about going back home."

I patted her arm. "Go, visit your family. But don't stay too long. I may be going to Padi soon, and I want to cherish our times together before then."

"I can come to visit you in Padi. My Aunt Mohini has asked me to visit her several times."

Riya's mother and Princess Mohini were sisters and my father's cousins. Mohini had married Prince Rudra, brother to King Verma of Padi.

We arrived at the temple, and the elephant kneeled, and we climbed down from the palanquin.

Prince Atul dismounted from his horse and waited for us. For a minute, I imagined Rish standing there with his hands on his hips, alert and intense. Then Atul smiled at us. His friendly gesture held none of the magic I felt when... I dragged myself from these futile thoughts and brought myself back to reality. We walked in through the temple doors together. The courtyard and flowers and the peacocks could not hold my attention now like they did the last time.

The priest awaited our arrival and started the *pooja* soon after. Afterward, he gave us the offering of bananas and milk. Handing it over, he marveled, "My lady, I told you your wedding day neared last time you visited. With Prince Atul here seeking your hands for his brother, Prince Amar, my words will come true soon."

He turned to Atul and boasted, "It is a boon for Prince Amar to marry our Princess Meera. She will bring prosperity to her husband and raise her children to be worthy kings and queens."

Atul glanced at me and said, "Padi is truly blessed then."

I remembered the story my father said earlier. There were fortune-tellers in Malla, who claimed to gaze at your face and foretell the future. My stepmother set a lot in store in the words of such. My father, though, was haunted by the words of a girl from his childhood. Did anybody really have the power to see into the future?

Atul called out me and brought me back to reality. We approached the temple pond. Riya climbed down the steps to sit at the bottom, facing away from us. Her slouched back and sagging shoulders whispered to me the pain she carried in her heart.

"This is a beautiful pond. The blooming lotuses remind me of you, my lady. While the water lilies are delicate and gently sway in the wind, the pink lotuses are majestic and spread its fragrance near and far. When your eyes fall on the lotus, all the other flowers fade in comparison. The color hues may be a gentle pink, but the flower is not a delicate beauty. It is a beauty to behold, beyond the reaches of mortal men," stated Atul, glancing at me.

My face lit up, "Careful, Atul. You may elevate me beyond the realms of men. Would you like to sit on these steps for a few moments?" He nodded, and we sat down.

"Coming back to the realm of men, did you enjoy the feast with the Vindhya clan?" I asked him, curious to see his reaction.

"The feast impressed me with the wealth and splendor of the Vindhya and the Malla kingdom. We in Padi can lay claim to a large land, but our wealth is no match to Malla."

"Were you fortunate to gaze upon Sudha Vindhya and ponder what flower she resembled?" I asked half mockingly.

"Sudha Vindhya is a beautiful flower with a sweet smell that draws the unaware in," he answered, matching my tones and pausing dramatically, "and if you are blessed, you would see the deadly thorns hiding underneath before it pricks your fingers.

"We have our own form of Vindhya in the Padi kingdom as well, a powerful family whose support the kingdom needs. It is like keeping a fire going. You need to add enough fuel to the fire to sustain it. A little too much, and you can burn your house down, and a little too little, and the fire is extinguished.

"Her family, though, were confused whether to mourn the missing Prince, pretend ignorance and hide it from me, or celebrate my visit. The conversation veered from her betrothal to the crown prince to find a worthy prince for her marry."

He understood the royal dynamics and had gauged in a short

amount of time where things stood between us. Maybe I underestimated this young man. His affable manner masked a sharp mind.

I headed to my father's chambers to share his mid-day meal. As I entered, I saw General Devan Biha conversing with father. I hesitated in the doorway. Father saw me and beckoned, "Come in, Meera. The General is taking my leave before heading to Saral."

The General bowed to me and said, "I am going to Biha first, my lord. My wife and sons would forget my face if I stay away any longer."

He turned to me, "Riya said she would visit you this morning, my lady. Her mother wanted to see her more than me. I am going to take her with me to Biha and allow the mother and daughter to reunite."

Riya had bid me farewell that morning. She promised to be back for my wedding, and we embraced and shed tears. I knew not if mine were for losing her or for my impending wedding.

Father asked the General, "How long are you planning to stay in Biha?"

General responded, "A few days to satisfy my wife, and then I will be on the road again."

Father nodded, "We have received very little news from Saral. If the Prince is captured by them, they have kept him hidden from all."

General agreed. "Our spies in Saral have not been able to locate him. Rish is there now heading the search. I hope to receive some news from him. Once I settle matters in Lukla, I will join Rish myself."

Father waved him off, "Tell my cousin Lata that I invited her to the capital. She has stayed away long enough, and there might be a wedding here in a short time. If Jay is found soon, we may celebrate more than one wedding."

With that, the General bowed and departed. The servants brought our food, and I settled down to eat with father. As I tasted the food, I said to father, "This spicy gourd, cooked in coconut and red chilies, is one of Jay's favorites."

Father mused, "Watching him eat reminded me of my youth. My brother and I were constantly hungry at that age. After eating a three-course meal with the king and the queen, we would later sneak into the kitchen to grab the sweets prepared for the evening."

I tried to imagine my father as a boy sneaking food. He must have been a favorite of the cooks. Even if he was not a prince, it would have been hard to say no to him, with his intense brown eyes and handsome face.

"My grandmother probably appreciated not having to cook the food herself to keep you both fed," I said, laughing.

Soon we finished our meal, and the servants cleared the plates away. I sat down next to my father. He looked at me and said, "Being born in the royal family has many privileges. But it also has many shackles on your freedom. Had she lived, your mother may have prepared you better for this life."

"Father, I have led a sheltered life, but I am no stranger to what is expected of me."

Father said, "When I left Kayal to meet with King Surya as Prince Vikram of Malla, I dreamt of being married to her and leading a blissful life. Little did I know my life would be thrown into turmoil with the loss of both my father and brother at sea.

"On the day they perished, fate entrusted me to protect this kingdom, with my life if needed. I have sacrificed many things for Malla while holding on to my life. You are dearer to me than my own life," said my father.

I leaned my head on his shoulders, which had been bearing the weight of this kingdom. He put his hands around me and continued, "So what I am asking is harder than anything else I have done in my life. I am asking you to consent to marry Amar."

"You are my king and father. You can command me, and I will obey."

"I am aware of that, my dear child. As a king, I would command you. Today though, I am a father who hoped for more for his children. I have failed my children, but I cannot fail this kingdom raised to power by my ancestors."

I sat straight and said, "You have not failed me. You have given me the wisdom and strength to overcome any obstacles. Father, I consent to this marriage to Amar."

He leaned over and kissed my forehead and said, "I will pen a letter to Verma, and I will summon a council meeting tomorrow to announce your wedding." He paused and added, "And I will do all in my power to ascertain positive news from Saral to put it off."

The next morning arrived, but the sun stayed hidden behind the clouds. The air felt cold and crisp on my skin. Kantha helped me get ready in a silk sari in the color of a banana flower with delicate flowers embroidered along the border and matching flower jewels. With the decision about my marriage made, I felt at peace. The king, queen, and the rest of the council were already gathered in the small throne room. I bowed to my parents and sat on a chair by the queen.

Atul strode in soon and bowed to the king. My father said, "Atul, King Verma sent you here seeking the hand of my daughter in marriage to his son Amar. I, the King of Malla, consent to this marriage of my daughter Princess Meera with Prince Amar of Padi."

Atul glanced at me briefly and said, "My lord, blessed is Padi to receive Princess Meera as our bride and future Queen."

He then addressed me, "Princess Meera, please accept my felicitations on this joyous occasion." His eyes studied me intently. I was tongue-tied but managed to nod.

The council and others joined in and expressed their joy for the occasion, and outwardly I joined in the celebrations.

Soon after, Atul prepared to leave the city. I gathered in my grandmother's chamber to bid him farewell. He came in, dressed for his long journey back. He touched my grandmother's feet, and she touched his head in blessing.

I stood next to her with a tray in my hand. As he came to me, I applied *tilak* to his forehead to ward off any dangers on the journey home.

My grandmother chided him, "Don't stand there. Touch her feet to seek her blessings. She will be your Queen one day."

"Grandmother," I protested, but he bent down and touched my feet. As he raised, I remembered sending Jay off to Saral.

"I hope this parting is not for long. I expect to be back in Akash soon with Amar and my parents for your wedding." Later, I watched him from one of the windows as he rode off with his men.

16

⚮

On the Road

The next morning, we rode out of Theni palace and were soon passing by the river Chambal on one side and farmlands on the other. We had good rains this year and could see farmers working in the fields. Chambal River flowed from the mountains in Padi through Malla and Saral and joined the Pune Sea at the end of its journey. Some of the women sang as they worked in the field, and their voices floated to us. The river brimmed with water and flowed with great speed. Small boats carried fruits and vegetables to the markets. When the people saw us, they stopped and stared. Some of them recognized me and bowed as I rode by. I waved but did not slow down.

Karan and Kapil rode beside me, and I searched for Rish. I saw him in front and guided my horse next to him. He said, "Prince Jay, because of the rains, the rivers are overflowing. We cannot cross here and will have to take a long way around."

He then continued in a low voice that would not carry far, "I found some trustworthy men to guard Princess Aranya." I nodded and mused that Aranya was capable of taking care of herself. When I took her leave this morning, she said she would wait for my arrival with a victory garland.

"Princess Aranya appears to have captured your heart, and the union will secure peace with Saral. Before I left Akash, the three chiefs appealed to the King for you to marry a girl from each of the noble houses. Sudha Vindhya is my niece and a wonderful girl. General Devan's daughter, Riya Biha, is Princess Meera's companion and groomed by her."

"I came to Saral just to get away from the parade of young women vying for my attention." I tried to keep my frustration out of my voice but failed. I'd found a girl on my own to love. A Saral Princess. My anger dissipated.

He said playfully, "You are like the sun." I stared at him perplexed. He explained, "The sun rises in the east every day without being aware of how bright and powerful it is. Moon and stars disappear from sight. Sunflowers in the field chase the sun's path in the sky, hoping for a ray of sunshine in their direction. You are like the sun, and these girls the sunflowers."

I laughed heartily and said, "I didn't know you were such a poet, Rish."

Kapil overheard us talking and brought his horse close to us. "Life is so unfair. All the beautiful girls happen to be my cousins, who I cannot court."

"That is the result of all our inter-marriages," Rish stated. "But not all cousin marriages are forbidden. Riya, who shares your family name, is."

"I have always acted as the big brother," Kapil said mischievously. I reached out to smack his head, and he ducked.

"My niece Sudha Vindhya, on the other hand, is a different story. You are quite eligible to seek this cousin's hand, apart from the little matter of her parents wanting her to be the Queen of Malla," Rish continued.

"You impress me with your prowess in matters of family relationships, Uncle Rish," retorted Kapil.

Would he be mad at me, like Vasu? "Kapil, all this attention showered upon me is for the heir of Malla. The girls love a shadow, a thought of crown and throne and glory, not the real Jay," I replied seriously.

"I know the real Jay and deem him worthy of all the attention," he said simply, dropping my title and addressing me as a friend. He had not done that in public since we were about eight, and his father cuffed him on his head and told him to learn to respect the prince. My heart swelled at his words, knowing I had a true friend in him. We rode in silence for some time.

For the rest of the journey, I rode alongside various men in my troop and talked to them about themselves, our journey, and some of my dreams. I remembered riding with Vasu on the way to Lukla, with him regaling us with battle stories. Vasu's betrayal still stung me.

That evening, we set up camp by the river, and I went to take a bath. Giri and Dev came with me. I had the same guards as before, but I neither saw nor heard them then. Here on this journey, I could not take a step without tripping over one of them. Kapil could sense my unhappiness with the constant tail, but he took his job of keeping me safe seriously and did not want to repeat Balan's mistakes.

I had taken off my jewelry and upper garments in the tent. I dipped my toe in the water. The river felt cool and refreshing in the heat. I stripped down to my loincloth, and I plunged in. A family of ducks floated nearby, and fish darted through. The trees by the shore had big roots and could hide a crocodile or two. I did not see any in the water, though. I swam a few yards from the shore when I heard some commotion. I saw Kapil along with all my guards. Were they yelling my name? I needed to have a word with Kapil. He was taking this too far. They pointed to some tall grass by the shore, and Giri had a bow in his hand. I looked where they pointed and saw a majestic tiger.

The Tiger was Malla's emblem and revered. Did Giri plan to shoot this animal? When Giri's arrow came flying by, the beast jumped in the water. I started swimming towards the shore and heard a lot of splashing. Some of my guards must have jumped in the water as well. Soon I got to shallow water and stood up, looking around. A tiger was a cautious hunter. They would sneak up on their prey and then jumped on them. With the element of surprise gone, the beast eyed us warily and swam off in a different direction. On the shore, Giri stood with his bow, ready to strike the animal.

I shouted, "Giri, stop." Dev and Karan stood beside him, and Kapil and Veer headed towards me. I swam to the shore without waiting for them. I tried to muster dignity in my loincloth, but I looked ridiculous. I got on the shore and grabbed my *dhoti*. I draped it around me and headed towards the tent.

Karan started to follow me, and I barked, "Stay. Kapil, my tent now."

When I got to my tent, I glanced at Kapil and huffed, "Wait here," and strode in. I remembered my father's words, "Angry men were fools," and I needed to calm down.

"Prince Jay, you are dripping wet," said Muthu, and he rushed to help me out of my wet clothes. I wished Somu was here. He would know the right thing to say.

I could see Kapil's shadow falling on the tent. He stood tall and still. His eyes were probably sweeping the area.

Muthu struggled with my upper garment and scratched my chest with his nails, and I snapped at him, "Watch what you are doing." With trembling fingers, he tried to tie the knots, but that only made it worse.

I sighed. "Fetch some food. I can finish my dressing."

"Yes, my lord," he said, his eyes on the ground.

"I will eat with my guards here. Send a man to get all of them. And ask Kapil to come in."

"There are some letters for you on the table, my lord," he said in a voice barely above a whisper. As he left, Kapil entered. He saw me tying the knot on my garment and came over to assist me. I let him help without saying a word, observing his steady hands. Then I went to the table and started reading the letters. One came from Minister Kripa. General Devan was on his way to Saral to help search for me. He must have written this before news of my escape reached Akash. I read several other correspondences. I had to sit down tonight and write my replies.

Then I lifted my head and eyed Kapil. He appeared a little resigned, and I tried to remember that he grew up with me and swore an oath to die for me. "I understand you want to protect me. But I have not had a quiet moment on this journey. There are two, sometimes three guards following me everywhere I go. I can feel their breath on me. If any of them drew their swords, my ears would be sliced. I like my ears. And one of them tried to kill a tiger."

He bowed his head and said, "My lord— I have been—" He hesitated and added, "My lord. Giri meant no harm to the tiger. He only tried to scare him. My first duty is to protect you. I will do so without—"

Before he could continue, I finished for him, "Without making me want to chop your head off?" He raised his eyebrows, and I grunted, "One tail close to me. If you want a second guard, station him further."

Kapil started saying, "My lord—"

I cut him off, "You swore to obey me as well, Kapil. If this arrangement puts my life in danger, we can discuss it again. Tigers can fend for themselves." Muthu brought in food then.

"I want to eat with all of my guards today." I went and sat at the table. The rest of them arrived soon. They came in and bowed, and I commanded, "Sit down."

Kapil responded, "My lord, one of us has to remain standing to guard you. The other four can join you."

I did not want to argue with him and said, "Have it your way." He whispered to Giri and waved at the rest. Giri stood while the others joined me. I looked at these boys. I'd known Kapil Biha the longest. The others I had gotten to know in the last year. Just a year or two older than me, Karan's short and stocky build helped him in wrestling, and he'd fooled me many times with his surprising speed. Giri and Dev were younger than me. Small for his age, Dev could climb trees like a monkey. He would rapidly climb on Balan's order and scout the area for us. Giri, a good archer, carried his bow and arrows with him everywhere. Mano Biha had picked Balan, and I'd picked Kapil and Karan for my guard, and Balan had chosen the rest. I hadn't gotten to know, Veer, the newest member of my guard yet.

Kapil said playfully, "I am not going to forget this morning, Prince Jay. The tiger prince of the forest came eager to greet the tiger prince of the land. We got in the way with our bow and arrows." The others watched this conversation. I remembered what my father said, *"Get to know your men. Share meals with them. Never forget you will be their king, though."* They were my shadows that are going to be with me every moment for the rest of my life.

I grabbed a banana and placed it on Kapil's head. "Giri, show us your mastery. Hit the banana."

Giri hesitated. "Prince Jay, he is my commander."

Kapil smirked, "Go ahead—"

I cut him off, "Don't move, or you might lose an eye."

Giri loaded his bow and appeared ready to release. At the last instant, I tossed the banana into the air, away from us. Giri responded quickly and turned with my hand and sliced the banana with his arrow. "Excellent shot," I shouted.

Kapil touched his head, "I love my hair. You showed me great kindness by saving it, my lord," and started laughing. I joined him, and soon the tent rang with our laughter. Growing up, Kapil and I challenged and pushed each other. He was the brother I never had. Foolish of me to be mad at him.

We exchanged horses before resuming our journey the next day. We covered a lot of ground and reached our destination sooner. I decided to camp overnight in the fields while waiting for word from the men on the cave mission.

My men pitched tents and started a fire to cook our meals. Soon we gathered to eat, and some men entertained us with stories. The stew of vegetables and rice, though simple, tasted better than the ten-course meals I had eaten in the last two days. Rish regaled us with stories of King Jay's conquest of Padi.

That night, as I walked back to my tent, I felt happier than I had been in a while. Traveling with friends through this beautiful land, definitely lifted my spirits. Kapil accompanied me to my tent. He went in ahead of me and checked the tent as I strolled in. My children and their children will be told these tales of King Jay. The names of King Jay's guards and their stories are not known to us and perished with the king they served. I remembered the oath my guards took, to protect me with their lives or die trying, as I fell asleep.

The next morning, I woke up early and called for my servant, Muthu. Kapil peeked into the tent and asked, "Can I help you with anything? He just went to get your food." He must have been standing guard outside my tent.

"Find Muthu and ask him to come here." I stared at the clothes and jewels he had laid out, enough to adorn half a dozen men. Somu knew me well, but Muthu being new, struggled to serve me. In a corner of my mind, I wondered about Somu's well-being. Would we be in time to release him? Had I made a mistake in not looking for King Surya first?

Kapil saw me looking at the clothes and smirked, "I can point to you where the hole for your arms and head go, my lord."

I muttered, "I would punch you, or better yet, find Balan, and ask him to kick some sense into you." As I said it, I realized Balan had killed himself. We both looked at each other.

"I will have someone fetch him," he said, his face solemn, and I nodded. I knew most men did the tasks themselves that I have servants to do for me. I wondered what life would be like if I was a common boy, getting dressed at first light and going into the forest to cut wood for the day.

Rish came in and interrupted my thoughts. "Prince Jay, we are heading into Saral territory. Should I ask Muthu to fetch your body armor as well?"

I felt exasperated. "Body armor in this heat will be enough to kill me."

Rish looked at me sheepishly and said, "I promised Princess Meera I would protect you."

I loved my sister and knew she always tried to take care of me, but I could not have my men thinking I needed constant protection. I clapped him on his shoulders and said, "Rish, I appreciate the advice. I am not going to wear my body armor today. I have faith in your ability to keep my enemies at bay." Did I see more than respect in his eyes when he mentioned Meera's name? I thought Meera beyond his reach, but something gave me pause. If we held a *swayamvara* for Meera, who would she pine for? *More likely, she will marry someone who would help me rule the kingdom*, I thought. She had always put my welfare and the kingdom's welfare ahead of her own.

Muthu came in shortly, and I pointed to the clothes and said, "Muthu, I am going to fight with my troops, not go to my wedding."

He replied nervously, "My lord, most of these men have never fought beside you, and you cannot appear before them looking like a peasant."

Poor man, he might die of fright if I didn't find Somu soon enough. I smiled reassuringly and said, "Let us compromise. I will wear half of what you laid out." With that, he helped me drape my silk *dhoti* and tie the sash around my waist, where I hung my sword. My crown, a necklace, earrings, armbands, and a few other trinkets completed my outfit. I wondered how you could fight in these clothes and hoped I would not find an unpleasant answer to that question today.

I told him I wanted to eat with my men and not inside the tent. The men seemed happy to see me, and the conversation flowed freely on various topics. I mainly listened and added a word or two here and there.

Just then, a guard came towards me and said, "Prince Jay, the Lt. Gen. requests your presence." I went with him and found Satya in the large tent we used for the council. Rish, Shiv, and the other men who went to Pullikadu caves were with him.

"Prince Jay, these men have brought some good news as well as bad." He looked at their leader, and he stepped forward.

"Prince Jay, after we left here, we made it to Pullikadu in good time. We split up and headed up the hills from four different directions. I led the men to the cave entrance. I positioned some men by the entrance, and our archers shot arrows through the holes, while the rest of the men rushed in through the concealed entrance. Saral men rushed at us, and my men and I fought them and slowly caused them to fall back.

"We headed deeper into the caves. It was difficult to fight in the narrow, poorly lit caves against men who knew their way around. I lost most of my men, but just then, the second group of men led by Shiv found another entrance to the cave and fought in with vengeance. They gave fresh lives to our cause, and we fought with renewed energy. We found Queen Anju housed in the caves, and she and her guards tried to escape through the back. But we gave them a fight for their lives. We reached the opening where we found about ten horses ready for their flight, and we tried to stop them from reaching the horses and bring her in as a prisoner."

Here he paused and looked at Shiv, and Shiv continued, "We had about ten men left, and they had three times that number. Our men still fought gallantly. When things looked hopeless, the third group of Malla soldiers reached the top and gave a boost to us. We had the Queen surrounded. I knew you did not want us to harm the royal family. By then, few of their men reached the horses and got on them. All of this happened in mere moments. We tried to stop them but were no match for men on horses. We fought with the remaining men on foot and killed most of them. We captured Queen Anju and her maid and headed back here."

I felt the tide turning in our favor in the war. "Where is Queen Anju now?"

"I have her and her maid in one of the tents under guard. I asked for food and clean clothes to be brought to them," responded Satya. "I don't have enough men to spare, to arrange for her safe transportation back to Theni, so she will have to remain here till we are back."

I praised the men for their deeds. "You all did well. Go and get some rest. I would like to discuss these matters further with Lt. Gen Satya."

After they left, I stood up, and when Satya started to rise, I motioned him to stay seated.

He continued, "I will send some men to scout King Surya's location. We have his wife and daughter in our custody. We should wait for a day or two to see if Surya sends us a messenger."

I did not correct him when he said Princess Aranya was our prisoner. It was better if Surya thought we held her against her wishes. He would not do anything foolish to endanger her life and ours.

"The escaped men will have headed to the palace and be on guard, but this is our best opportunity to attack."

I stopped and thought about things. Having made up my mind, I said, "I would like to speak with the Queen."

Giri, with his bow and arrow, followed me. Two men stood guard outside her tent. They bowed as I walked past them and into the room. The small, dimly lit tent held a bed in the middle. I asked Giri to wait outside. He inspected the room first and then left. The queen sat on the bed with her maid near at hand. I approached the queen. "Queen Anju, I wish we could have made our acquaintances under different circumstances."

She rose on seeing me, and I found myself looking at a girl barely older than myself. She hailed from a wealthy family, and her father supported Surya's war. Surya had a grown son. Why didn't he have Prince Nakul marry her? Did he still hold out hope that Prince Nakul would marry Meera and heal the rift?

Queen Anju had married a man old enough to be her father. Life on the run must not have been easy on her. Scars marred her arms, and her face appeared damaged from the sun. She wore simple earrings, a nose ring, a plain necklace, and a few bangles, not jewelry fit for a queen. I was adorned with more gold than her. I said, "Please be seated, my lady," and sat in the only chair in the room. Her small and scrawny body sat on the edge of the bed, and she eyed me nervously.

"I hope you find these accommodations comfortable, Queen Anju," I said.

"I lived in a cave before you brought me here," she snarked. Then she softened and said, "Your men have been kind to us. We have no want for anything, except being sent back home. What do you intend to do with us?"

"That would depend on your husband, King Surya, my lady."

She sighed and turned away from me. I felt sorry for her. She came from a minor Gomti branch in Saral. King Surya had married her for wealth, but a spare heir would not have been unwelcome. My glance dropped to her naval briefly seen through her sari. I could see no telltale bump of a pregnancy. Still, he couldn't abandon her after taking her for his wife.

Her maid, an older woman, put a hand on the queen's shoulder for comfort, while staring at me intently. I glanced at her, and she said, "You have your mother's eyes."

Then realizing she'd spoken out of turn, she covered her mouth with her hand.

"You knew my mother?" I asked. She had a weather-beaten face and could have been the same age or a few years older than my mother. She nodded, afraid to say more.

I had a thousand questions in my head. "Where did you meet her?"

She looked at Queen Anju, who inclined her head. She then said, "I worked in the palace when King Surya brought his new bride, Queen Lata, to Lukla. Your mother, Kayal, came to visit her cousin for a few fortnights, and that is when I saw her. She was beautiful." She paused and stared into space as if remembering.

"In a year, Queen Lata conceived a baby. The royal astrologer said a child born in Kadal would rule the world. So, she went home to Kadal to give birth. That is the last I saw of the Queen. Few days after giving birth to Prince Nakul, Queen Lata died of fever. Your mother took care of the baby, and King Surya wanted to marry her. But King Vikram came to Kadal and abducted her."

King Surya must have the same disease that plagues my stepmother. She cannot take one step without consulting the court astrologer. He knew this and used it to fatten his own purse. He claimed he could tell our future by looking at the alignment of stars when we were born. My stepmother consulted him before my father left for Lukla, and that did not stop him from coming back on a sickbed. The common man looked at the sky to gauge when it would rain, but kings and queens gazed at the stars to tell the future.

I had heard whispers in Akash that King Surya expressed his displeasure that my father married my mother Kayal. He wanted to marry her himself. He had held that grudge through the years and started this war for vengeance.

I tried to remember my mother, but my memories of her had faded over the years. Her face appeared in my mind, obscured by the smoke of passing time. Meera said she would sing to us. Try as I might, I could not recollect her voice. But I could vividly remember Meera singing to me the songs she learned from mother. I had a sudden longing to see my sister but told myself I was no longer a child.

I looked back at the woman sitting in front of me. I needed to send a letter to my father that we had captured Queen Anju. Whether I heard from King Surya or not, I had to wait for my father's command on this matter.

"Queen Anju, do you know where King Surya may be hiding now?" She shook her head. Would she tell me if she knew?

"Is Princess Aranya here with you?" she asked, and I did not respond.

"That girl is wild," snarled the queen suddenly. They were close in age, and I sensed some animosity. She continued, "Since her mother died, she rides horses and swims in the rivers. She is of marriage age, but there are freckles on her face, tangles in her hair, and dirt underneath her fingernails."

That is quite a crime in a girl my age, I thought. The Aranya I knew understood her role as a princess.

"The king loves her. He will come for her, if not for me," she finished with resentment.

"If you are in want of anything, my lady, ask the guards," I said and left them.

As I walked back to my tent, Shiv joined me. "Prince Jay, what did the Queen say?"

"Not very much," I responded as we approached my tent. Giri checked the room while I sat down at my table. Shiv stood on the other side.

"There are ways to get her to talk," he said with a sly grin.

"What do you mean?" I asked suspiciously. Giri left us to stand guard outside.

"Well, if you threaten to strip her naked—"

"Shiv," I interrupted him, angrily, "She is a queen and my guest. I am not threatening her with such vile things."

He jeered, "Prince Jay if you want to be King, you need the courage to do these things."

I growled. "Courage? Threatening women does not require courage. Protecting them does. Say no more on this subject to me."

He relented, "Pardon me, my lord. I thought you cared as much as I did about winning Saral back."

"I care about ending this war. Do you have any other idea that does not involve the queen?" I stormed.

"I will lead the battle of Maram. Or you can lead it yourself. It will be like old times. Though we can both beat our enemies bloody now instead of each other." He laughed.

I joined him in his laughter, half-heartedly. I remembered Meera's words, "To serve the realm, you need to be alive."

Shiv looked at me eagerly with a grin on his face, and I said, "Let us do it. First, I have to ask the council's permission."

"You don't need their permission. You are the Prince of this land. Satya should be obeying your orders," Shiv said.

"It does not work quite that way," I replied. When I left Akash, my father wanted me to consult General Devan on all matters. That order still held with Lt. Gen. Satya in charge. "Let me finish some correspondence. Meet me outside Satya's chambers."

After he left, Kapil entered. "Kapil, double the guards around Queen Anju's rooms," I ordered.

"Yes, my lord. I will immediately. Did something happen?"

"No, not yet. I want to prevent any danger befalling her when she is under our protection."

Kapil nodded. "I will take care of it."

We left together for Satya's tent. Inside, other men had already gathered. Satya said, "We need to attack tonight, my lord. We can surround the palace. There are two vulnerable walls, one on the western side and one on southeast that we can breach. Once breached, our men can open the doors for us into the palace."

All eyes turned in my direction, waiting for my approval. I thought back to father's words to me before I left. *Spare the lives of Prince Nakul and Aranya. Kill or capture King Surya.* Neither men were at Maram.

I pulled my sword out and raised it, "Let us march. Victory to Malla!!!"

The room echoed with battle cries.

17

Battle of Maram

We left that night, darkness giving us cover. Before approaching the castle, our men split into several groups and then surrounded the palace. I mounted my horse and watched the action unfold with Kapil and Giri on either side. My face remained a mask while my stomach had twisted into many knots. The enormous weight of sending men to die for me clogged my throat. I gripped my sword handle tightly. The Saral men saw us arrive and shut all the gates. Their archers stood ready on their towers to shoot us down.

Our archers and spear throwers lined up at the western and south-eastern gates, to provide cover for the warriors breaching the walls. Men arranged six deep rushed the barrier while a fierce battle of archers ensued. The soldiers held a single long shield over their heads as they approached the palace. Our information turned out to be accurate. The western side had a blind spot that their archers could not cover. As our soldiers got closer, they formed human ladders to hoist men on to the wall. They were immediately attacked by spears and arrows from within, but my men responded with their bows. Some stood atop the tower, shooting down arrows within, while others jumped in swords drawn.

With the first group of men fighting fiercely, the next set ran towards the barrier, repeating the same steps. When the third group climbed atop, we breached their outer keep.

"Now is the hour come, soldiers of Malla," I thundered, getting ready to ride in. "I have been itching to fight the Saral soldiers since the day I came to Lukla, and I could not have chosen better men to fight by my side. The glory that we reap here will be ours forever. Are you ready to defeat our enemy on this glorious night?" I shouted, raising my sword. The men raised their swords and spears towards the sky.

With a roar, the door burst open, and we rode in furiously. "For King Vikram," I trumpeted as I raced towards them.

"For King Vikram," echoed my men. "For Prince Jay," some chanted.

Wielding the sword of my great-grandfather, I cut through men left and right as I went through them. In the flaming torchlight, swords and spears glinted. Arrows flew through the air, weaving in the light and dark. Rish and Kapil fought alongside me, acting as my shield, deflecting weapons headed my way, striking first before a sword could strike me. We fought all night, drenched in blood and sweat. Soon, sounds of metal against metal were replaced by human moans and groans.

As the sun rose, I surveyed the carnage. The smell of death hung in the air. Blood and body parts covered the courtyard. We'd lost half of our men, but the enemy was routed. Most had died, and we imprisoned the rest. I got off my horse, handing the reins to Karan, and went around making sure our wounded were taken care of.

The men appeared in good spirits and regaled me with tales of their bravery. Most had minor wounds and would recover soon. Some had lost a limb or an eye or their nose. These would have to get used to a life outside the Malla army.

A boy about my age sat in a corner. He had lost his leg in the fight, and a heavy bandage covered the stump. He tried to get up as I approached him, and I put my hand on his shoulders and said, "Stay seated," and sat down next to him. "What is the name your parents gave you?"

"Selva."

"Selva, tell me how you came to be at Lukla."

"I'm from a fishing village in Thari. My father died; my brother got his boat. So, when men came asking for boys to fight, I said aye."

"Did you go fishing with your father?"

"Yes, many times." He got a dreamy expression in his eyes. "The water is blue, cold in Thari. In Saral, a man told me the seawater is warm."

A lump formed in my throat. "When you get better, I will give you money for a boat, and you can go back to your fishing village."

"My lord. I fish with a boat, and there is a girl—" He stammered, "I'm going to marry her if she will marry a man with no leg." He laid his head on my feet and wept. I let him for a few moments and gently touched his shoulders, "She would be a fool not to."

Dusk settled around us. Kapil and Rish led me to a modest room in the palace, a small area someone cleaned up for me. They moved an old wooden bed into it. A servant came in with some banana and milk for us. I had very little appetite, but I poured myself some milk.

Before the cup reached my lips, Kapil screamed, "Prince Jay!" I brought the cup down and scanned the room for an intruder, and Kapil grabbed the cup from me. He sniffed my milk and drank some himself and waited.

"Well, it has not killed me. Safe for you to drink, my lord," he said and poured me some milk in a new cup. "If you want to eat the banana, let Uncle Rish eat it first," he added. I stared at the milk and laughed.

"It would be funny if I survived the battle and keeled over from drinking milk," I said to Rish, and he laughed with me. The laughter felt odd after the horror we unleashed but allowed me to break out of the battle mode momentarily. I drained the cup and put it on the table.

"I have not thanked you both for saving my life today," I said to Rish and Kapil.

"Just doing our duty," quipped Kapil. He added, "I have never seen you fight like that before. You were ferocious and brutal."

"I pledged to serve and protect you, my lord," Rish said simply. Before I could say anything, he continued, "My father served in the King's guard and gave up his life protecting the king. He died an old man with grown offspring, having fulfilled his oath to king and land. Greater glory he could not have asked for. As a second son, I had to carve out my own path in life. I don't want to speak ill of my blood, but some of the actions of the Vindhya Chiefs do not inspire respect or loyalty. When I met you, I anticipated being in the company of another royal who cared only about power and wealth.

"After being with you and seeing how you take time to get to know your men, truly care about the people, and how loyal they have become to you in such a short time, I can understand how there can be no greater value for a second son's life than to die protecting his king. My choice is clear."

I opened my mouth to say something and then closed it. His words had a powerful effect on me and left me speechless. His sincere tone touched me, and I experienced immense gratitude to have found such a loyal friend. I clapped him on his shoulders, thinking about what he said.

"We have a long journey back to Theni, my lord. Let us get some sleep," he said and found a place on the floor. I laid down on the bed. Kapil stood guard.

I flashed back to the battle. I'd struck down several soldiers, but I'd killed only two men. No, not men, boys. My first time committing this act, and it wouldn't be my last. Instead of feeling triumphant and brave, I felt hollow. When I closed my eyes, their faces swam before me, and my sword slicing their throats. I regarded Kapil. I could not discuss this with any man who needed to respect and obey me. Meera would not understand my feelings either because she did not have to lead men into war. My father would be the only person I could voice my feelings, and he lived in Akash. I could not pen him a letter describing my thoughts, feeling grievous after killing enemies. What was happening to me? If I gave in to such thoughts, how could I make even tougher decisions as a king. How did my great grandfather conquer the three kingdoms?

Along with these thoughts, I sensed the room grow stiflingly hot. I still disliked the heat here in Saral and longed for the cooler nights in

Malla. Sweat dotted Kapil's forehead as well. I said to him, "Even after the sun has set, warmth lingers in these lands."

"Yes," he said as he observed me and then stepped out.

I leaned back against the pillows and closed my eyes. I disappeared into a world that began with men fighting and peacock feathers, which morphed into horses. I ran among them, slaughtering them to screams and tears when I woke up in a panic. A cool breeze blew, and I opened my eyes. Karan stood guard, and I could see Kapil asleep on the floor on a mat. And a man I had never set my eyes on before fanned me with a peacock feather fan. Kapil must have fetched him last night.

Karan's forehead furrowed, and he said, "You muttered something about horses, my lord." I looked at the man, and Karan followed my glance. "He is deaf, my lord." I raised my hand to ask him to stop. Karan also asked him to stop, using hand signals, and sent him off.

I sat up on the bed. Images of the men I'd killed and the horse I'd lost as a child flickered through my mind. "Just a dream," I muttered, and Karan did not press on.

Leaving a hundred men behind in Maram to keep control of the castle, we readied ourselves to set off for Theni. As we reached the campsite, we saw the tents dismantled and the men ready to depart. Queen Anju and her maid were locked up in a horse-drawn cart. With the cart and our supply wagon, we progressed slowly through the dense forest.

Men not at the battle wanted to hear the details, and as we rode, Shiv and others regaled them with stories. Each time the story got told, the tale grew larger and our victory bigger, and my fight more heroic than before. My first battle and a triumphant outcome. Hearing the men's reactions to the tale caused a surge of elation in me.

Soon we came across a herd of female elephants and their calves on their way to the water. We halted to let these magnificent beasts pass. A couple of baby elephants played with each other, and it reminded me of sparring with Kapil and Vasu as a child. Could I have prevented his betrayal by being a better friend?

Once the elephants passed, we resumed our journey. Suddenly one of the scouts came back and said he spotted a lone bull elephant heading our way. Lt. Gen. Satya appeared worried, and I understood why. Just then, Giri asked, "Didn't we just pass a herd of elephants? Why does a lone bull concern us?"

"Lone bull elephants in a rage can charge and leave us unhorsed and hurt or worse, dead."

"Satya, the supply wagon cannot outrun an elephant. We need to divert him from heading towards us."

Shiv joined us and chimed in, "Prince Jay, you and I are fast on our horses. Let us go and divert the elephant and then come back and join these men. We can take your guards along."

Shiv had proved his worth to me with his prowess at the caves and this idea of his held merit.

"That is a good idea, Shiv." Then I addressed the others, "Lt. Gen., I will take Shiv, Dev, and Giri and divert the elephant and join you soon." Kapil frowned at me with his brows together, not wanting to let me out of his sight. "Kapil, come looking for us if we are not back before the shadow grows longer." Before he could answer, I ordered the scout, "Soldier, lead the way."

Shiv, Giri, Dev, and I followed the soldier. After a few minutes, we saw the elephant in a distance. "Giri, blow the conch."

He took out the conch shell and blew it. The full-grown male with long tusks stopped and eyed us and then headed towards us. "We need to take him at least a few miles from here, so he will not come back," I said.

"I know the way, Prince Jay. Please follow me," said Shiv and galloped off. We went after him, and the elephant trailed behind. For such a huge beast, he ran fast. He trumpeted, and the noise scared our horses. Still, our mounts were able to better maneuver the tree roots and trunks. After what seemed a long time, I guessed we had covered enough ground. I scanned the forest and eyed the majestic birch, ficus, and teak trees.

Making a decision, I said, "Dev, the rest of us will stay stationary and hide among the trees. You make some noise and take the elephant further into the forest. Then jump off your horse and climb up a tree.

Horses are very intelligent and will get away from the elephant safely. Then, we will find you and the horse and get back to the group."

Dev nodded. I slowly stopped and hid among the trees, and Shiv and Giri followed. Dev roared and continued, and the elephant ran after him. Dev rode away from us, trying to take a straight path to make it easier for the elephant to follow him. He shouted periodically to keep the beast's attention. After a little while, the horse and the elephant disappeared from view. We could hear hoofbeats for a few more moments, and then that sound receded. The elephant's trumpets stayed with us for a while longer. When all the sounds dwindled, I told Giri to go pick up Dev and find his horse.

"Do it quietly. I don't want our big friend back."

I saw Giri ride his horse slowly. When he reached the spot where Dev vanished, he stopped and waved. Then he disappeared from our sight. The scout remained with Shiv and me.

As Giri's hoof beats slowly receded, I inspected the area around us. The elephant had uprooted some trees and pulled down some branches. The lone bull had caused havoc on its path, like a storm moving through the land.

I could feel Shiv's stare on me and turned to look at him. A strange gleam appeared in his eyes.

He took out his conch and blew it three times in short bursts. A smirk touched the edges of his mouth. The hair on my neck raised. I immediately put my hand on my sword.

"What are you doing, Shiv?"

In response, he took his sword and sliced down the scout in one quick movement. The man barely had time to breathe, much less defend himself. Before I could react, I saw men on horses riding towards us. They wore nondescript clothes, but I guessed these were Saral men.

I unsheathed my sword. I'd been wrong. Shiv must be the spy. He betrayed me earlier in Saral. I would not be captured again. Ten of them and Shiv against one. Against me. Alone. I could not wait for Dev and Giri. They may have been too far away to hear the conch.

I grabbed my spear with my other hand and tossed it at Shiv. Fury and hate giving it speed I'd never felt before. It hit his stomach and un-horsed him. I went to Shiv and yanked the spear out along with innards, and he yelped. I had no time to think about this traitor. The men came at me. I decided to meet them.

I raised my sword above my head and yanked my horse to the left. I rode towards the last man. With my sword, I cut off his hands and put my spear through the man behind him, yanking it out with a grunt. Two out and eight more to go. The rest of the men tried to form a circle around me. I pulled back from them. My horse was tired after the ele-phant chase, and I hoped she would hang on.

The lone archer in the group took aim. His arrow whizzed past my head, nearly taking off an ear. I charged straight into the middle of the group and plunged my sword into one of the men. The man next to him brought his sword down on my shoulder. Pain seared through me. Blood seeped out of that wound. I bellowed in pain and rage and sliced his head off with my sword. The remaining men came towards me, and one of the arrows hit my horse. She neighed in distress, the arrow sticking out of her flank.

To serve the realm, I need to be alive, I told myself. I could not give up now. I tossed my spear at the archer, and it pierced his heart, and he went down. An attacking spear sailed through the air and sunk into my thigh. I let out a wail and plowed my horse through the line, swinging my sword. Death had me in its sight.

Suddenly arrows came flying by and took a man out. Then another. I saw Dev drive his spear into one man from the corner of my eye. With renewed energy, I plunged my sword into the man nearest to me. His blood splashed onto my face, stinging my eyes. The last remaining man tried to escape, but Giri's arrow hit him in his neck, and he fell over, dead.

Dev jumped off the horse and ran over to me. "Prince Jay, are you all right?"

"I am alive," I rasped.

Giri took out his conch and blew it five times, to signal that I was hurt. I got off my horse, and she went down on her knees. She would not survive this. With my heart in my throat, I took my sword and plunged into her heart to put her out of misery.

Pulling the spear lodged in my thigh would cause me to lose blood. Instead, I broke off the handle and then wobbled towards Shiv. Giri got off his horse and went to check on the fallen men. Dev stayed close to me, alert, with his spear ready.

"You coward! You breached my trust," I growled, my eyes narrowed to slits.

Shiv hissed, "You were a kid that I beat up. You are weak and could not even order us to kill King Surya. How can you be the king of this land? I saw Prince Nakul fight in a battle, and he would be the king you can never be. King Surya promised me riches if I delivered your head. I could have taken it off in your sleep. But I did not want to die at the hands of your guards. My plan today would have worked. You would have died, and I would have been hurt. I could have blamed it all on Saral men when the Lt. Gen. and others came." He laughed like a mad man.

Giri spoke, his voice cold, "Prince Jay, a nod from you and my arrows will put him to death."

I glared at Shiv, and a surge of hatred rose in me. I wanted to rip his innards off and wear them as a garland and wash my face in his blood. I took a few breaths to calm myself and walked away from him. He'd committed treason, but he was the son of Chief Bhoj Thari. Only the king could punish him for his crimes. And he did not deserve a quick death.

I looked around and saw five horses. Shiv's horse neighed, unharmed in the ambush. I decided to ride him.

"Giri, wrap Shiv's wounds as best as you can and get him up on one of these animals and take his reins. Dev, ride one of the others. Let us head back to the rest of our group."

I patted Shiv's horse and mounted him. I grabbed the reins of another and headed back. My bleeding had slowed, but the wound on my shoulder and my thigh throbbed with pain.

I rode slowly and asked Giri to tell me how they got back to me. "I found Dev south of here, and we were heading back to you. Then we saw deer, rabbits, and monkeys running towards us. That made me suspicious, so I asked Dev to climb up a tree," said Giri.

Dev continued, "I saw birds flying above the trees, north of us, disturbed by something below on the ground. I led the elephant south into the forest, so I worried about the source of this commotion. We should have never left you without any personal guards, so we galloped back."

Suddenly I heard sounds of horse hooves. I stopped and drew my sword. Giri loaded his bow, and Dev held his spear ready for a strike. As the horses came closer, I could see the tiger emblem on the flag, but we did not let our guard down. Kapil came into view, galloping ahead of others, and stopped in front of us. He took in my wounds and Shiv's and our drawn weapons.

He gasped, "Prince Jay, what happened? I worried when—"

Satya came behind him and exclaimed, "You are hurt. And not by the elephant. What happened?"

I told him what occurred. Kapil glared at Giri and Dev and scolded, "You both left the Prince alone and went off. What part of your oath to protect him did you not get?" They appeared chastised and bowed their heads.

"Prince Jay, you fought against ten men. That is extraordinary," marveled Rish.

They brought the Physician with him. As Kapil helped me off the horse, I said, "I will live. Treat him first," and pointed at Shiv. Most of the physician's supplies were in the wagon, so he just wrapped the wounds as best as he could. After he treated Shiv, he came to me. He gently removed the spear from my thigh and applied an herb mixture on it and wrapped a cloth around it. "This wound is not deep and should heal in a few weeks."

He applied the same mixture to my shoulder as well. He handed me a drink, and I gulped it down.

I got back on my horse, and we headed back to the river. Satya came to me and said, "Prince Jay, I suggest you get on the boat and come up the river. You need the rest. I will meet you north of Pullikadu tomorrow, and we can discuss our plans." I nodded in agreement.

I boarded the boat with my guards, the physician, Muthu, and Shiv. The captain of the boat led me to his room. I thanked him and gazed out through the windows. The vessel started moving, and the men on the shore receded from us. Muthu came in with a basin of clean water. I glanced down and saw my blood-splattered body and clothes. I let him help me while my thoughts wandered. Why did Shiv betray me? He called me weak. Was that what others thought of me? He mentioned Prince Nakul, and I had a sudden vision of the prince, tall and regal. My father wanted him to rule Saral after he agreed to pay homage to Malla. Nakul seemed to have other ideas. He was a dangerous opponent to have. I should try to make him an ally through marriage or kill him in battle before he did.

Muthu asked me if I wanted to eat my food in my room, and I told him I was not hungry. He left to get me some milk. Kapil came in and regarded me. "Prince Jay, you need to rest, so I will not take too long. Dev and Giri failed their duties when they left you alone."

"They came back and saved my life, Kapil."

"My lord, I failed you as well when I let you go without adequate protection."

My head ached. Why hadn't Kapil followed me immediately into the forest? Had he colluded with Shiv? I tried to stop these train of thoughts. *I cannot let Shiv win*, I thought sternly. If I succumbed to them, I would start doubting my own shadow, or worse, my sister.

"They left my side for a few minutes. Do you want me to stay chained?"

He sensed my anger and stayed quiet, and I took a deep breath. Does a prince apologize? "Kapil, I gave them the orders, and they simply followed them."

He looked at me and said, "Prince..."

He hesitated, and I said, "Kapil, I should have taken you along when I took off with Shiv." I wanted to add I was young and confused, but I did not.

"Prince Jay, you single-handedly defeated seven men today. If that is not bravery, I don't know what is. I am not a man of words. You are destined for greatness, and I have been putting up roadblocks in your path. I have forgotten the meaning of my oath. There are going to be many times when you must put your life in danger. My duty is to protect you, not stop you. Your guards remain loyal to you. I have talked to them, and..." he paused and cleared his throat. "We want to renew our oaths to you." I studied him as he said it. "If you assent, I will bring them in."

I understood what he'd tried to do and could only nod. Kapil knew me well and sensed the doubts that plagued me. All five came in. They placed their swords on my feet and said the oath in unison, and it washed over me like cold water from the rain.

18

Betrayal

I saw Shiv on the boat corridor the next day, chains wrapped around his ankles and wrists, and he smirked at me. Dropping all pretense of cordiality, he jeered, "I was right. You are too weak to even kill me."

Karan jabbed his face and told him, "Keep your mouth shut and speak only when spoken to. Otherwise, I will make you rue the day you were born."

"Is your prince too feeble and sends his minions to do his bidding?"

Karan raised his fist to punch him when I said quietly, "Karan."

He stopped and dropped his arm. I glared at Shiv. I forgot my earlier thoughts about taking him to an Akash court and having the king serve him justice. I could not let him go unpunished for what he had done. My men would never respect me.

I glanced at his guard and ordered, "Cut his chains and bring him to the top. Karan, get Kapil and Giri." Then I limped to the top of the boat. Kapil and Giri came immediately, and I beckoned my guards close to me and whispered, "I am going to fight Shiv. Stay out of my way."

Kapil gazed at me in a new light and nodded. Since our conversation, a new understanding had sprung up between us. I trusted him to keep me safe, and that gave me an unfair edge. Shiv had betrayed me. He did not deserve fairness.

Shiv rose and rubbed his hands, getting the blood to flow back into his chain-shackled limbs. He wobbled a little, and with his wild eyes, appeared like a drunken beast. He sneered at me, and anger exploded in my chest. I took a deep breath to clear my head.

"Give him a sword," I said menacingly and unsheathed mine. "You coward pig, this has gone on long enough. One of us will perish today, and I don't think it will be me. Grab the sword and fight with me." My thigh still throbbed from my wound. Well, we were about even then.

He picked up the sword. "Remember, I used to beat you in our fights." Saying this, he thrust his sword at me, and I sidestepped. I could not move fast, so I used that to my advantage. I watched with my eyes and ears. I parried his blows, waiting for the right moment to strike. It came soon when I fell on the floor. Shiv raised his sword and swung at me, and I rolled and got on to my feet. Pain shot through my thigh, but I ignored it. Shiv laughed monstrously and lunged at me. Rage coursed through me, and I swung my sword at him, screaming.

His head rolled for a few feet and came to rest near a drum. His body went limp and collapsed.

I came to my senses and looked around. Giri stood on top of another drum with his arrow nocked. Kapil had his sword drawn, and Karan remained near at hand too. Other soldiers all looked on, and suddenly they broke into a shout, "Long live, Prince Jay."

What had I done? I'd killed a man without a trial. Yes, he'd committed treason, but the king settled these matters. I'd acted impulsively, worried about how I'd look, rather than doing the right thing. I felt ashamed but tried to hide it. I asked Kapil to preserve Shiv's body. In this heat, the corpse would decompose quickly. I owed it to his father to give him his son's remains.

I then went to my room with the men cheering me. Honor, family, and duty. All so confusing. I'd tried to make him an example, so no one else would dare to betray me. Are loyalties won through fear or friendship?

Kapil came into my room. I was covered in blood, but that was not what gave him pause. He knew me too well to be fooled by my stoic face. He could sense my conflict. I wished I could talk to him about the doubts that festered in me. About Shiv poisoning my mind. Something stopped me. "I will get you some water to clean up," he said softly and left.

The boat would dock soon, and I needed to compose myself to speak to Satya and Rish. I would look like a boy unable to control his emotions. In a while, the boat stopped, and I heard the sound of horse hooves outside. The heat stifled me, and sweat dotted my forehead. Waves of emotion threatened to drown me. I went up and breathed in big gulps of air.

I searched the shore and saw Rish. I asked the men to drop the ladder, and I climbed onto the land. Rish looked ready to get off his horse, and I told him, "Let us go for a ride." I rode with him along the shore and stopped by some rocks. The current in the river caused the water to swirl around the rocks and reflected the confusion in my mind. I briefly told him what happened.

"Prince Jay, you had good reasons to do this, but Bhoj Thari is one of the pillars of Malla, and he is not going to be happy to hear that the crown prince beheaded his son. It is difficult to predict what a father's heart might do. I will send a messenger to King Vikram immediately."

My father would understand why I did it. But as a king, he avoided bloodshed. He would not be pleased I'd decided to take justice in my hands. A normal sixteen-year-old could make mistakes and learn from them. A prince though rarely gets a second chance.

When we arrived in Theni, General Devan Biha waited for us at the fort entrance. Seeing him on his feet, I dismounted. My herald announced me to the General, and he came up to me and bowed. "Prince Jay, I am heartened to see you. When I learned you had escaped captivity, my joy knew no bounds."

I inquired after my father and sister and the General attested to their good health. Kapil waited for the formalities to be done and then stepped forward and touched his uncle's feet, and the General embraced him. After handing off the horses, I walked in with the General. A tall man with broad shoulders, his beard peppered with grey and scars on his face, arms, and shoulders, paid testimony to his prowess on the battlefield. He ruled Biha, one of the key territories in the Malla kingdom.

The General asked me to join him for my meals, and I headed to my chambers to clean up.

I thought about our journey along the river, the last few days. I had enjoyed swimming with the fish and the ducks. There was something liberating about being in free-flowing water. Though we built dams to contain the flow of the river, she found a way to break free and flow where her mind desires. Not completely free, though, as she flows with one destination in mind, reaching the sea. For now, I dipped a cloth in the water basin and cleaned myself. Muthu came and laid out some clean cotton clothes and helped me out of my dirty clothes. Kapil waited outside for me when I came out, and we walked to the General's quarters.

The General seemed unhappy about me leading the fight and about Shiv's death.

He looked at his nephew Kapil and said sternly, "You failed in your duty as head of the Prince's guard."

"He also swore to obey me. I am the one responsible for this misadventure, not Kapil or Rish," I responded.

"My lord, I am an old man, and you will one day be king of this great land, but I pray you listen to me. Your father sent you here, entrusting your safety to me. You are the sole male heir to this kingdom, and news of your disappearance plunged the Capital into turmoil. If anything happens to you, chaos and despair will rule the land."

"Uncle Devan, I apologize for sneaking off to Maram earlier in disguise. If I had sought your advice, we may have avoided the ambush. But this battle was a necessity."

"Though my youthful days are behind me, I understand its earnestness. Patience is a virtue that comes with age." He added kindly, "Princes though do not have the luxury of time if they want to grow old."

Shackles of prince hood. I needed to accept it gladly. "Say no more, General. I hope to be wiser for this."

The General then said, "I see all the good qualities of a ruler in you. I still remember your birth. The king held court when the maid came in and announced that your mother gave birth to a boy. Your father rejoiced in the news. He ordered lamps to be lit all over the palace, heralding your arrival. Temples performed special prayers, and the people of Malla rejoiced by lighting lamps in their houses as well. All of Malla celebrated." He paused for a moment, reliving the past. I had heard some of these stories from my grandmother before. My father had been a just and able ruler of this land. So had been his forefathers. I could hear my ancestors whispering in my ears, "*The fate of Malla rests on your shoulders, Jay. Do us proud.*"

The General continued, "You have won the hearts of the men in the short time you have been here. You are surrounded by many loyal men in your service. I am one of them. I will give my life for this land and you, my prince."

At times, I would have to call on loyal men like him to put their lives in danger. For me and Malla. When I did, it could not be for petty reasons. I thanked the General and asked, "General, we captured Queen Anju. Do we have any word from King Surya or the scouts we sent after him?"

"Prince Jay, one of the scouts, came back. I have asked him to give his account to us. With your permission, I would also like to move Queen Anju to our fort in Lukla. We would be able to better protect her there." I agreed to that. *It would be wise to put some distance between Queen Anju and Princess Aranya*, I thought

While waiting for the scout, I asked, "Tell me more about King Surya."

"King Surya's actions are that of a mad man. He nourished a grudge against your father ever since he—" He hesitated and then continued, "Prince Jay, I am not privy to what happened. Only two men alive know the details, and they are both kings. I am just narrating what I have heard over the years. Surya married your mother's cousin. Some say your mother was betrothed to Surya, and others disagree. After your father's coronation as the king and his marriage to Queen Charu, he made a journey by ship to Kadal. Very few people knew of this. Veera Vindhya went on the journey with your father as his guard. King Vikram came back with your mother. Surya has held a grudge since then."

My father never shared the complete story with me or the reason behind Surya's grudge. I pondered what secrets both kings held.

The scout who had searched for King Surya walked in, along with Satya and Rish, and bowed to us. He had a lush beard and mustache and only three fingers on his left hand. The general asked the man to narrate his story, and he said, "We went to Pullikadu and tried to trace King Surya's path. We chased several false trails. Ultimately, we spotted one of his guards south of Pullikadu and followed him. Surya and Nakul are on the move, trying to find shelter."

Satya said, "There is a castle south of here where we could allow him to take shelter. It is a castle we can easily capture back."

We spent hours discussing our next move and a plan crystallized.

Later that day, I went to meet Princess Aranya. As I walked in with Kapil, she waited for the doors to be shut, and then she came to me and held out her hands.

Kapil said, "I will wait outside my lord," and left us alone. I pulled her into an embrace. She looked up with tears glistening in her eyes, and I bent down to kiss her. "I missed you," I whispered against her lips. I forgot the world around me, Shiv's betrayal, and my duties as a prince, wishing to hold her in my arms forever.

Slowly she pulled back and said quietly, "I am not leaving your side again."

I thought about the men I slaughtered, my mud and blood-splattered body and clothes, my doubts and rage. She felt like a sanctuary away from it all.

19

March

We departed on the morning of the fourth day, due to delays in gathering the men, after the last battle. With a troop this large in Saral lands, the news of our march would be difficult to hide from King Surya. Our spies informed me he would be able to gather 500 men, but he would still be vastly outnumbered. To prevent him from escaping to the islands with Prince Nakul, I sent 300 men to the coast to block him from boarding his ship.

The general split the men up. He had 20 men board two boats on the river and tasked one of them with meeting us south of Pullikadu and the other to follow us. He had 30 men head southwest, and the rest of us headed to where men last spotted Surya.

I rode on my horse beside Kapil and Rish. Giri and Veer spread out among the other men on horses. I decided to bring Aranya along because she insisted on joining us. I did not have the heart to refuse her request again. If her father or brother got hurt, I did not want her to find out through a messenger ten days after. Dressed in male clothes, she rode beside Karan and Dev. This way, she drew less attention among my men and remained hidden from Saral spies.

The fields were filled with paddy crops, and the young plants danced in the winds. Men and women worked in the fields. The men mostly wore no upper garments. Some wore their *dhoti* similar to me, draped around their waist and going between their legs and tucked in the back, to be able to ride and fight. Others draped the cloth around their waist. A few months back, I would have been envious of these farmers for their simple lives. Not anymore. I had a destiny to fulfill.

The rains fed the plants and kept the scenery around us green. The shower also hampered our progress. We rode mostly in wet weather that soaked us. With the breastplate and my upper garment, I would have been suffocatingly hot, if not for the downpour. The roads, though, were in need of repair. When this area came under Malla rule, I would have the roads repaired.

We had spies throughout the region, tracking King Surya's movements. I let him take shelter in an old castle and then surrounded the castle. Somu remained a captive of Surya. The thought of losing him caused my stomach to twist into knots. I wanted to rescue him without letting Surya know how much he meant to me. I hoped, maybe foolishly, that Surya would keep him alive to get information about me.

My men surrounded the castle, and we pitched tents in the open fields. From our spies, I gathered Surya had enough food for a moon month or perhaps a bit longer if he put his men on half ration. I let it be known that I would pardon his men who chose to pledge loyalty to me. These were not men I would want on my side, but I could chip away Surya's resistance. Any man who surrendered would be kept in confinement for a while, till I could ascertain their loyalty, or use them as hostages.

I paced in my tent, discussing our strategy with General Devan, Rish, Satya, and others when Giri entered.

"My lord, there is a woman outside who claims to be Somu's sister. She seeks your audience," he said.

"Bring her in. She may have some news from her brother. And ask Princess Aranya to join us. She served as their maid for many years, and the Princess would recognize her."

Giri brought in an older woman with a lined face and grey hair. She wore a simple sari, and walked with a straight posture, and her build indicated a woman used to hard work.

She approached me, and I saw tears glisten in her eyes. Had I failed to save Somu? Before I could ask the question, she cried, "Prince Jay," and fell at my feet.

Taken aback, I quickly bent down and lifted her back up by her shoulders. Controlling the tremors I felt with great difficulty, I asked urgently, "Is Somu still captive at the castle?"

"Yes, my lord," she said, not sounding very concerned for his safety.

"What brings you to here, *Ma*?" I asked, hiding my confusion.

"When I heard you started marching against King Surya, I traveled day and night to arrive here. I seek your promise to protect Prince Nakul, my lord," she said, peering at me through her tear-filled eyes.

She continued, "I have raised the Prince since his mother's death. He is a kind-hearted boy and would be a good king to his people."

Aranya strode in, saw her, exclaimed, "Thangam," and ran forward to embrace her. The two women stayed for a few moments with their arms around each other, shedding tears. Then slowly, they broke apart, and Thangam turned towards me again. "Spare the life of my Prince, my lord, as you did with my Princess," she requested pleadingly.

"Prince Nakul is a fortunate man to have been raised by you. My intention is not to harm the Prince, if I can avoid it," I said.

I said to Aranya, "Princess, we traveled without any female companions for you. Would you—" before I could finish my question, she replied, "Yes," and took Thangam's hand. "Thangam, let us go to my tent. There is much I need to talk to you about."

Thangam bowed to me and walked out with her. "Your hair, Princess. It will take me hours to fix it."

Thangam's arrival distracted me, and I paced the room for a few minutes. Prince Nakul and I had at least one thing in common: the loyalty of the sister and brother who raised us. What actions of our mothers earned it because it could not have been for any of our actions?

Slowly, I brought my attention to the matter at hand and the men in the room.

"My lord, in a moon month, Surya's supplies will dwindle, and he will be forced to surrender," said Satya.

"Satya, in a moon month, I would like to be back in Akash, not waiting here."

"We could attack the walls. We allowed him to seek shelter here because the castle defenses are weak."

Others chimed in, "If we use our elephants, we could break in through the door."

"Our archers can be positioned to fire at any men attacking from within."

Slowly a plan emerged. We would wait for a few days for the men to recover from our march and our foot soldiers and supply wagons to arrive. Then, early in the morning, we would attack. I told the men to keep our plan a secret until then.

As others left, Rish stayed behind.

I said, "I have set on this battle without the king's blessing. Even with the fast horses that the messengers were on, we may start our attack before the news reaches Akash."

"My lord, when I left Akash, the King and the Princess feared they had lost you forever. They would be overjoyed to receive news of your survival, and I do not believe this battle of yours will change that," he said, smiling slightly.

"My return has not caused much joy in you. Where did you lose your cheerful ways?" I asked, studying him.

He laughed sadly and said, "You did not see me before your return, my lord. Men avoided me for my dark and gloomy spirit. In Akash, I failed miserably to save Balan from plunging the knife in his heart. I could not stop my Uncle from plotting. And I could not offer reassurances to the Princess that I would find you. And, my Prince, I played no part in finding you."

"Rish, you and I can sit all day here and trade tales on who had the worse few months. The trials of the last months have made me stronger and more resolute. I have clarity on what kind of ruler I want to be. Rish Vindhya, I am sure you were a great comfort to my sister, and you must have earned her respect for her to send you to find me. These are difficult times, and I need brave and loyal men at my side. You are one such man. I am not going to allow you to wallow in self-pity."

"My lord—"

"We have difficult times ahead of us. After the immediate battle of Saral, we have to head to Akash and face the Padi princes. King Jay ruled the three kingdoms of Magadha under one umbrella, and the kingdoms prospered peacefully following one ruler. Prince Amar wants to be that one ruler, and we cannot let that happen. Are you with me on this?" I asked.

"My prince, it would be my honor," he said solemnly, standing a little straighter.

20

Prince in Akash

Prince Atul left for Padi with my father's consent for the wedding. Soon, the Padi royal family would be headed to Akash.

On the inside, my mind struggled to make sense of all I knew. No news of Jay had reached us, and I did not know what to make of Nakul being my brother. How would he react if he knew he was the rightful heir to the throne? And what about Jay, could we deprive him of what he believed was his? In my dreams, what I feared while awake happened, my brothers, fighting each other for the throne. Father seemed less sorrowful since he'd shared what must have been a heavy burden with me. Two sons, one raised as the heir of our perpetual rival Saral, and one lost to the world.

On the outside, I anticipated my wedding with the right amount of eagerness and shyness. Kantha came to me on a gloomy day and said, "The king requests your presence, my lady."

With a sense of dread, I trotted to my father's chambers, my mind racing faster than my footsteps. When he saw me, he put my mind at ease. "We have good news from Saral, Meera." He asked me to sit beside him. As I did, he commanded, "Repeat what you told me earlier," to a messenger in the room.

"My lord, Prince Jay escaped captivity with Princess Aranya's aid, and reached the safety of Theni palace."

Upon hearing those words, a sob escaped me, and my father put his arms around my shoulders. Jay alive. My prayers answered. One of the knots in my stomach slowly unwound. I longed to see him. To make sure he was okay.

My father then asked him to tell us what happened since General Devan left, and the man launched into a long tale of despair and hope.

"My lord, Prince Jay is preparing to capture King Surya and Prince Nakul to bring Saral under Malla rule. He said he would return to Malla victorious." On hearing these words, my stomach turned.

Father said, "Meera, let us not forego the hope of victory. These young men may succeed where older men like me have failed." I assumed he included Nakul and Jay in the young men group. Didn't he worry his sons would face each other in battle and try to kill one another?

The queen and I went to the temple that night to offer our prayers for Jay's safety. I prayed silently for Nakul's safety, as well.

Within days, news of Shiv's betrayal and death reached us. Saral had been far more dangerous than I expected. Father strangely chuckled and boasted, "Nakul knows the weakness of men and how to use them." He relished both his sons' triumphs. "And what about Jay's bravery? I wish I had witnessed him fight ten men on his own."

I would never understand men and their love of war.

After a pause, he muttered, "I need to send a personal message to Bhoj Thari. His son's defection is reason enough for the punishment, but I understand a father's heart. It does bleed no matter the reason."

Shiv Thari had spent a few years in Akash, learning, and training with Jay. Thari ties with Malla went back many generations. Shiv was no fool. To entice him to abandon Jay, the prize must have been great. But he would not have wanted the deception to become known. He'd planned for Jay's death in the ambush and to emerge as a loyal wounded warrior, unable to save the crown prince. If that had come to fruition, I could not bring myself to think of the consequences. Jay, how had he taken a betrayal from someone so close to him? If he let this mistrust take root, he would have no peace as the ruler.

Father added, "It appears they have captured Queen Anju. She is the young girl King Surya married in recent months, mostly for her wealth, from what I hear. This girl is of little value to us as a hostage, but we will have to keep her safe under our guard."

A few days passed since this incident, and I kept busy getting the palace ready for Prince Amar's arrival from Padi. News of Jay's survival had kept my spirits lifted during that time, but the impending arrival of Amar dampened it. My earlier fears crept into my body, twisting my stomach.

Malla chiefs and other important families gathered in Akash to participate in my wedding. People of Akash decorated the city for the occasion. Banana trees adorned the entryways to the city and the palace. Strings of flowers and mango leaves adorned the thresholds.

On the day of his arrival, the sun rose gloriously, as if mocking my fears. I decided to take courage in the warmth and light to get rid of my dark thoughts. I had nothing to fear until we exchanged our wedding garlands. Even then, I could control my destiny if I used my skills wisely.

Kantha woke me early and helped me get ready. She laid out a fine silk sari in the shades of a peacock feather along with jewels inlaid with sparkling blue sapphires. Peacocks were the symbol of Padi and my outfit in outward appearances at least, would symbolize the embrace of my future home. When my heart would be ready for this merger was a different matter.

After draping the sari, I sat down in front of the mirror, and Kantha worked her magic on my hair. I stared at the reflection, and it stared back at me with a twinge of sadness.

"Every girl is sad to leave her home, Princess Meera," said Kantha sagely.

"Yes, it is even harder when it is such a beloved place. I will have to take some of Malla with me to Padi."

Saying this, I paused and glanced at Kantha. My marriage loomed over me, and instead of facing the inevitable, I had been wallowing in pity.

"Kantha, I should have asked before. Would you come with me to Padi?" I asked in a rushed voice.

Before I could continue, she blurted out, "My lady, I know you have been busy these last few days. So even though you never asked, I have been getting ready for Padi. I wouldn't part with you."

She paused here and wiped her tears with the end of her sari, and it brought tears to my eyes. My heart let out a sigh. One less parting to worry about in the coming days.

Soon, I waited with my companions on the castle steps, along with the King and Queen. Since the news of Jay's escape, my father had made a remarkable recovery and walked on his own to greet the Padi guests. Elephants, horses, and chariots arrived at the city doors and made their way to the King's castle.

I caught sight of a splendid young man in his royal outfit with long hair framing his face. Tales about Prince Amar's looks were not a lie. As he came closer, I realized his gaze rested on my person. Our eyes met briefly, before I averted mine, as tradition dictated. No smile reached his lips or his eyes. Was the grim satisfaction I saw in his face due to my appearance? Or perhaps he still grieved for his previous wife? My eyes alighted on a warm face, and I returned Prince Atul's smile.

Men jumped off their horses and stood to wait for a horse-drawn carriage to approach us. The carriage came to a stop, and King Verma and Queen Radha descended from it. Padi King Verma had joined forces with the Malla men to fight the Sunda kingdom. As a prize for his victory, Verma married Sunda Princess Radha.

The Padi family walked towards the castle, and my father climbed down the stairs to greet his cousin. We followed a few steps behind him. Heralds from both sides announced the royal members and greetings were exchanged. One of the girls handed me an *arati* plate, and I waved it in front of Prince Amar to ward off any evil. Then I reached up to put a tilak on his forehead, and his cold eyes looked into mine, and my heart tightened. I saw a scar on his cheek that had faded with time and was visible only at close quarters.

Later in the day, after the visitors washed away the dirt and weariness from their travels, we gathered to eat our midday meal. The feast and the festivities would happen that night. For now, only the families gathered to celebrate the union of the two families, already twined by blood and marriage. I sat next to Queen Radha, and grandmother asked her from across the table, "What do you think of my granddaughter, Radha?"

The Queen looked at me kindly and replied, "She takes after you, Aunt Priya. I heard her wit matches her beauty, so Amar is indeed fortunate."

At the mention of his name, Amar looked at us. I kept my gaze down to not look into his eyes till after the wedding. I saw that he had not touched his food. What was on his mind?

The Queen leaned in and said in a whisper, "Meera, I heard your brother Jay went missing in Saral."

I nodded. "Even the sun hides behind the cloud at times. We have news that he is on the march to capture Saral. I do hope he returns to Malla soon."

"Sometimes, hope is all we have," said the Queen and turned to talk to my stepmother. I saw my father and King Verma in deep conversation on the other side. The young Prince Parth sat beside me, and he struck up a conversation, "I feel like I already know you, Cousin Meera. Atul has been talking about you continuously since his visit here."

"I hope he found some good things to say about me."

"Good things? No. Great things, Yes. For the past fortnight, we have only heard how great you are. Everything in Padi has been compared to your beauty, kindness, and grace and failed to live up to it. We have all been shunning him for fear he would launch into another of his praises. Amar forbade him to mention your name in front of him, on the way here."

As soon as he said this, he realized he might have said too much and added, "Seeing you in person, I realize his praises were not unjust."

I wondered why Atul risked his brother's wrath. I got the sense he had not done me any favors with my betrothed. I responded with a smile, "I hope I can win the acceptance of the people of Padi with such ease."

He did not seem to hear my words and asked me instead, "Before we left, we thought your brother died in Saral, my lady. His survival put Amar in a foul temper."

His blunt words shocked me, and as I recovered, I said slowly, "All of Akash celebrated his recovery, Parth." The young prince had two older brothers and had not been groomed to rule. I forgave him for his bluntness. Jay's reappearance would dash any hopes of Padi ruling the Malla kingdom. A knot of worry crept into my belly for my brother's safety.

At night, as the darkness fell, we gathered to watch Malla dancers depict the history of the two kingdoms. I sat beside Prince Amar. He quietly watched the first few performances and barely acknowledged my presence. Then he leaned across and whispered in my ear, "My brother has been singing your praises ever since his visit here."

"I am not sure I deserve all his kindness."

He jeered, "Opening your door to him would have ensured this."

Before the meaning of what he said sunk in, he continued, "You can open your doors for me tonight, and I can taste some of your kindness as well."

Anger coursed through me, and with great difficulty, I controlled it and responded, "My lord, such language is beneath that of a Prince of Padi and brings shame to both our families."

He seemed to delight in my anger and brushed his lips against my ear as he spoke, "You look beautiful when you are annoyed. Forget my brother. In a few days, you will be mine. Why wait till the wedding? Open your heart to me now, and I can show you pleasures as you have never felt before."

For the first time, he terrified me. Icy tendrils of fear crept up my spine. I would have to ask Kantha to sleep in my chambers tonight. "My lord, the words you speak to me are not worthy of either of us, and that is not the way of a Malla princess."

New dancers came on stage Madhavi among them. Amar turned to look at them and whispered, "If that is the case, I will have to find my pleasures elsewhere tonight."

The next day, I sought the solitude of the palace gardens to make sense of what had happened. I found myself near the same place where a young man once held me in his arms and kissed me. I wondered if Rish still thought of that night. Why did this heart that welcomed the embrace of one shun that of another? Before I found an answer, a hand grabbed my waist roughly and turned me to face him.

Prince Amar held me in a tight embrace with both his hands, leaving me no room to move. I opened my mouth to speak, but before any sound came out, his lips crushed mine. With no warmth or love in this kiss, I felt the pain keenly. I struggled against his hold, fighting the tears threatening to flow when I heard footsteps.

"Amar," bellowed Prince Atul. He glared at his brother, his nostrils flaring, and ranted, "She is your betrothed and will be your Queen one day and the mother of your sons. She needs to be treated with respect by you because others will follow your lead," while trying to break his brother's hold on me.

Amar let go of me, spun towards his brother, and hit him hard across the face. He sneered and strode away. I sat down on the bench and clenched my fists. Shame and anger at my helplessness bubbled in my throat. I refused to give in to my emotions and sob.

Atul stood in silence for a few moments and then said kindly, "My lady, allow me to escort you to your chambers."

I stood up and regarded him. His brother's hand had left a mark on his cheek, yet he made no move to show any pain. Had this happened before? Atul gazed at my face and said softly, "There is blood on your lips."

I walked to the pond stating, "Your brother has left a mark on both of us," and washed my face and wiped it with the end of my sari. Then, Atul and I headed back to my chambers.

Atul departed in the hallway to my room, and I ambled towards it. In my chambers, the Queen waited for me.

"Mother," I exclaimed, hoping she could not sense my distress.

Her eyes wandered over my face, and she said, "Meera, come and sit next to me." Once I did, she said, "Prince Amar is no different from your father."

Shocked, I looked at her, and she continued, "After your father and I wed, he never came to my chambers, and rumors swirled around the palace. One day, Queen Mother came and spoke to me. Like a naïve child, I cried when she asked me about the king. I had not seen him since our wedding day. That night, King Vikram came into my room, drunk, and consummated our marriage. Worse, he cried out the name *Kayal*, while with me. The next day, the King took me out on a chariot ride and drove the chariot himself. People gathered in the street to watch us ride by. He said he had treated me poorly and would make amends, but my mind fixated on one thing. I blurted out my question, *who is Kayal?* His lips tightened, and he said curtly it was a ghost he'd buried."

I sat in shock that my father would do this to a woman.

The queen took a deep breath and continued in hushed tones. "We lived a loveless marriage for months and did our duty as king and queen. But after a while, I saw a glimmer in your father's eye and felt a softness in his touch. His fondness for me had started to grow. Then my castle came crumbling down. That wretched servant Somu came from Saral and spoke to your father. He left in a hurry with his guard, my Uncle Veer Vindhya. He told me he had a promise to keep. And he came back with your mother, Kayal, who he claimed he had married before he had ever met me."

She gripped the chair tightly, and her knuckles turned white. "He remained still the dutiful husband to me, but performing that duty was a heavy burden on him. I saw him and Kayal in the palace gardens one day, and for the first time, I saw your father laugh. His face lit up and his lips curled, and I longed for the day he would smile at me. My stomach quickened, and I prayed to God that I would bear a son to the king. But I bore a stillborn girl. Your mother gave birth to you, and as I held you, I thought the gods could not have been crueler towards me.

My stomach quickened again, and my child died a few days after birth. Then your brother came into this world, the heir to the throne. After that, I stayed queen in name only. Your father and mother rode in a chariot through the city with you and Jay, and the people cheered and showered flowers on them as I watched from the balcony."

I remembered my father's laughter on several occasions while my mother was alive. Once, we traveled by boat on a river, and my mother said something, and my father laughed out loud. Jay and I watched the fish in the water and shrieked out when we saw one of them jump. Our mother sang afterward in the evening while holding Jay in her lap. I sat next to my father with his arms wrapped around me, listening to my mother sing. The younger and happier father in my memory vanished with my mother's death. Only a shell of his former self endured for his children. My stepmother's voice brought me back to the present.

Her brows furrowed as she said in clipped tones, "Your father stopped visiting my chambers after your brother's birth because he did not want a rival tiger cub. I spent many a dark night alone with no tears to express my grief. Your mother's eyes filled with pity when she saw me and your father's with pain, and I did not know which felt worse. Your mother named her third child, Charu, after me, and that baby died along with your mother.

"I became a childless queen to play mother to the two of you. Princes pursue glory on the battlefield. Princesses live for duty and honor and, if blessed, for their children. Your father honored me as his queen, but he did not love me as his woman."

She regarded me intently and said gently, "Love is for fairy tales. Amar is bound to break your heart. You still need to carry on, performing your duties as a queen, wife, and mother."

As I heard my stepmother's words, a grim determination came over me.

21

Battle for Saral

I spent my days with the men, overseeing preparations for the campaign, listening to the advice of veterans, and offering words of encouragement to the young men facing their first battle. I also trained with my guards, regaining my strength and sword skills. The days flew past, and our attack would unfold at dawn tomorrow. As night fell, Satya and others left my tent after our conversation.

As I paced, thinking through our plan, Dev entered and bowed. "Prince Jay, Princess Aranya is here."

She sauntered in. Dev left us alone. My men treated us like we were betrothed, though we had neither parent's blessing. Aranya came and stood in front of me. Though I saw concern in her eyes, her face stayed composed. I took her hands in mine and said, "I will keep my promise to you. I will do my utmost to protect the lives of your father and brother."

She nodded and let go of my hands. She removed a long gold chain with a fish-shaped pendant from her neck and held it in her hands. "Jay, when my mother passed away, my brother gave this to me. This was his mother's, left to him as a baby. He told me our mothers would watch over and protect me. I have nothing else to offer you—"

I interrupted her and said, "You have already given me the most precious gift of all, yourself."

This brought a smile to her face, and she said, touching the pendant, "Please wear this to battle tomorrow as a token of my affection then."

She then held out the chain, and I bent my head so she could put it around my neck.

Sleep eluded me that night, and I lay awake thinking about Somu, King Surya, Prince Nakul, and most of all Princess Aranya. I could feel her chain against my skin. I liked wearing a piece of jewelry that previously adorned her neck. As I lay thinking about her and what lay in store for us, dawn broke. I rose and got dressed in a state of agitation. I took a deep breath to still my thoughts.

Soon we mounted and stood in the fields facing the castle. I had been training all my life for moments like these. Calmly, I watched the action unfold in front of me.

The first task was to breach the castle defenses. Archers stationed in the fields provided cover for our men who guided elephants holding tree trunks to break open the castle front doors. Other men tried scaling the castle walls in various spots. One or two succeeded and then attacked their archers stationed in various alcoves in the castle walls.

All of this went according to plan and looked orderly to my eyes. A passerby observing this might have only seen chaos and confusion. Two of our elephants were brought down by spears from above, and two more took their place. The fourth set of elephants broke open the doors.

As the doors opened, I walked my horse a few paces ahead and faced my men. I took a few moments to view their faces staring at me in anticipation.

"Men, we have an opportunity to create history today and bring this beautiful land under Malla rule. After months of hiding, we have trapped King Surya and his heir, Prince Nakul, in this castle. March with me into it and let us capture both men and put an end to this fight. Let the sunrise this morning pave the way for the rise of the tiger."

Then I turned my horse and raised my sword into the sky and thundered, "Victory to King Vikram," and galloped ahead. I heard an echo of voices shouting, "Victory to Malla" or "Victory to Prince Jay," and the men followed me.

When I got closer to the door, I jumped off my horse and rushed in, surrounded by my guards. We fought our way through the weak Saral resistance, my eyes searching for Prince Nakul or his father. I soon found the prince at the head of stairs, fighting off men below, and headed that way.

Prince Nakul fought fiercely, and many Malla soldiers fell victim to his sword. I stood at the foot of the stairs and moved up, as my men made way for me.

Prince Nakul noticed me and said, "I don't fight with boys. Send me your men." I did not waste my strength responding to him and soon approached near enough to let my sword speak. Fighting him from below proved difficult, and I tried to push him back into the halls, but he showed no sign of fatigue. Suddenly though, he appeared distracted as he looked at my armor, and that allowed me to push him back. He continued to fight me absently while gazing periodically at my chest.

As our swords clanged, he asked, "Where did you get that chain?"

I realized what had distracted him. "This is the princess's token of her love," I said savagely, continuing to fight.

Nakul stopped my thrust with his shield and said, "Stop. I don't want to hurt you."

"Hurt me?" I laughed. "Don't worry about me. My men have surrounded your castle and—"

He did not appear to pay heed to my words. "Jay, stop fighting and listen," he ordered me in a voice that caused me to obey him. I did not lower my sword, but I paused and regarded him.

"Order your men to cease fighting, and I will do the same. I will take you to my father's chambers, and we can resolve this peacefully."

"What kind of jest is this? I know you take me for a naïve boy but—"

"But my sister has chosen you and I assume your intentions are honorable?"

Confused, I nodded, and he continued, "Peace through marriage is better," and lowered his sword and shouted at his men, "Stop the fighting."

I studied him for some time and then shouted the same to my soldiers. Then, surrounded by my guards and Satya and a few others, I followed him and a few of his men to the King's chamber.

As we neared, Satya and Rish looked at each other and whispered to me, "Prince Jay, this could be a trap."

Prince Nakul overhead and said, "Only if you think Princess Aranya would lead you to one." I did not doubt her feelings for me.

We reached a heavily guarded door, and Nakul said to the guards, "Tell the king I am here with Prince Jay, who has come seeking a truce."

The soldier opened a small window in the door and spoke to a man inside.

Nakul said, "You can bring two escorts with you."

Satya started speaking, and I raised my hand to stop him and turned to Rish and nodded at him and then at Giri. My best swordsman and best archer.

A voice from inside shouted, "Go away."

Nakul ignored this order and said to the guards, "Open the door."

"My lord. . ." One of the guards hesitated but then regarded Nakul and opened the door.

Nakul entered, and then Rish followed. When Rish gestured for me, I strode into the room. The King sat at a table, eating an elaborate meal and drinking toddy. I glared at him in disgust. Enjoying a meal while his men perished all around him. He revolted me.

When he saw me, he staggered to his feet, "*Him.* How dare you bring him into my chambers? Kill him!" he said, pointing to his guards.

The guards observed Nakul and hesitated again, this time waiting for his command.

Nakul straightened. "Father, we are surrounded. We can resist for half a day, but that would only prolong the inevitable."

"You are still alive," the King spit at him, "and I ordered you to hold the castle or die trying."

"I would gladly die for Saral, but there appears to be a peaceful way to solve this. Aranya has chosen Jay, and with your blessing, this marriage can save our kingdom."

"Save our kingdom!" the King exclaimed. "It would sell us to Vikram, and you want me to be a slave to him."

"Father—"

"You are no son of mine," he shouted. He grabbed a knife off the table and threw it at Nakul. Nakul's eyes widened in shock, and I did not think. I pushed him aside, and the knife clattered to the floor, grazing his left arm. Nakul appeared rooted to the ground, unable or unwilling to move. The king threw his plate at him. I was ready for it and knocked it away with my shield.

"Kill him," the king shouted at his guards, pointing towards his son. Swords drawn, eyes darting between the king and their prince, they seemed to wait for Nakul's commands. Nakul continued to stare at his father, his mouth twisted into a grimace.

The king stood up and threw his lighted oil lamp, and it fell on the rug a few feet from us, setting it on fire.

As the drama unfolded in front of me, I understood I dealt with a madman. I jumped over the fire and approached King Surya on a run. His guards sprang into action and attacked me. As I sparred with them, I shouted, "Satya, bring our men in."

Rish guessed my intention and held his sword at Nakul's neck, who made no move. Giri followed me with his bow and shot his arrow at a man who fought me. I thrust my sword into another's arm and knocked his sword out of his hands.

I moved to King Surya's side in the blink of an eye and held my sword at his throat. "Prince Nakul spoke the truth. I have more men than you, and I have surrounded this castle. Tell your men to drop their swords," I said and pressed my sword at his neck.

He looked at me with quivering eyes and shouted, "Kill them all!"

By then, Satya had overcome the guards outside and rushed in with the other men. Soon, it was over. Seeing Nakul standing still, the Saral men gave up the fight quietly.

I stepped back from the King and let my men hold him. "King Surya,

I would like to seek your blessing to marry your daughter. Please come to Akash and bless us and pledge your alliance to King Vikram. You will be allowed to rule this land in peace."

"I would kill Aranya with my own hands rather than marry her to you," he screamed at me.

"I cannot disobey my father," said Nakul glancing at me.

I sensed a hint in his words. "Arrest them both. King Surya will remain in this room until we can find better quarters for him. Post guards inside and out. Bring Nakul to the tent," I said and left.

Two men tied Nakul's hands. There were pockets of fighting, and I yelled, "Stop the fighting. Your King and Prince are in my control."

Nakul echoed me and said, "Stop the fighting," to his men, and walked behind me.

I halted to talk to Satya. "Ask the men to look for Somu and bring me news of him."

When I reached the castle doors, Giri ran towards me and said, "My lord, they have found Somu in the castle dungeons. He is weak but alive."

"I will go release Somu myself," I stated, my heart pounding.

Kapil and I went to the dungeons. Rooms stood mostly empty, and Somu laid down on a straw mat in one of the cells. Kapil took the keys from the guard and opened the door. Somu looked at us when he heard the keys turn.

"Prince Jay, you are back," he exclaimed and staggered up. As Kapil opened the door, I stepped into the cell and approached Somu. He said softly, "I prayed to the Lord Muruga that I would shave my head—" He raised his hand as if to touch my face, but suddenly, he seemed to realize there were other people around us and dropped his hand.

"Is that all I am worth to you? You were going to give up your hair for my safe return?" I teased, smiling at him.

He smiled back, "At my age, hair is a precious commodity. It does not grow back easily."

I put my arms around his shoulders and embraced him. Instead of smooth skin, my fingers touched bumps on his shoulder. "Somu, turn around," I ordered, barely suppressing my anger. He obeyed, and I saw his back crisscrossed with whip marks. I clenched my fingers. "Let's go," I barked and stormed out. I raged at Surya for doing this, but I blamed myself for putting Somu in this position. I'd acted like a spoiled boy seeking an adventure, rather than a Prince thinking of the welfare of his people.

Somu half-ran to keep up with me. Once outside, one of the men brought us horses, and I climbed on it and rode off with Kapil and Somu, to the shouts of greetings and cheer.

Once in my tent, I asked Karan to send for the Physician.

The Physician came in and asked, "Prince Jay, are you hurt?"

My pride, I thought to myself but said, "Not me, it is Somu."

He looked at Somu's whip marks and said, "I have an herb paste for this. Come to my room to get it." Somu left with him, and I settled in my room. Somu had taken care of me since I was a young child, and in return, I almost got him killed. I could sense Giri moving around the room, checking the doors and windows. I owed the victory today to Aranya. Old guilt and doubts raised its head, and I squashed it. I did not have to carry all the burden of ruling Malla. Aranya, Kapil, Devan, Satya, and others would aid me.

I asked a servant to bring Princess Aranya. Rish and Dev brought Prince Nakul into my tent, and I ordered them to untie him. Aranya scurried in, her eyes lighting up when she saw me. Then she noticed Nakul. She ran to him and threw her arms around him, burying her face in his chest. He held her tight and kissed her forehead.

Slowly, she let go of him and whispered, "Father?"

Nakul responded, "He is alive, but a prisoner, as I am."

I smiled and said, "Prince Nakul, I owe it to you for stopping this battle with very little bloodshed. Come with us to Akash and bless our marriage in place of your father."

He looked at his sister, and Aranya came to me and took my hands and stepped forward, gesturing me to follow. We stood in front of Nakul, and she touched his feet. He placed his hands on her head, blessing her. When she raised, he put his hands on my shoulder and said, "Jay, you are my brother now. Let my mother's protection extend to you," he said, gesturing at my chain.

That night, I invited Prince Nakul to share my meal with me.

"Kapil, I would like to talk to the Prince in private."

"Can we trust him, my lord?"

"I am going to marry his sister, so I would answer in the affirmative." He nodded and talked to the other guards. Two of them, Karan and Giri, stood on guard outside when Prince Nakul came in.

I rose as he came in and asked him to sit at the table. Somu brought in steamed rice cakes, spicy vegetable stew, porridge made of millet sweetened with jaggery, and many kinds of fruits, including bananas and mangoes.

He looked at Somu intently and said, "You are Thangam's brother."

"Yes, Prince Nakul. My sister and I were in the service of Gomti Chief Arul. Thangam went to Lukla to serve Queen Lata when she married King Surya. I stayed behind in Kadal to serve her cousin, Queen Kayal."

His devotion to my mother outlived her life. Meera believed his feelings for my mother to be beyond that of a devoted servant for him to leave Saral and make his home in Malla. After my mother died, I had asked him once about what happened in Kadal when my father came to bring my mother home. He said, "Prince Jay, I am your servant now as your mother's before. I am here to serve. As I go about doing my duty, I hear and see many things. Those are not my stories to share. The story you are asking is your father's to tell."

"I heard Thangam is staying back in Saral?" I asked.

"Queen Nila had left her some farmlands, so she does not lack for comfort, my lord."

Somu left us to eat, and I studied Nakul. Once, I pictured him like the demon king Ravana with his ten heads. He did not have ten heads, nor did he look like a demon king. On the contrary, he looked like how one would picture a prince – tall, strong, and handsome. No crown adorned his long curly hair, but I imagined it would fit well.

"Aranya is my half-sister, as we have different mothers, but I am deeply fond of her. I would seek revenge if any harm befell her."

"Princess Aranya saved my life several times. My duty would be to protect and cherish her."

He looked at me and then satisfied with my response, continued eating.

Observing him, I stated, "Cousin Nakul, I beheaded a friend who you turned against me."

"Jay," he said, "that was in war. Shiv Thari was greedy and dishonest. I used him to spy against you but never trusted him. I intended to capture you, not kill you. My father had other ideas, though."

"How about Vasu? Did you use him to spy on me as well?"

Puzzled, he blurted, "Who?"

Waves of emotions spread in my throat, and I cleared it. "An old friend who I thought had turned."

Nakul shook his head. "Never heard of him."

Vasu had not betrayed me. The thought that he had, after growing up together had burned a hole in me, and now learning otherwise would allow that wound to heal.

22

Heading Home

From the Lukla fort set on top of the hill, I surveyed the land north of me. I saw the river snaking around in the distance. The sky had cleared, and flocks of birds flew towards the water. My eyes feasted on the forest ahead, a green carpet with bright yellow and red spots from blooming flowers, and I felt happy to be on my way to Akash.

In Lukla fort, carved out of the hills, General Devan held King Surya and Queen Anju in separate heavily guarded rooms. My father had previously captured the city when he fought with King Surya. While escaping, Saral men had set fire to the various quarters, destroying furniture, doors, windows, and many inner structures. Only the defensive walls and towers remained relatively undamaged. In the ensuing months, the main quarters had been cleared of fire damage with doors affixed to the rooms. Most of them were sparsely furnished. The forest around the fort provided wood for the repairs. When I arrived in Lukla many moon months ago, men had just started restoring the adjoining quarters. They'd completed most of the work recently.

General Devan had set out earlier with our important guests, Prince Nakul and Princess Aranya. Traveling in supply carts, to hide from spies, their journey north would be slower. Leaving Lt. Gen. Satya in charge of Saral, I made my way home with Rish, Somu, and my guards.

The narrow path down the north side of the hill slowed our descent with all our horses. Then it started to rain heavily, and Rish asked us to halt under the trees. I agreed. I gazed at the majesty in the heavy dark clouds and the pounding rain while soaking in it. The forest came alive, and an earthy aroma exuded in the air. In a little while, the rain slowed to a steady drizzle, and I told my men to start moving again.

Soon we reached the plains. Setting the horse at a steady pace, I rode beside Rish.

I said, "My sister is betrothed to Prince Amar, and I heard he has arrived in Akash."

Rish gave a curt nod but said nothing.

Then I asked him, "Do you know Prince Amar?"

He cleared his throat. "I visited Padi with my father and brother. My father expected us to play with the prince, but he was a brute and a bully, and he taunted us. He let his dog loose upon us. My brother climbed up a tree, and I tried to as well, but I fell. The animal took a chunk off my thigh, and I used my dagger to cut its throat. I heard Amar's laughter, and something snapped inside me. I took the same blade and jumped on the prince and pinned him down and drew my weapon across his cheek. If you meet him in person, you will see the scar he bears from my cut. Men pulled apart us and took me to the king.

"My father begged the king for mercy since I was only a boy of eleven. A boy from Padi would have been hanged for treason. My father came there on behalf of the Malla, and we owed no allegiance to the Padi royalty. King Verma relented and ordered me to be whipped twenty times in the hands of his son as my punishment. I made sure I did not cry when the whip sliced my skin raw, though I still carry the scars. From what I heard, as a grown man, he has added drinking, gambling, and women to his list of transgressions."

I have seen and heard worse stories, but Amar letting a dog loose on young boys his age for no apparent reason horrified me. And that he had no care that the animal had been slaughtered either? I knew my father promised him Meera's hands in marriage, but had Rish only told this tale to turn me against Amar? I suspected Rish cared for Meera, though he could never hope to marry her. How much was the above tale truthful? What benefit would there be for him to lie?

He continued, "His younger brother Atul, a boy of eight or so at that time, seemed a normal child, and unlike his brother, I've heard he has grown into a valiant young man of excellent disposition."

Could I halt Meera's wedding to this monster if I wanted to? The rain stopped, and the whole hillside came alive with birds and animals leaving their homes in search of food. "The wellbeing of this beautiful land has been entrusted to me, and I only hope I am up to the task," I said more to myself.

I studied him. "You know all about me, Rish. I hardly know a thing about you. Tell me more about your life in Vindhya."

He mused, "You already know my father's story. He could have requested to be released from the guards when he got married but considered it his duty and an honor to protect his king. So, he stayed in Akash, and I grew up in Vindhya. As the youngest of three, I led a carefree life until recently. After my father's death, I realized I'd wasted my life and mended my ways."

"No girls pining away for you in Vindhya?"

He laughed. "Not all of us have the same pressure to produce heirs to carry on the family."

He continued more solemnly, "After my father died, my uncle wanted me to marry the daughter of a newly wealthy trader. The trader, once he acquired the wealth, wanted the connections and the name of an old family. Right now, my name is my biggest asset. I could not refuse my uncle, but told him and my mother that I wanted to see the world before I settled down."

"The girl must have been hideous," I mocked him.

"No," he denied laughingly. Then added, "I don't know, honestly. I never saw her."

"Why did you not marry her, then?"

He paused for some time and replied, "My uncle has his ways, and they were different from my father's. I do not want to be a pawn in my uncle's games. I chose my father's way."

And you met my sister, I thought to myself. When your world is lit by the moon, the fireflies hold less attraction.

That night we camped in the open fields, and Somu served me a steaming bowl of my favorite rice pudding made with rice cooked in milk, swimming in butter, and sweetened with jaggery. I suddenly realized I was hungry. As I ate, he cleaned the room. I wanted to say something to him, to thank him, but every word seemed insignificant. Instead, I handed him my empty bowl.

While Kapil worked out guard duties for the night, I went to take a bath. I let Somu scrub my back while my thoughts wandered to my guards. Like a shadow, these men stayed beside me day and night. I'd received them when father crowned me heir apparent. I had no secrets from them.

Somu chattered about getting the barber in tomorrow to cut my hair while I dried myself. He accidentally dropped the copper pot that he used to pour the water, and it rolled on the floor with a loud noise. Karan opened the door immediately and looked in. He saw Somu picking up the pot, made sure I was okay, and turned to shut the door. I asked him to leave it open and draped the dhoti around my waist. I entered my bedroom thinking I had a guard when I bathed, a guard when I relieved myself, and a probably a guard when I would be with my wife as well.

Somu glanced at me as if he understood my thoughts and said, "Your father and mother once traveled to Padi for the coronation of King Verma. While there, they pitched tents, and the king shared one with your mother. The guard outside heard some noises and rushed into the tent." He paused and regarded me. "The king grew furious with him and almost dismissed him from his duties. The same guard, Veera Vindhya, died saving your father's life in Lukla. As a young child, you sought solitude by hiding in the palace. That is no longer wise. I have watched Kapil. He is very loyal to you, my lord. And he intends to keep you safe."

I cherished having Somu back. He understood me like no other and guided me in his unassuming way. Somu left soon, and I settled in my bed.

The sun had set by the time we reached the Vindhya palace. As we approached, I saw Uncle Mani waiting outside the palace gates surrounded by his men. I slowed the horse down, and the royal herald blew his horn and announced my presence. "Prince Jay of Malla, heir to the throne of the great kingdom of Malla, brave as a tiger; son of the noble and just King Vikram, conqueror of Saral; grandson of esteemed King Karan, keeper of the peace in Malla; great-grandson of the warrior King Jay, ruler of the three worlds."

Mani approached me and said, "Prince Jay, I am delighted to welcome you to this humble abode." Humble would not be my first choice of word to describe this palace. In the setting sun, the marble stairs and granite walls shone, symbols of wealth, and stability.

I replied, "I am honored to be your guest, Uncle Mani." Mani was bedecked with more jewelry than the Goddess Durga idol at our temple.

I noticed tents being pitched outside, and following my glance, Mani said, "When the soldiers on foot arrive, they will be provided accommodations and a feast. They can rest here overnight and then resume their journey." I nodded at him and thanked him for his service.

My friends and I rode through the gates and dismounted outside the main palace. Rish dismounted as well and touched his older cousin's feet. They embraced briefly, and Mani asked Rish to take us to our rooms. Mani crowed, "It is not every day the crown prince visits us. So, I have arranged for a musical play after the feast."

I wanted to get some rest after the long journey, but instead, I smiled and complimented him, "Vindhya is renowned for its dancers and musicians. I am sure it will be a feast for my eyes and ears." As Rish led me and my guards into a spacious room, I scanned it and asked, "Where is Somu?" Before Rish could answer, Somu came in and inspected the space.

"This room is inadequate for the prince," he proclaimed.

Somu did not let anyone forget what they owed a prince. I had more pressing things on my mind, so I said, "We are here for one night, Somu. I am sure you will find ways to make my stay pleasant. Draw me a bath."

Somu muttered about sheets and pillows and went about his duty. After freshening up, Rish came to take us to the feast. At the start of the meal, Mani and his wife Nidhi welcomed us, and I thanked him and asked him about the King and the Queen. Mani served us an elaborate meal on a banana leaf. It started with bananas and jackfruit dipped in honey. Then we were treated to fish stew cooked in coconut, deep-fried banana flower, greens cooked with lentils, spicy green and yellow beans with chilies and cashews, pumpkin in tamarind sauce, and aromatic rice. Multiple sweet dishes made with milk, cashews, and mangoes followed the spicy course. We ended the meal with cooling cucumber in yogurt, plain rice, and buttermilk.

After the feast, I met with Rish and asked him to leave that evening with my message to Akash to announce my impending arrival. Having fought along my side in two battles, Rish would be able to answer the king's questions better than a messenger.

Uncle Mani grumbled, "Prince Jay, I have several fast messengers that we can send, instead of Rish."

Vindhya pride, I thought. "Uncle Mani, is it beneath Rish Vindhya to carry my message?" I asked in an even tone, standing up straight. Time had come to assert myself and put an end to any notion that I was a docile boy to be domineered.

Before he could respond, Rish said, "It is an honor, my lord. I will be on my way."

I left them both to make the necessary arrangements and headed back to the others. I mingled with the guests and spoke to the men gathered in the room. Most had received the news from Saral and wanted to hear the battle stories from me. Traders concerned about the Saral men controlling the Pune Sea took the long route with our trade ships. Vindhya was the only territory in the kingdom to have a coastline on both east and west coasts. This has enabled them to prosper through trade. They wanted to know when it would be safe to travel the seas, and I made appropriate remarks to them. A few months back, I would have been tongue-tied in front of such a setting. Now, instead of being nervous, I listened to various people to understand their problems. I remembered my father saying, men who talk only hear themselves, men who listen, hear others.

Kapil spoke to his Aunt Nidhi Vindhya at the head of the table, and I approached them. Aunt Nidhi covered her plump body from head to toe in gold, not to be outdone by her husband. Nidhi said, "Kapil, my brothers Devan and Mano have forgotten their sister in their quest to serve the kingdom. But we women do not take part in these matters of the crown. Tell your father that I pray for his health and safety." Though born in the Biha family, she bore little resemblance to her brothers, General Devan and Chief Guard Mano.

"Aunt Nidhi, I will pass on your message to my father," he said and joined me. Out of her sight, he rolled his eyes at me and whispered, "You rescued me in time from a boring sermon."

I smiled and said, "Nothing compared to what you do for me."

Mani then led us to the open courtyard where the play would be staged. With no moon, the stars shone brightly in the sky, and a light breeze blew. I sat in the front with Mani, his wife Nidhi, their young sons Darsh and Dayan, and others.

Mani leaned and whispered, "My daughter, Sudha, will sing a prayer first." I viewed the stage, and a young girl appeared. She looked about my age. She had draped a blue silk sari and the jewels she had adorned herself with shone in the light from the lamps. She sang a mesmerizing song about Ganesha, the elephant god, and remover of obstacles. Afterward, she came and sat down next to her father. I could smell the jasmine she had braided in her hair. I wondered about marriage to her. It would keep the Vindhya house firmly on my side. I leaned over and addressed her, "You sang melodiously, my lady. My sister loves to sing as well. She would be delighted to hear you perform."

She blushed at my comments and said shyly, "You are too kind, Prince Jay. I visited my Aunt, Queen Charu recently and had the great pleasure of hearing Princess Meera sing. My ability is nothing compared to hers."

How many months had it been since I heard Meera's voice? Soon, she would be wedded to Prince Amar and headed to Padi. She'd acted as my guide and confidante, and I had relied on her advice all my life. What would I do without her? And, Meera. How did she feel about leaving her beloved Akash and marrying Amar? I felt the sudden urge to leave that night to Akash to see her and father. I took a deep breath to calm myself.

The play began and depicted a battle scene during King Jay's rule and showed how the Vindhya family helped the king. Our plays mostly portrayed battle and glory from the Malla royal history. Our poets wrote love stories about common men. In ancient times, poets composed a great many love stories about the royal families. Once upon a time, when a king organized a swayamwara for his daughter, princes near and far came to compete in a conquest to win her hand. The princess would pine for the one who'd stolen her heart and hoped he would win the contest. I didn't know why that practice had stopped. Prince Rama of Ayodhya won Princess Seetha's hands in a swayamvara when he strung an inhumanely big bow. It evolved into a story of duty and responsibility and moral values. Prince Rama gave up his kingdom for his younger brother and went to live in the forest with his wife Seetha. As life sometimes turns out, the years in the forest happened to be the best in his life, before the demon king kidnapped his wife.

That night I dreamt of standing in a fort and being attacked by a Saral soldier. I fought gallantly with the soldier but was unable to stab him. When my sword finally pierced his heart, the soldier morphed into a young woman with a garland of jasmine who approached me shyly. One turned to many, and I ran desperately to hide. Somu came in and woke me the next morning, and I woke up with sweat dotting my forehead.

23

Crown Prince

I woke up with a start, confused and afraid. The cause of this became apparent when I heard a knock on the door.

My heart pounded, fearing Amar had come again, seeking entry into my chambers. Earlier that night, he'd stood outside my door, yelling to see his future wife and trying to break in. For the first time, I wish I had learned how to wield a weapon. The palace guards gently urged him away, not knowing how or whether to stop him. I sat quivering in my room with Kantha, hoping the solid wooden doors would withhold his assault. Following what seemed like an eternity, I heard Atul's voice moving him on. After loud protests, he left, but I lay awake for a long time, dreading his return.

The knock on the door sounded again, but these were more measured, unlike Amar's. "Kantha, wake up and see who it is," I whispered urgently.

She ambled sleepily to the door and then exclaimed, "My lady, it is one of the King's guards."

"King's?" I asked, confused. "Open the door."

She did, and the guard strode in. I sat on the edge of my bed, and he bowed to me and said, "My lady, the king requests your presence in his chambers."

What was it that could not wait till the morning? I asked him to wait outside until I dressed.

After the guard escorted me through the halls, I entered my father's chambers, searching for him. When my eyes found him, I uttered, "Father," and rushed towards him. Then, I sensed another person in the room. I spun around, and my gaze landed on Rish. He bowed his head slightly, staring at me with a big grin on his face.

My heart leaped from the warmth of the smile and in anticipation of his news, and my stomach plunged from his earlier betrayal. The twin emotions became caught in my throat, and I swallowed them down.

"My child, come and sit beside me," said my father from behind me, and I obeyed.

"Do not keep us waiting any longer," he commanded to Rish.

Rish immediately launched into his story. "I come with good news, my lord. Prince Jay is at the Vindhya palace. He has conquered Saral and imprisoned King Surya. He is on his way to Akash, and his travel companions include Prince Nakul and Princess Aranya. He will arrive in the city soon, and he wanted me to alert you to the news."

As Rish told his story, tears poured down my cheeks unchecked, and I held my father's hand in silence. After a few moments, my father asked Rish to tell him all the details, and Rish launched into the extraordinary tale.

By the time Rish finished and was dismissed to refresh himself with some rest, the first light broke through in the eastern sky. Many thoughts ran through my mind, creating a web of chaos. I clenched my fists and forced myself to focus on the most important matter.

"Nakul is coming to Akash," I whispered to my father.

He mused, "Meera, Jay has been groomed to rule Malla. If he finds he has an older brother, what do you think he would do?"

The same question had been on my mind many days. I answered, "He would abdicate for his brother."

"Nakul, though my blood, has been raised as the heir for Saral. He cannot be the king for both. The secret has to stay with us for now, so that each may rule the land they deserve."

"Jay and Nakul can become brothers through marriage if Rish's tales about Princess Aranya are to be believed," I added. All along, in the back of my mind, I had been thinking about my pending wedding with Amar. I waited for the right moment to bring it up.

"Father, I know we have fixed my wedding day for the day after tomorrow, and all the preparations are underway. Not one, but both of my brothers are on their way to this city. And a girl only gets married once in her life. I would like my brothers at my wedding."

My father nodded his agreement. "I will talk to King Verma and move your wedding."

He smiled at me and said, "You can greet your brothers as the Princess of Malla."

* * *

Strong arms circled my waist and lifted me off my feet. I looked up and smiled at the dark chiseled face.

"My lady," a voice interrupted me.

"*My lady*," said a deeper voice, and the man placed me in front of him on his horse.

"My lady," a female voice persisted and gently touched my shoulders, waking me from my sleep. I turned at the touch and curled up to go back into the arms of the man in my dreams.

"Lady Meera, Rish Vindhya is here and has requested an audience with you," my maid Kantha carried on. On hearing his name, my eyes fluttered open. Wiping my dreamy eyes, I sat up. With her help, I dressed quickly and headed to the gardens to meet Rish. The day dawned with the sun reluctant to leave his cloud blanket. The gloomy weather did not dampen my anticipation, and I walked with mixed emotions in my heart. My old feelings for him surfaced. I longed to be held in his arms. Then anger erupted at him. For violating my trust. For crushing my love.

The young man stood by the lotus pond and wheeled around to face me as I approached. Pink lotus buds in the water faced east, awaiting the sun's arrival. When I stood within an arm's length, he bowed to me, and I inclined my head while studying him in the pre-dawn light. The few fortnights at Saral had hardened his palace-grown body. He contemplated my face as if he wanted to etch it in his memory. I resisted my desire to embrace him and let my anger wash over me.

I glared at him and blurted, "You spied on me. You gained my affections to further your family's interests and betrayed my trust."

His eyebrows raised, he gazed at me questioningly.

"Don't deny it. I heard you in my stepmother's chambers before you departed for Saral."

"Is that why you never came to bid me farewell?" he asked softly, a frown on his face.

"Do not change the topic, Rish."

After some moments, he said, "Spy, that is one of the roles I played, my lady. I have never betrayed you, though, and my feelings have always been genuine."

"What did you tell Chief Kasu and my stepmother about us?" I asked scowling.

"The truth for the most part," he replied without hesitation this time.

He paused then and stared into my eyes with a raw hunger and added, "I have concealed details from them. I never shared my true feelings for you. And I would not tell them how in the morning light you look like a golden goddess and how it takes all my will power to—" he stopped and bit his lip. "I told them only what they wanted to hear; what they needed to hear."

"I am betrothed to Prince Amar," I said shakily. My heart thumped inside my chest. My desire to touch, to be touched, echoed his. I twisted my sari end.

"I heard the news," he lamented in a troubled voice and lowered his eyes. He then smiled ruefully and added, "Spending time with royals has been nothing but trouble for me."

I assumed he included me in the list of royals he wished he had not met. I replied starkly, "I can set you free at this moment."

His eyes clouded in pain. "I apologize for that outburst, my lady. I would be honored if I were bonded in your service for life."

He stepped closer and whispered, "Did you think I betrayed you, while I remained in Saral searching for Prince Jay and then fought beside him?"

I could feel his warm breath. I wanted to kiss the young man in front of me. To wipe the pain in his eyes. My heart raced. I took a deep breath and mumbled, "I doubted you. That sent me into despair."

His lips parted, and he said urgently, "Meera, you were never out of my mind. Everything I have done was with the goal of bringing you happiness."

I gazed down and said, "You did. You brought me out of my wretchedness by bringing Jay back safely."

I was about to marry my nightmare, and now I'd found out Rish stayed loyal to me. If I had known earlier— It was too late to dwell on the past. I had a duty to fulfill, to Malla. Thinking it made it no easier. Bitterness coated my tongue at the thought of giving up my love. The unfairness of it. I thought of my stepmother. Her words to me. This would be the first of many hard decisions in my life.

Gathering my strength, I uttered, "Rish, I do set you free. I am betrothed. I am going to Padi and may never see you again. But before I depart from my home, be my ally over the next few days. I need friends around me."

He stayed silent, and I did not trust myself to look at him. Slowly, he took a step back and murmured, "I pledged myself to you, my lady. I don't want to be free." He paused, and I sniffed, still staring at the ground.

Do not make this more difficult for me, I thought.

He continued, "But I will respect your wishes. Always." I heard his footsteps as he left. Sadness and despair brimmed over, and I struggled to squash it into a tiny ball and hide it along with other secrets I carried.

We expected Jay soon, and the city readied to welcome her son back. Along the main street of the capital, people lined up to catch a glimpse of him and to wish him well.

Rish came to escort me to the steps of the palace. After our initial greeting, I asked, "Tell me more about the Saral Princess."

"My lady, she appears to have saved Prince Jay's life and escaped with him. They spent several days together before they arrived at our palace. She seems devoted to the Prince and him to her." My feelings on hearing this confused me. Happiness yes. For my brother. Also, jealousy. A marriage that would serve our kingdoms also took the form of a love match. I shook my head to clear my thoughts.

We arrived at the steps, and I joined my maids who waited to welcome the Prince with flowers and lighted lamps. One of the girls handed me a plate filled with turmeric water. Soon, Prince Amar and his brothers joined me, and Amar came and stood next to me.

"Your brother could have stayed dead for the sake of our sons," he whispered in my ear. All my learning had not prepared me for dealing with this man. No response came to me, so I stayed quiet, surrounded by four men, Amar beside me, his two brothers on either side of us, and Rish in the back. Amar noticed Rish, and an ugly smile curled on his lips. Rish's eyes darted to the scar on Amar's face for a moment. I wondered if they knew each other already somehow.

Soon, I heard the gallop of horses, and a group of men came into view, with Jay in the middle and flanked by his guards, Dev and Giri. Prince Nakul and Princess Aranya were not with him. When the Saral royals arrived, they would be escorted into the palace through a side entrance.

When he came closer, Jay jumped from his horse and climbed the stairs. It had been only a few months since I'd last seen him, but the boy who left the city was no more. Instead, I found myself watching a young warrior, marching towards me. Girls showered him with flowers on each step, but his eyes studied each man around me.

They then came to rest on mine, and tears glistened in my eyes. When he stood at arm's length, I raised the plate and moved it in a circular motion around his face to ward off any evil. Then I applied tilak to his forehead, and he bent to touch my feet, and I gathered him in an embrace. Months of worry in my stomach dissolved. I barely reached his chin now, so I rested my head on his chest, enveloped by a pair of strong arms. His rough palms shocked me, and I gazed up into his face. Tears welled up in his eyes as well, but he smiled at me warmly. For all his physical changes, I recognized my brother in his smile.

Jay had my mother's eyes. He appeared taller than my father already with more years to grow. He'd adorned his short dark curly hair with a simple crown made of gold. He emanated a majestic quality that would inspire loyalty in those around him. A boy, afraid and needing guidance, no longer stood in front of me.

He'd truly become the Crown Prince.

24

New Alliance

As we proceeded to the throne room, I realized my sister had not uttered a word since my arrival. On the long walk there, Meera of the past would have asked me about my capture and escape and teased me about Aranya. She now seemed a shadow of her former self.

I'd missed her as a friend and mentor. I knew her marriage would take her away from Akash. While being groomed to be a king, I could not admit this to anybody, but I worried about losing her. She had been the one constant presence in my life since our mother died. I could not imagine what must be going through her mind about leaving her beloved city.

In our land, we cherished women for their beauty and not their wisdom. I did not remember my mother very well, but a portrait of her hung in my sister's chambers. Queen Kayal looked beautiful with her long dark hair and delicate features. Meera inherited some of these features, but bolder and more regal. Her spirit and courage matched my own, but her wit exceeded mine. She studied the affairs of the state. Most important of all, she cared deeply about the people of this land.

I would have to find time alone with her, to consult my closest friend, and to talk about all the changes coming to pass.

Soon, we arrived in the hall leading to the throne room.

Huge iron double doors that needed at least two men to open them led us into the impressive throne room. Pillars elaborately sculpted with scenes of Malla victories in the battlefield lined both sides of the hall-way. Flaming torches mounted on each pillar lit the path. As I entered, the ornate gold throne placed at the end of the hall drew one's eye. Each armrest of the throne had a ferocious tiger head, representing our tiger emblem.

Today I entered through the royal side door and viewed Father sit-ting on the throne. He had stopped wearing the heavy royal crown em-bedded with rubies after his injury and wore a simpler one instead. To his right, on a smaller seat, sat Queen Charu. She rarely attended coun-cil meetings, leaving the governing to my father. In the audience were also the Malla chiefs and members of the King's council and the Padi royal family.

As I strode in, the many assembled stood up. I reached my parents and touched their feet. Then I sought the blessings of the elders in the room.

My father surprised me by getting up from his throne and taking a few steps forward to embrace me. "Son, I had feared I lost you forever," he whispered in my ear. Then stepping back, he said in a louder voice, "Jay, where I failed, you have succeeded. You have captured Saral and set us on the path of glory my grandfather, King Jay, paved for us. You have rekindled the Malla fire, and I hope it continues to burn long after my demise. Long Live, Prince Jay!"

The audience echoed his cry around the room. My father beamed at me proudly, and my heart swelled.

At his command, I narrated the tale of our conquest and ended with King Surya imprisoned in Lukla. As I spoke, my gaze wandered towards Amar and Meera. Meera never looked at him. Her eyes stayed on me. Amar's face betrayed no emotion, even when he peered in her direction.

Later, after the others had left, I met with my father in the small council room.

The sun poured in through the large windows.

"Father, grant me permission to bring the Saral Prince and Princess," I asked, and he nodded. They'd arrived earlier today, and I felt anxious to bring them in front of the king. Would he bless my marriage? Would he accept Nakul's offer of peace? I stepped outside and sent Rish to bring them and came back in.

"Rish told me the Saral princess helped you escape," my father said. I narrated the tale to him, leaving out my indiscretions.

My father regarded me kindly and asked, "Is she bearing your child?"

I stammered a, "No," and then recovered enough to say, "However, I do seek your blessing to marry her. Aranya is a brave and kind-hearted girl."

"Beautiful as well, I imagine," interjected my father, his lip curling up.

I smiled in embarrassment, and my father said, "Son, I can see this girl has bewitched you. But you can never belong to one person. You will be the king of this land, and you will belong to her people. You may have to marry other women if this princess does not bear you a male heir."

"And to strengthen existing alliances," I replied. "I have already thought about it. Father, I know how important it is to keep our alliance with the Vindhya clan. Sudha Vindhya is a bridge to that family, and I fully intend to claim her hand in marriage as well."

My father contemplated me and said, "I was never groomed to rule and made mistakes. You, on the other hand, were raised as my heir. You will make a better ruler than me."

My father continued, "Some kings go on conquering quests and ravage the people and plunder the lands. If you only want to fill your coffers, that might work. In the long run, a king cannot rule without the goodwill of his people. That is why I asked General Devan to rebuild the Saral villages savaged in the battle. We have nothing against the people of Saral. My goal is to sign a peace treaty with them like King Jay did with Padi and seal it with your wedding to Aranya. King Jay knew killing royalties just sprouts two more in their place who want to seek revenge. Prince Nakul can rule Saral, while our ships obtain access to the Saral seas. Keep this in your mind. I have heard he wants peace with Malla and the Saral people would follow their prince."

Before I could respond, Rish brought in Prince Nakul and Princess Aranya. Nakul took a few paces and looked at my father and said, "Great King of Malla, accept the greetings of this Saral Prince. You married a Saral girl, but that caused a rift in our relationship. I am here to offer my sister's hand to the Prince of this land, to mend that rift."

Father gazed at the Prince, tears welling in his eyes. I felt confused at the show of emotion. After waiting for him to say something, I slowly prompted him, "Father?"

He reacted as if coming out of a dream and shook his head.

"Prince Nakul, does King Surya pledge his allegiance to the Malla crown?" he asked.

"My Majesty, my father still seeks vengeance for acts committed before my birth."

"He is my prisoner now," Father muttered, glancing at Aranya. "Come closer to the lamp, child, so I can look at you." She took a few paces forward, her face betraying no emotion.

He sighed and then turned to her brother. "Would the king agree to this match?"

Nakul shook his head. Father returned his attention toward Aranya. "Princess Aranya, I heard how you nursed my son back to health after his injuries. He sought my blessing to marry you, but no such blessing would be forthcoming from your father. Do you consent to marry Prince Jay of Malla?"

Aranya's gaze darted between her brother and I. Nakul inclined his head, and Aranya then said, "My Majesty, I bound my life with Prince Jay when I escaped with him to the Saral forest." She stepped forward and touched my father's feet.

He touched her head and said, "Rise, my daughter. Good things should not put off. Meera's wedding to Amar is in a few days, and we will hold your wedding on the same day."

My lips curled up as I regarded Aranya at these words. Her eyes twinkled as she stole a glance at me. My father's words brought me back.

"Nakul, with Surya in prison, we can crown you King of Saral, once you pledge your allegiance—"

Nakul interrupted him before he could continue, "My Majesty, I understood the desires of Aranya's heart and knew the marriage would end the enmity between the two kingdoms. Ruling Saral is a different matter. My allegiance is still to my father and king."

Father studied him thoughtfully and said, "Let the wedding take place, and I will discuss these matters with Jay and my council."

We left my father shortly, and I took the brother and sister to their quarters. Before I left, I whispered to Aranya, "I will send word for you to meet Princess Meera," and headed to my sister's chambers.

Meera stood up to embrace me. "Jay, you had us on sword's tips these past few months."

We sat down facing each other, and I said, "Can a man grow years in months? The naïve young boy who left on the journey died in Saral lands."

She urged me to tell her what happened since I'd left, and I narrated the tale of Shiv's betrayal and Surya's descent into madness. I paused, and Meera grasped my hand and blurted, "Jay, you inspire loyalty in your men. Do not lose faith in them because of the lone act of one treasonous boy."

I nodded, remembering those dark days. "I did lose faith initially. Every spear, arrow, and sword in my presence caused me to panic. I imagined they were meant for my heart. I could not tell friend from foe. Princess Aranya restored my faith and trust.

"When we were on the run, we hid in the fields when her father passed us by. She could have stood up and joined them, and I lacked the strength to fight. But she stayed behind with me. My guards allowed that trust to take root, and the actions of my men allowed it to flourish. And Somu," I paused here, remembering. "My men found him in the dungeons, and I went to free him. When he saw me, he shed genuine tears of joy. He forgot his place, and I mine. He called me by my name and embraced me and touched my face several times as if to make sure I was alive."

Meera smiled for the first time since I'd arrived and said, "When we heard you went missing, we placed our trust in Somu finding you. You may have supplanted mother in his affections." She poked me in the chest. "I've also heard tales about Aranya's beauty and bravery. She appears to be the rare princess who knew her heart and let it guide her. When will I meet her?"

"Soon." I beamed. "First, tell me what you think of the Prince of Padi."

Meera became pensive and mused, "If our mother lived, she would say princesses do not choose their husbands. They are married to strengthen the ties between her birth kingdom and her husband's."

"Our mother, who married for love, would say no such thing."

"It is the truth, Jay, and there is no need to pretend otherwise." She looked at me with resigned eyes and continued. "And what is not to like about marrying the heir to the Padi throne? I would be Queen one day and my son the King."

Her words were tinged with sadness. I felt guilty about being captured in Saral and forcing this choice on her.

"Enough of me. Go bring me your bride," she ordered, and I obliged.

Soon, I strode in with Aranya. Meera greeted her warmly, and Aranya stepped forward to seek her blessings. We sat at the table, and I watched the women closely for their reaction.

Meera gazed at Aranya and said, "Malla is forever in your debt for saving my brother's life."

Aranya replied, "I thought not of Malla when I helped him, my lady," stealing a glance at me.

Meera followed her glance and smiled. "Jay is fortunate to have won over your heart, Aranya."

"The fortune is all mine, my lady. When I nursed him back to health," she paused, smiling shyly, "he would murmur in his feverish sleep. He begged the forgiveness of his father for failing in his duty. He begged your forgiveness for failing to restore Malla's greatness. He kept saying he had to be willing to die for his lands if he expected others to die for him and his kingdom. Words I have heard spoken before, but not seen anybody try to live up to it."

I chimed in. "There, my secret is out. I am irresistible when I am unconscious. A wonderful trait for a Prince."

Both broke out laughing, and I joined them, glad to be with the two most important women in my life.

I had been in Prince Amar's company a few times since I had been back. Each encounter deepened my mistrust of him and increased my concern for Meera.

The worst though happened the previous night. After dinner, while Meera and I conversed with Nakul, Amar approached us, drunk. He gripped one of Meera's arms and tried to kiss her. She took a step away, only to have him grab her waist from behind and hold her captive against him. He then took a dagger out and held it carelessly against her stomach. Meera's eyes widened in shock, confusion, and anger. Before I could recover my senses and decide what to do, she spoke calmly, "Go ahead and kiss me, my prince." He let go of her and turned her around.

With a sly smile, he approached her. I signaled to Rish, and we both took hold of one of his shoulders before he could act. I forced the dagger out of his hands and made it drop to the floor. Meera looked at the dagger for a moment and then spun and left the room, her head bowed. With barely controlled rage, Rish and I escorted the Prince to his chambers, and I ordered guards to be posted outside. Father would not allow a palace maid to be treated that way, let alone the princess of this land. Anger simmered in me.

In the morning light, several thoughts passed through my mind. I could take the Prince on a hunting expedition. In my mind, I pictured myself aiming arrows at his back. Accidents happened, but it would be my luck that I would cripple the man rather than kill him. Meera's fate would be worse than before.

Somu walked in with clean water for my basin and an idea formed in my mind. As I got dressed, it crystalized, and I approached Meera in her chambers with a plan.

As her chambers came into my view, my footsteps slowed. For many years, she had been the strong one and protected me after our mother's death. Under a different circumstance, I would have been happy for the role reversal, but today I felt unsure of her feelings. I knocked on her locked door. Footsteps approached the door, and Kantha's voice asked, "Who is it?"

"It is Jay," I responded. She threw the bolt open, and I entered. My sister lay on her bed, and I asked Kantha to leave us alone.

She faced the wall away from the door, and I sat on the foot of the bed. Her many lamps glittered in the sunlight. Sensing my presence, she slowly turned to look at me.

"Don't pity me, Jay," she muttered in a wrenching voice that brought a lump to my throat.

"All these years, you have sheltered and protected me and now that you are in need—"

"You cannot help me, Jay. He will be my lord soon, and then I will be his slave."

"Don't speak like that, Meera. You are the Princess of Malla and are nobody's slave. I have an idea that I would like you to hear."

She rearranged her pillows and sat up, listening to my plan.

"Somu came to Malla with mother and stayed to serve her and her son after. What if I send a Queen's guard with you from Malla, to serve and protect you? Five Malla men sworn to you?"

She considered it and said, "Amar would oppose it."

"Leave that part to me. I will convince Father and King Verma. What do you think?"

"What can five men do against a kingdom?"

"Padi would rejoice in you. It is only Amar that these men need to protect you from."

"How can anybody protect me from my husband? They cannot hurt him. He will be king. He will be the father of my children."

"Meera, they can spy for you. Help you avoid him. And you are right. They could not always protect you, but their presence will remind him he would have to face my fury if any harm befell you."

Slowly she nodded her assent, and I stood up.

"I have the perfect person to be head of your guard: Rish Vindhya. In Saral, I learned he is devoted to you. He is brave and insightful. I will . go ask our father for his permission."

25

Queen's Guard

I sat dazed on my bed for a few moments at the thought of Rish being my guard. Jay, I don't know if you want to tempt me or protect me. Somu served my mother with devotion, but as a plain man, he did not cause a flutter in a girl's heart. My mother's feelings for him were probably that of a queen's gratitude for her loyal subject. Rish's face floated into my memory, and I felt a sudden longing. I jumped from my bed to clear my thoughts. I needed to go and stop Jay before he acted on this.

As I headed for the door, Kantha entered. "My lady, Prince Nakul waits in the gardens to meet you," she said as she came to help me. "He says it is urgent."

I had not had a chance to see my long-lost brother alone. As I stood there, I was torn between stopping Jay and meeting Nakul. Jay would not have rushed to the kings straight from my chambers, and even if he did, King Verma and Prince Amar would not agree to his mad scheme. I decided to see Nakul first and headed to the gardens. As I walked down the path, I saw him standing straight with his hands clasped behind his back, staring into the distance. With his long hair framing his face, he reminded me of the painting of my father in his youth. Nakul turned to face me when he heard my footsteps, and I smiled at him tenderly.

He walked towards me, and as he reached me, he said quietly, "I worried about you, my lady."

I looked into his face and saw true concern in his eyes, and my heart swelled. I had a sudden urge to tell my older brother all my worries and let him protect me. I pushed that thought away.

He went on. "I wish I could be of help to you. I would be willing to fight an army to seek the hand of the most beautiful and talented princess in the land."

As he continued, I realized I had let my knowledge cloud my judgment. He saw me as a Saral Prince would, a princess to rescue and marry, not as a sister.

"You have a matter to discuss?" I asked.

He said, "All my life, I have sacrificed my needs and wants for Saral and her people. My father let his fury get in the way of ruling, and I vowed to myself that I would be different. I surrendered to Prince Jay when the fighting would have destroyed my land. I am here to give my sister away to strengthen our political ties. But seeing you has weakened my resolution."

He hesitated, scanning our surroundings first. "Many Saral women have vied for my affections, but none match your beauty. I have seen your father and brother rely on your judgment. You are a diamond among rocks, one who is willing to sacrifice herself for her land with this marriage to Amar. You have been tormenting my dreams, though that is no fault of yours. One word from you, and I am willing to elope with you to the nearest temple."

He regarded me intently, and his anguish and affection reflected in his eyes. Anger rose in me at my father for leaving him in Saral. At the mercy of King Surya. Of keeping the truth from him about our family ties. Nakul should never have had to feel like this about me.

I needed to tread carefully. I murmured, "My lord, all the virtues you have bestowed on me would be for naught if I led an honorable man astray. I am betrothed to the Padi Prince, and you and I running off would lead to war with that kingdom. Neither of us would want to plunge our lands into chaos. I hope Jay is not the only one who gains a brother through his marriage to Aranya."

His shoulders sagged for a moment in defeat, but he nodded, understanding in his eyes. "Your words have only increased my esteem of you, my lady. I wish we'd met under different circumstances. I cannot think of you as a sister yet, but you can count on me as an ally."

With that, he bowed, and we parted ways, and I gave a sigh of relief. I sensed a sadness in him as I walked back slowly to the castle, wishing I could share our family secret with him. When father told me the truth, it weighed on my mind like a feather in my hair. Now, with Nakul in Akash, it carried me down like a rock tied to my ankle in deep water. I hoped I could guard this secret while both my brothers lived.

Deep in my thoughts, I did not see Prince Atul approach in the garden until he spoke to me. With worry lines etched deep in his forehead, he searched my face and spoke urgently, "My lady, please accept my apologies for my brother's actions last night."

"He is a grown man, and you cannot be responsible for him."

He flushed angrily. "The time for secrets has passed. Father asked me to make sure Amar did not fall into his old ways, and I succeeded for a time. While he slept, I thought it safe to leave him. To my horror, upon my return, I heard he held a knife against you. I will tell you now what I did not allow myself to say when I came to Akash earlier. You have seen what Amar is. Padi's hopes rest on you, my lady. You have to make an able ruler out of him, succeed where others have failed."

Padi would be better with you as its ruler, I thought. "Atul, I have been off to a bad start then," I said, smiling ruefully. As I walked with him, a seed got rooted in my head. An idea. A plan. I tried to uproot it, but my efforts were in vain.

In calmer tones, he replied, "My lady, the books I have read celebrate the bravery of men in war. True bravery lies elsewhere. The kind needed to marry a rogue prince and tame his dark side."

I laughed out loud. "Bravery? I am coming to the realization I am a coward. And you a dreamer. Miracles do happen in books, but the reality is ugly."

Before Atul could defend himself, Kapil appeared before us. "Princess Meera, the king commands your presence. Prince Atul, you may want to come along as well."

I'd forgotten about Jay's plan. Had a decision already been made?

The palace was overrun with princes, and none had been very helpful to me this morning. Jay, my dear brother, had grown into a man. Before he would run to me to solve his problems, now he was taking charge. Had there ever been a Queen's guard before? He mentioned Somu when he spoke of his thought, so he thinks Rish would be devoted to me. But he did not know my heart, and I could not blame him because I barely knew it myself. I hoped I wouldn't rue not talking to Jay sooner.

I walked into the small throne room with Atul and Kapil. My father and King Verma sat on the two thrones. Amar stood next to his father, a frown on his face during the proceedings. I went and stood next to Jay, who turned to look at me. His lips were pressed together, forming a thin line, and his chin jutted out.

King Verma started speaking, and I turned towards him. "My daughter, I heard what happened. Let me assure you it is not how we treat women in Padi, let alone the future queen. My son here regrets his ways and would like to make amends. Prince Jay proposed sending Malla guards with you. The day Padi is unable to protect her Queen will be the day ruin befalls us. I hope it does not happen while I live." He glared at his son as he spoke, and I briefly looked at Amar to see if he expressed any remorse. He kept his eyes focused on the ground, and as I glanced away, his eyes rose to meet mine for a brief instance. His stare poured such venom at that moment, and it caused me to lower my eyes. The idea I'd had before while speaking with Atul surfaced again, and I tried to drown it, dismissing it as a path unbecoming of a virtuous princess.

King Verma continued speaking with my father, some words about allowing Prince Jay's other request, but their meaning did not register till Rish stood in front of me.

Jay spoke, "Rish Vindhya, I relieve you of your oath to me and forever will be grateful for your service to this kingdom."

With the eyes of the men in the room on me, I did not trust myself to look up at Rish.

Rish laid his sword at my feet, and as he rose, our eyes met briefly. His face remained a mask like mine, and he swore his oath in a clear voice. "I pledge my allegiance to Princess Meera and swear to obey her commands. I swear to protect her with my life or die trying. I devote myself completely to this duty, this day, and all days thereafter. I swear to take my own life if any harm comes to the princess during my watch."

My stomach twisted into a knot. *Jay, what have you done?* I could not decide what would torment me more, being married to Amar or having Rish by my side as a shadow and pretend he meant nothing to me. I wanted to stomp out of the room and sob into my bed. Instead, I stood silently, steadying my breath.

I walked to my chambers with Jay. Rish and Kapil followed a few feet behind. Jay said, "Kapil is my head guard now. He drove me crazy initially, but Rish is very discreet. You will forget he is around in a few days. I am glad I convinced King Verma to see the merit in having a Queen's guard. Rish and I will help you pick four more loyal men to serve in it."

From ten feet away, I sensed Rish's eyes on us. I had listened to stories of God testing his devotees. By placing obstacles in their path for them to deviate from the path of morality. This must be my test.

After Jay left, I paced alone in my room with Rish standing guard outside. I took some time to get my thoughts in order, and then I called him in. "Rish Vindhya."

He strode in, alert, and I said, "I would like to speak to you in private."

He regarded me, then shut the door and came forward.

He stared at me for a few moments, his face reflecting the confusion I felt. He opened his mouth several times as if he intended to say something, but never did. Then he took a deep breath, cleared his throat, and said, "My lady, when Prince Jay proposed the idea, he mentioned he had your blessing. I would not have taken this position otherwise. Prince Amar and you will be married, and I understand my place in this. I spoke ill of him to Prince Jay, but those words were formed by old angst."

"Are you saying he has some redeeming qualities?"

He paused as if searching for virtues. "His mother is astonishingly beautiful. From what I have seen, he has inherited her looks. Most women would consider him attractive."

"Being attractive can make up for a lot of other faults," I said and gazed at him. His hair appeared disheveled like he had raked his fingers through it. Resisting the urge to smooth it, I brought my mind back to the perilous path I had chosen. "Rish, can I depend on your undying loyalty?"

"My lady, I am sworn to protect you with my life. My life and loyalty are yours to command."

"Would you obey me if my command is unscrupulous?"

"I am here to serve, my lady, not judge. You are the author of this tale, and I will play my part to make it a reality," he said with a frown.

The tale I want to weave might start a war, I thought. My glance fell on his lips, and I remembered the warmth of them on mine. I shook my head to chase these thoughts away. I had more pressing matters to deal with.

"Rish, do you remember the dancer, Madhavi?" He nodded, his eyebrows drawn, wondering as to where this conversation was headed. "Bring her to me in the gardens by the lily pond. I would like to speak to her alone."

26

Death in the Palace

I found Kapil in the courtyard, training. He smiled at me and asked, "Prince Jay, I have knocked down all my opponents today. Do you want to be next?"

I grinned back and took my sword out of its sheath. "You forget you are talking to a tiger."

Kapil had good legwork and strong arms. We circled each other and parried a few blows. My mind wandered to fighting on a battleground with men screaming, horses running everywhere, and arrows flying. I got momentarily distracted, and Kapil did not take advantage of it. He seemed to hesitate, as well. I brought my attention back to the fight and knocked his sword out. "I would have been dead in a battlefield if I fought like that," I said aloud, angry with myself.

Kapil said sheepishly, "You are my prince. I took a vow to protect you. I cannot hurt you in a real or imaginary fight." I remembered him guarding me fiercely with little regard to his own life in our last battle. I smiled at him reassuringly.

A voice spoke from behind me. "You need to fight real men to get a measure of your strength, Jay."

I turned around to see Prince Amar and Prince Atul striding towards us. "We are going to be brothers soon, Prince Amar. I wouldn't want to fight you."

He mocked me. "Spoken like a man with no brothers. Ask Atul how many times I have beaten him bloody."

Just then, Rish appeared, and Amar sneered at him, "Better yet, I can fight him."

"I have just appointed him to Meera's guard. Any harm that befalls him would be an act of war," I warned.

Atul said, "Amar, father is waiting for us" and led him away.

I watched them leave, my shoulders heavy. Amar wanted nothing more than to bully others. Soon he would be wed to my sister. Had I done enough to protect Meera? My glance fell on Rish. Rish stared at the back of the Padi prince, his mouth drawn into a thin line. I had never felt more helpless, relying on Atul and Rish to protect her.

Tomorrow at dawn, I would be wedded to Aranya, and the thought should have brought a smile to my lips. Instead, I worried whether my love for her would prevent me from making sacrifices for Malla. I hoped not, but as my eyes fell on her walking in front of me with Meera and Sudha, I worried about my resolve.

We strolled back after seeking the blessings of the Goddess Durga at the temple. Queen Charu had organized a special prayer, and I had joined in the celebrations at my sister's insistence. Sudha turned and looked back at me, and I remembered the events of the past few days.

Father had held a small council meeting to discuss recent matters, and Chief Kasu Vindhya, General Devan Biha, and Chief Bhoj Thari were among the gathered. As soon as Chief Bhoj arrived, I visited him and conveyed my regrets regarding what happened with his son, Shiv. Losing a son was a wound that would take years to heal, but he held me mostly blameless.

I'd met with Minister Kripa earlier, another grieving father, and recounted how Vasu fought bravely to protect me and died as a hero. I also had written to Balan's family, praising his service to me. None of this would bring their sons back, but empty words were all I had.

General Devan and Chief Kasu expressed unhappiness with my upcoming wedding to Princess Aranya. Both had girls of marriage age in their families, Riya Biha and Sudha Vindhya. I'd spoken to Meera about Riya, and Meera suggested a marriage alliance between Prince Nakul and her. I trusted Meera in these matters, and she expressed her views to Father to get his blessing. Riya was the daughter of Princess Lata of Malla, and the more I thought about their marriage, the more I viewed it favorably. Father agreed with that sentiment. He made his wishes known to General Biha, and the General sent for his wife and daughter. They would arrive soon in Akash. Meera spoke to Prince Nakul and extolled the virtues of Riya. Whether that convinced him remains unknown to me, but Father also commanded the Prince to marry Riya or be thrown in Akash dungeons. Harsh, perhaps, but a king needed to be cold-hearted. Given no choice, he agreed to a life sentence of marriage.

There were no other first in line for the throne princes around to offer in marriage to Sudha Vindhya, and Chief Kasu made his displeasure known at the council meeting.

"My Majesty, my advice would be to crown Prince Jay as the heir apparent in Lukla. Letting Prince Nakul rule in his father's stead only weakens Malla's hold on Saral."

"Jay will marry Prince Aranya of Saral soon. Prince Nakul will pledge allegiance to Malla when he comes to power," said my father.

"Which may not happen for decades if we hold his father in prison."

Father turned to Minister Kripa and asked, "What are your thoughts?"

"Your Majesty, I heard Prince Nakul does not want to usurp his father, but the throne is not his father's anymore. Prince Jay won it for Malla. That crown is now Malla's, and as the Malla King, it is yours to bestow my lord. If you so wish, you can crown Prince Nakul as the Saral King and command him to pledge his allegiance to Malla."

Father listened to this advice, and I could sense him turning this in his head to find any weaknesses. Finally, he nodded and said, "Excellent advice, Kripa. This provides a way out of waiting for the crown to pass to Nakul."

Prince Nakul could be ordered to rule Saral, but I wanted to make it easier for him to obey. I had one way of doing just that. "Father, holding King Surya prisoner in Saral does not help. Nakul would abhor being crowned in Lukla, while his father languished in the dungeons there. We should move him to Akash, and then Prince Nakul would be more open to being crowned." With his father in Akash dungeons, Nakul would see this as a way of keeping Surya alive and governing for the welfare of Saral in his stead.

We discussed this some more and had the consensus of all gathered except for Chief Kasu. He took my pending marriage to Aranya as a slight against him. After Father dismissed the assembly, he and I stayed behind.

Chief Kasu cleared his throat and requested, "My king, my grand-daughter Sudha is a girl grown, and I seek your blessings to offer her hand in marriage to Prince Atul of Padi."

Father glanced at me and stated, "I would if my son was not set on marrying her himself."

"My lord, I gave my daughter in marriage to the Malla King and have nothing to show for it. With the Prince marrying Princess Aranya, Sudha, as a second wife, would be relegated to a housemaid, and I don't want her to be visited by the same fate that befell my daughter."

There was anguish in his voice, and my father remained silent on hearing it. Then slowly, he spoke, "Uncle, Charu is my wife and the Queen of this land." Then with some anger, he added, "What you see as horror, I see as honor." Chief Kasu sensing he'd crossed a line tried to speak, but father cut him off. "This is not a request. I command that Sudha Vindhya be betrothed to Jay at the next auspicious day. I don't want to hear any more talk of marriage to Prince Atul."

He dismissed us both, and I went to find Aranya to convey the news to her.

"You are not even married to me and already seeking other women," she teased.

I reached out to hold her hands. "Vindhya is our richest territory, and I need their support to rule this land. The easiest way to gain that support is through marriage."

She regarded me and nodded. "I understand, Jay. Nakul has said many times that our father placed his interests ahead of Saral, and he hoped not to make the same mistakes. You placed Malla ahead of you, and I knew that when I fell in love with you."

My heart swelled. I had to make many hard decisions, as the ruler of this land. It would be easier to do it with her support and love.

"Though while my father will be in a dungeon, hers would be filling your coffers," she added, gazing at me.

"There is only one throne next to the king's, and you will occupy it as my Queen one day," I said, leaning in to kiss her. Could I do what my father failed to do, keep two women happy?

My thoughts were brought back to the present with a question from Prince Atul. His brother refused to join us and asked Meera to pray on their behalf. Meera did pray, whether, for deliverance from him or strength to lead a life with him, I did not know.

We reached the halls of the castle and having to choose between accompanying Aranya or Sudha to their quarters, I chose Meera. Some might say I acted cowardly, and I would agree. Meera and I walked to her chambers with Kapil and Rish following us at a distance. Atul departed us to go to his chambers.

"Tomorrow, you will be married to the Prince of Padi," I said.

She did not reply immediately. I glanced at her, and her eyebrows were drawn together. Exhaling slowly, she said, "As a young girl, I dreamt about my wedding. I imagined I would be dressed in a rich silk sari and marry a handsome young Prince. That part of my dream will come true tomorrow."

She did not continue about what part would not come true, but I could guess. Prince Amar was a cold-hearted man, and while the wedding would match her dream in splendor, her life afterward would not be a dream come true.

Before I could respond, I heard a loud curse in Atul's voice. We paused, and my hand instinctively went to the sword's hilt. Then I heard footsteps running.

"Rish, take my sister to her chambers and stay there. Kapil and I will go investigate."

Without waiting for his response, I trotted toward the sound. Kapil joined me, and we turned a corner and came to the hall leading off to the quarters given to the two older Padi princes. Prince Amar had requested chambers in a secluded corner of the palace, and Atul had his rooms in the same hallway. As we got closer I heard a woman's scream followed by indistinguishable noises in Amar's voice. I saw Atul ahead of us bursting open the door to a room, and we followed him in our swords drawn.

Half-clothed Prince Amar lay on top of a woman, and the screams came from them. In the dim light, I tried to make sense of the scene while Atul ran forward. Amar had his hands wrapped around her neck, slowly draining the life out of her, her screams becoming feeble.

"Amar, stop!" His brother tried to pry his fingers open. Kapil and I rushed to help Atul, and between us, we loosened his fingers. Then I spotted the blood slowly coming out of Amar's side, and I groaned, "Atul."

Kapil cursed under his breath and whispered in a shocked voice, "Prince Amar has been stabbed."

Atul and I yanked him off the woman and laid him on his back. I looked at her for the first time, and her eyes found mine. She tried to whisper something, and I leaned closer to hear. "Tell her. . ." she mumbled before she gasped her last breath. A thought tried to form in my head, but it disappeared before it could take shape.

Atul peered at me with tears in his eyes. "Amar is dead." All of this happened within a few moments of our arrival, and before I could make sense of it, I heard a cry. Meera stood at the threshold with her hands covering her mouth. She and Rish must have followed me.

"Meera," I blurted, hoping to stop her, but she came forward. Seeing the state of undress of the man and woman on the bed, Atul draped some sheets over them. Meera's glance fell on the Prince and then the woman. A cry escaped her lips again. I went to her and held her elbow. "Meera, let us go."

I ordered Rish and Kapil. "Help Atul while I take Meera to her room." I led her out, closing the door behind us. Tears ran down her cheeks, but the moonless night kept us in the dark. Rumors would fly, and the less Meera was involved, the better.

Once we entered her room, Meera lay on her bed and wept into her pillow. She would have married Amar when the sun dawned, but now he lay dead in bed with another woman. I felt lost as to how to comfort her.

"Meera," I said feebly, waiting for the sobs to subside. Past the initial shock, my mind raced to the future. Death of Amar before the wedding meant Meera would not be tied to that monster for life. But her tears troubled me. Had she come to love her betrothed?

Meera slowly turned towards me and wiped her tears. I pulled a chair close to her and sat down.

"That woman with Amar," I said, recalling a faint memory, "she looked familiar to me."

Meera nodded and said slowly, "You know the dancer, Madhavi? She performed the other night."

"Madhavi, I remember her now. She spied for you."

She nodded again, and fresh tears flowed down her cheeks now. Were the tears for the Prince or the dancer? Did Meera have a hand in his death? No, I could not allow my mind to go there.

"Meera, I need to go inform Father of what happened and make arrangements for tomorrow. I will find Kantha to come and spend the night with you."

"Jay," she said urgently, and I regarded her. "We still need the alliance with Padi," she whispered, her eyes urging me to understand her.

"Yes, that is why we proceeded with the marriage alliance despite—" I did not finish my words, not wanting to cast aspersions on a dead man.

She continued to stare at me. My mind worked slowly today after the long tumultuous night. What could we do to strengthen our ties in the face of death? With Amar dead, Atul would be the heir. Prince Atul!

"Meera, Prince Atul would be the crown prince," I said, watching her face. She nodded imperceptibly. I continued, "Under normal circumstances suggesting marriage to the younger brother, when the older one just died would be abominable. These are not normal circumstances. The future of two kingdoms is at stake. If we can avert disaster by you marrying Atul, would you agree to it?"

She sighed softly and nodded. I'd underestimated my sister.

"I did not wish for Madhavi's death," she whispered. "I sought her help knowing Amar's propensity for women. I cannot mourn his death, though. My life would have been hell married to him. I had to act before that life sentence."

Her eyes reflected her pain and courage. I reached out and squeezed her hand. "I dreamt of leading a hunting expedition and purposely showering Amar's chest with arrows. You are not the only one who wished him an ill fate." I'd failed to act, but she hadn't. She would be a better ruler than I.

"Who else knows," I asked her?

"Rish. He does not know all the details, but he can guess. I spoke to Madhavi in private."

"Let us keep it among us then, Meera. You did the right thing. You found a way to get rid of Amar without starting a war. I wish I had your courage and intelligence."

She laughed without mirth. "Courage? I acted like a coward, Jay. I performed my duty when it posed no burden. When it became hard, I abandoned my duty and let someone else's hands be bloodied. More so, as she is now lost in death."

I shook my head. "No different from me sending men to die on a battlefield. You are still doing your duty. To Malla and Padi. By marrying Atul. He will be a much better ruler and more inclined to listen and follow your advice."

I got off the chair and bent down and kissed her forehead and departed her room.

27

Royal Wedding

I stared at my reflection in the mirror numbly. The flurry of activities last night left me in a state of shock. A knock sounded on the door. Kantha, who'd helped me with my wedding jewelry, went to open it. My grandmother, the Queen Mother, entered. I rose from my seat and went to greet her.

"Grandmother, I would have come to you—"

My grandmother interrupted me, "Today is your day. I brought you something. Something from my past and your future." She handed a jeweled box to me, and I opened it gently. Inside sparkled a beautiful crown with a wing-spread peacock. She took it from the box and crowned me with her shaking hands. She took a step back, tears glistening in her eyes. "You look beautiful, child."

The crown perched on my head brought me back to reality. Part of me worried someone from the Padi family would snatch it and throw me in the dungeon for murdering their Crown Prince. Malla still commanded the largest army, so no one would dare to do that. But Atul could learn about my hand in his brother's death, and it might poison his mind against me. I took a deep breath to let go of these thoughts.

No one I knew mourned Amar's death. I was freed from marrying him with my honor intact. I decided to savor that.

I touched my grandmother's feet to seek her blessings, and she embraced me tenderly and said, "May the Goddess Durga give you strength and wisdom."

My father came to see me a few moments later, and my grandmother took her leave.

Alone in the room with me, he said, "The events of last night kept me busy and awake. King Verma mercifully agreed to your marriage to Prince Atul. I wanted to see you for myself and make sure you are fine with this wedding."

I looked into his kind face and nodded. Words escaped me at the moment. My mixed emotions with death and being free of Amar overwhelmed me. He gently kissed my forehead. "That boy Atul is beside himself. He came to see me at the first light of dawn. He is blaming himself for his brother's death and is not sure if he is worthy of you. I convinced him that the alliance is in the best interests of both families."

Atul, an unwitting victim in the drama that was unfolding, and thrust into the role of the crown prince and into marrying his brother's betrothed in a one-night span. I wished I could talk to him before our wedding.

"I understand how Atul feels," continued my father. "My life took a similar turn. Before I could mourn the father and brother I lost to the sea, the council crowned me in place of my father, and I took my brother's place at his wedding. Atul, though, still has a king, so he has time to learn. You were raised to be a queen, my child, while he lived in the shadows of his brother. Your role as his wife will be to help him learn to rule, so one day he can successfully take his father's place."

"You made a fine king, Father," I said, and he smiled at me. My thoughts turned to Atul. I liked him well enough when he'd come to seek my hand for his brother. Given time, my admiration of him may turn to love, though that was not a required ingredient in a royal marriage. Still, not staring into the abyss of marrying Amar gave me hope.

I straightened and took my father's hands, "Do not worry about me, father. I know my place in this. I will fulfill my role as a wife and help Atul navigate the royal sea." I remembered Atul's sharp mind masked by his affable nature. He would make a fine ruler.

Sitting in front of the fire, Atul and I exchanged flower garlands, while the wedding guests showered us with turmeric coated rice. The eyes that looked into mine echoed the same questions. Atul took my hand tentatively and led the walk around the fire, and I followed him. Seven steps tied us for life.

With our ceremony done, we walked over to bless Jay and Aranya. Smiling at his bride, Jay took the flower garland from his neck and placed it around hers. Aranya beamed in return and gave him her garland. Their joy brought a flood of emotions into my heart, and I glanced at Atul briefly. Where do we stand, his eyes seemed to question? Not knowing the answer, I looked away towards the guests. My eyes were drawn towards one face. Rish. Suddenly, all vanished except for that face, which grew so that it appeared close to me, almost kissing my lips. The warmth that filled me caused me to panic, and I quickly averted my gaze.

The four royal brides and grooms were escorted to our wedding feast. We accepted the blessings of the esteemed guests from all three kingdoms. Prince Nakul came over to me, and I touched his feet to seek his blessing. He seemed stunned initially and then recovered to bless me.

He presented me with a pair of fish earrings. "Something of your mother's land to take with you," he said, and I thanked him. With the secret my father entrusted to me, weighing heavily on my mind, I looked at my older brother.

"Prince Nakul, Riya is as dear to me as a sister. Bring her along and visit us in Padi." I turned to look at Atul, and he extended the invitation, "Riya and I share an aunt through marriage. Princess Mohini would be delighted to see her sister's daughter as well. As for me, I welcome any chance to show off the treasures of Padi."

Nakul smiled. "Well, you have your beautiful bride to take around Padi and reveal all the splendor. And I am not married to Riya Biha, yet.

I do wish to see the snowcapped mountains of Padi and may infringe on your hospitality. King Vikram rules Saral now, so you don't need my invite to visit. The people of Saral, including me, would welcome Princess Meera to her mother's land with open hands." With that, he left.

Servants served a seven-course meal to the wedding guests, and Atul, and I barely touched our food. We still hadn't said a word to each other, and I longed for some time alone with him. To understand what he thought of the turn of events. Of marrying his brother's betrothed.

Later, the newlyweds were taken around the city in an open carriage for the people of Akash to bless us. Jay held Aranya's hands in the carriage and waved at the crowd, pointing out to her the various sights. A city she would rule one day. Aranya's face shone with genuine happiness, and she greeted the people cheerfully. Atul and I did our part and greeted the crowds, the smile never quite reaching our eyes.

Exhausted, I reached my chambers to see it decorated with flowers. The meaning slowly dawned on me, while Kantha helped me undress and slip into my bath. Dressed in simpler clothes, I waited for Atul. I heard voices outside and a knock and went to open the door. My eyes fell on Atul and then on Rish. Confused, I mumbled, "Rish, what are you doing here?"

"I am your sworn sword, my lady, and I am doing my duty," he said, without meeting my eyes. He swore to protect me. How had I forgotten that?

Atul smiled at him and said, "I don't have my guards yet, so you will be doing double duty today."

Then, he walked in with me and shut the door behind him. Trying to put Rish out of mind, even though I knew he stood right outside the door, I scanned the area. My bed suddenly loomed large in the room, decorated with jasmine and lilies. Their fragrance threatened to overwhelm me. I turned away from it and walked to the chairs and sat on one of them. Atul followed my lead and took the chair next to me.

He turned to me and said, "This morning my father came to my chambers, and asked me to marry you. Did—" he hesitated slightly.

Understanding what he meant to ask me, I nodded and said, "Jay asked me as well."

He gazed at me with gentle eyes and said, "My father raised me to serve our future king, my brother. Now I have taken his place, and I have so much to learn."

Sensing his need, I said, "Atul, I am your wife, and you don't have to do this alone. I will be beside you every step of the way."

At my words, he regarded me with a fresh set of eyes and said, "When I visited earlier, my feelings for you evolved as I spent more time with you. I started feeling resentful of my brother. There were times I dreamt of marrying you myself."

He paused, and I finished his thoughts, "And now, you feel guilty about that, and about his death." I added slowly, "Your dreams and my prayers brought us here then." *Not just prayers,* I thought, but I buried that notion deep inside.

He held out his hands to me and I stood up and slowly took them. He pulled me down on to his lap and held me around my waist. "I feel like I can face any challenge, with you by my side," he murmured.

I rested my head on his chest, forgetting all my worries for a moment, letting my breath synchronize with his.

The next day, I went to meet Riya Biha, who had come to Akash for my wedding.

"My lady, my father has consented to my marriage with Prince Nakul."

I searched her face to see if there were any misgivings and found none. Instead, she smiled shyly and said, "Prince Nakul shared his evening meal with us yesterday."

Nakul had won a place in her heart. Given his looks and manners, that did not surprise me. I hoped he found a worthy consort in her. I had groomed Riya myself to be a queen for my brother. It just turned to be a different brother than the one I had in my mind initially.

The day of their wedding arrived, and General Devan and my father went to a lot of effort to make sure the ceremony befitted a future king and queen.

Our father and mother had arranged for the three royal pairs to offer gifts to the people of the city. Many Akash residents lined up to bless us and receive our giving. Jay and Aranya stood in the middle, as future king and queen of Malla. Atul and I stood to their right and Nakul and Riya to their left. An old woman approached us. She took the bag of grain held out by Riya and said, "Crown, I see on your head."

Nakul raised his eyebrows at that and turned to the man behind her. She approached Jay and took the sari held out by Aranya. She repeated, "Crown, I see on your head."

"Thank you for your blessing, *Ma*," said Jay.

She approached us and held out her hand. I handed the bag of coins, and she looked into my face, "Crown, I see on your head." As she moved, she spun around to look at me and said in a louder voice, "*Your son will rule the three kingdoms.*"

All eyes were on her and me.

Father invited me to his chambers for lunch and as I sat down, Somu arrived to serve our food. Surprised to see him there, I waited for Father to reveal why he had brought us together. As Somu set our plates, Father whispered to him, "She knows the truth." Somu glanced at me, fleetingly. With a brief nod, he continued to serve us our lunch.

After he left, Father turned to me, "Somu and his sister Thangam in Saral will take their lead from you after my death. I am entrusting you with tremendous responsibility. The fate of Malla rests upon you."

Two brothers and two future kings. Would I take the secret to my grave, or would I one day need to reveal it?

"Father, I believe the old lady who prophesized to you came to the royal giving."

"What did she say?" he asked excitedly.

"For each of us, she said she saw a crown in our future." He nodded.

In a trembling voice, I said, "For me alone, she said my son would rule the three kingdoms of Magadha." I hesitated for a moment. "Father, I fear this knowledge you have entrusted with me. I fear harm falling on my—" I did not finish the thought.

"My child, Malla, Saral, and Padi are at peace with your marriages. There is nothing to fear. Settle your mind and help Atul learn to rule."

I wished I shared father's view. My fear centered on my unborn son and what actions I would take to ensure his future.

Jay and I went horse riding the next day, along with Rish and Kapil. Jay did not travel anywhere without his shadow, and it was still strange that I now had one as well.

We stopped under a big banyan tree and sat on its thick roots, side by side. Our guards were out of earshot. We did not say anything for some time. I could not share the doubts that gnawed at me with anyone but him.

"I plotted to get rid of my betrothed. Does that make me a monster?" I asked, looking ahead.

Jay turned to face me. "By that reasoning, I would be a monster for slaughtering my enemies on the battlefield and for beheading a traitor. Even a merciful ruler needs to be ruthless against his foes. I wish I had your courage, Meera."

I'd acted mostly in my self-interest. If I had thoughts about Padi or Malla's future, they were relegated as secondary goals. I knew I had to forgo that in the future, for the sake of the kingdoms.

"I did not mean for Madhavi to die." I sighed. Her death weighed heavily on me. She tormented me in my nightmares, and I woke up in a panic last night, being chased by her ghost. Atul comforted me by stroking my back, and I fell into a fitful sleep on his chest.

Jay laughed when he heard me say that. Surprised, I regarded him.

"I do not mean to laugh at your pain, only that we are even more alike than I ever thought. Guilt tore at me after I slew two young men in Maram. I hadn't spoken about it to anyone. I did not believe anyone could understand, except Father. But you do."

"Jay, that is not the same. You are duty-bound to fight for Malla. And Shiv committed treason."

"Amar was a monster. His rule would have hurt our kingdoms. And you are not duty-bound to suffer for Malla."

I twisted my sari end. "Do you have battle anxiety now? About killing men?"

Jay jutted out his chin and said, "I spent one sleepless night thinking about it. Then, I slaughtered half-a-dozen Saral men who tried to kill me and cut the head off the traitor who plotted behind my back. Rage supplanted my guilt."

"I don't feel guilty about Amar."

I'd only experienced a sense of relief at Amar's death. Padi and I would fare better without him. But doubts plagued me still. Would I continue to commit acts in my interest, even if it went against Malla's or Padi's? I found no ready answers.

Even with this turmoil, my mind attained some peace. I lost the sense of dread I felt at the thought of marrying Amar. In the last few days, I had regained my love for life.

"Your life with him would have been odious, and you did the right thing."

He paused and put his arm around my shoulders. "Our guilt is good for the three kingdoms. We will think before we act."

"Since when did you become so wise?"

"I have always been. You were just wiser."

I smiled at him, and he squeezed my shoulder.

"Jay, I have not had a chance to talk to you about Sudha. Two women vying for your attention, and fighting over it can turn ugly."

He sighed, "Tell me something I don't know."

"You may be tempted to put off your wedding to Sudha, but I would suggest otherwise. Marry her soon. Travel with both to Saral, and there you can crown Prince Nakul."

"Meera, I don't know how to handle one, let alone two women. If you had asked me to single-handedly defeat the Padi army, that would be easier than this."

"You may not know, but Aranya does. There is no question about Aranya's loyalty, so take her into your confidence. Ask Aranya to help you win over Sudha. Away from her Vindhya family, Sudha will not have anyone whispering dark words in her ears. When you come back to Akash, you will need to have two women loyal to you."

He was quiet for some time and then requested, "Sing that song about the rivers of Saral."

"The one our mother taught us?"

"I don't remember her, let alone her voice. I only remember you singing to me."

I shook my head at him and sang in a low voice. He sat back against the tree and hummed along. At that moment, I was transported to our childhood, when neither of us knew or understood our duties and could simply enjoy each other's company.

Several days later, Atul and I readied ourselves to leave for Padi. I, however, still had one unfinished task: Rish Vindhya.

Faithful to his sworn words, he followed me around, keeping his distance from the newlyweds. His role in Prince Amar's demise and our history together led me to believe I needed to release him from his vows. Neither Jay nor Atul agreed with that sentiment, though I never revealed the entire truth to them. In their minds, Kantha and Rish would represent home in a new place. I could not divulge my reasoning to them, so I decided to talk to Rish himself.

I attended the small council meeting with Atul, Jay, and others. When the conversation veered towards making our seas safer, I left them with Rish in tow. As I approached my chambers, I slowed and waited for him to come nearer.

"There are matters regarding our travel I would like to discuss with you. Please join me in my chambers," I said and entered my rooms. He followed behind and closed the door. I sat down on one of the chairs and asked him to sit across from me. The tension in the room felt like an elephant sitting on my chest, hard to ignore.

"Rish Vindhya, you have faithfully served me, and my brother. I believe your place is beside Prince Jay. He needs brave and loyal men like you to help him win the seas."

With his arms crossed, he regarded me. "My lady, your brother released me from his service, and I am sworn to you now."

I shook my head. "Amar is dead, and I don't need protection from Atul. Here in Akash, you can marry well and serve the Malla kingdom."

"Marry someone else?" He pushed his fingers through his hair. "My lady, once the sun comes out, the moon and the stars fade away. You are my sun, and my destiny is to serve you. Please allow me that pleasure."

"Rish—" I said softly. "You would be seeing me in the arms of another, my husband."

"The alternate is not seeing you at all, my lady."

"Oh, Rish!"

He stood up. "My lady, some men sail the ocean while others walk along her shore. I am fine with walking along the shores, just do not banish me to the desert. And, I may be of service to you in the Padi court."

With that, he walked towards the door.

"I can find you a girl to marry in Padi," I blurted out.

He bowed and smiled. "If that is your heart's desire...I swore to obey you, my lady."

Did I want to see another girl in his arms? I did not want to know the answer, so I remained silent.

"Will there be anything else?"

I shook my head, not trusting my voice. I don't deserve such love and devotion. He bowed again and left.

Thoughts swirled through my head. Can I trust myself to not succumb to my temptations? Infidelity in a queen is punishable by beheading. I shook my head to clear these images. Atul had been nothing but kind to me. Rish was an honorable man. And I was no ordinary maid to give in to her urges.

Rish would have his uses in Padi. He could go places I could not and see and hear things I would not. While I had to learn the palace intrigue, I didn't have to question his loyalty. It would be nice, having his familiar face by my side, in the sea of new ones.

The day to bid farewell to my beloved city came far too soon. The last few days were a whirlwind of action.

Nakul and Riya headed to Saral after their wedding, accompanied by General Devan. My father relieved Devan Biha of his Southern Commander role, now that his daughter was married to the future king of Saral. He promoted Satya to that role and appointed Giri Thari as his Lieutenant-General.

Giri headed to Saral with them. After losing one son, Giri's appointment offered some solace to Chief Bhoj Thari. After setting up his daughter in her new household, my father tasked General Devan to bring King Surya to Malla.

Jay wedded Sudha in a simple ceremony and planned to follow Nakul with Aranya and Sudha like I'd advised him to.

I had visited all my favorite places and said my farewells to countless friends and family. Now, I sat with Jay and father in his chambers, recollecting old stories when mother lived. With tears in his eyes, Father looked at me and said, "My dear child, you have been the Queen of this city for several years. While I will miss you, your rightful place is by your husband. I know you will win over Padi and help Atul rule it in the years to come."

Jay looked at me. "I hope all your lessons stay with me, Meera. I will come to visit you in Padi soon after I return from Saral."

Looking at my gaunt father, with his sunken eyes and mop of grey hair and then at my brother, with his bright eyes, dark curly hair, and the strength of youth, the contrast could not have been greater. Jay would shoulder many of the king's duties going forward, relieving Father of some of the burden he carried. It was no longer my duty to take care of either of them.

I hugged them both, shedding tears.

Back in my chambers, I hummed a song and looked around the familiar room reliving the memories of my childhood. Kantha came in, making sure all the things were packed and loaded onto carts.

"My lady, your mother sang that song. She had a magical voice."

"It is about a girl's love for her home. Kantha, I am leaving my home and childhood behind."

"True, but you have a new journey ahead. That is the way for every child who grows up. Your journey will already be smoother than most.

I have seen the way Prince Atul looks at you. He worships the ground you walk on. You will have all of Padi singing your praise soon."

Outside in the palace courtyard with Atul by my side, I bid farewell to my family.

Father seemed in good spirits after having commanded his oldest son to rule Saral. Jay and Nakul had come a long way from the days of facing each other on the battlefield. With Aranya as the bridge, their mutual respect and affection had grown. I hoped Jay's trip to Saral to crown Nakul will cement their friendship and earn him a brother.

Atul helped me into the chariot, and I gazed at him fondly. His feeling for me ran deeper than I'd realized, and he had showered me with love since our wedding. I held secrets that I could not share with him, about my brothers, my feelings for Rish, and my role in Amar's death. Notwithstanding that, my respect and attachment for him had grown. I smiled at Atul warmly, and he returned it with equal fervor. Secure in his affection, I looked forward to making my home in Padi.

Atul and Rish mounted their horses. I bid farewell to Jay and Father, and in the company of two men who loved me, I began my journey north.

The End

Acknowledgements

My first inspiration was my grandmother. As a young child, I spent several summers with her. Mealtimes were storytimes, and I remember prolonging it so I can hear one more story. Her stories based on Indian mythology would bring characters to life. She had excellent delivery for comedy and would have my brother and me laughing at the funny stories. She passed away many years ago, and her memory lives in me through these stories I write.

Christa Yelich-Koth: *Thanks for your patience and for your valuable feedback to help make this story even better and the cover art*

Holly Kammier: *Thanks for introducing me to the writing community and for your encouragement and support*

R.J. Van Wart: *Thanks for taking my back of the napkin scribbling and transforming it into the Map of Magadha*

*I could write a book thanking my **family**, who allow me to indulge in reading and writing stories. Maybe I will one day. For now, thanks for being my biggest cheer squad.*

*Grateful to my **friends**, who believed in me and supported me through this process.*

*And to my dear **readers**, without whom this would not be possible, many thanks.*

About the Author

The stories I read growing up inspired me to write. I am interested in historical fiction and within that society, examining the human heart in conflict. I like to place my female characters in difficult situations and see how they learn to survive with no actual power. And watch my male characters fall in love while fighting for king and land. I love exploring the struggle between love and duty.

I live in California with my family. Visit me at annabushi.com to learn about upcoming books.

Reviews are priceless to authors like me. Your reviews would introduce my book to other readers. Thank you for supporting me by posting a review.

Follow me:

@anna.bushi.book on instagram

@annabushibook on twitter

Turn the page to read the blurb from book 2 of the Land of the Magadha series . . .

War of the Three Kings

Coming soon!

News of her father's death shatters Queen Meera's peaceful life. King Nakul is invading Malla, while her brother Prince Jay is fighting a battle in neighboring Sunda. Can she stop Nakul without revealing the deadly secret she holds? She makes a fatal mistake, allowing her heart to rule her head. Will it destroy everything she cherishes?

Prince Jay seeks revenge for his father's death. But he cannot tell friends from foes. Can he save Malla and his crown? Or, will a secret revealed destroy him forever? Magadha is at war, and kings are being hunted. Who is next to fall?

* * *

Want to know when I release a new book? Sign up for my new release notification at https://annabushi.com/contact-me/

Made in the USA
Las Vegas, NV
27 January 2021